PADOSKOKS

AMERICAN INDIAN LITERATURE AND CRITICAL STUDIES SERIES

PADOSKOKS

A Jacob Neptune Murder Mystery

Joseph Bruchac

UNIVERSITY OF OKLAHOMA PRESS : NORMAN

This book is a work of fiction. Names, characters, places, and incidents are either the product of the author's imagination or are used fictitiously, and any resemblance to actual events, locales, or persons, living or dead, is entirely coincidental.

Library of Congress Cataloging-in-Publication Data

Names: Bruchac, Joseph, 1942– author
Title: Padoskoks / Joseph Bruchac.
Description: First. | Norman, OK : University of Oklahoma Press, 2021. | Series: A Jacob Neptune murder mystery | Summary: "Abenaki detective Jacob Neptune and his best buddy Dennis Mitchell find themselves on the Northwest coast investigating a series of murders and disappearances that may be linked to the monster known as Padoskoks, the giant underwater serpent"—Provided by publisher.
Identifiers: LCCN 2020026487 | ISBN 978-0-8061-6842-5 (paperback)
Subjects: GSAFD: Mystery fiction.
Classification: LCC PS3552.R794 P33 2021 | DDC 813/.54—dc23
LC record available at https://lccn.loc.gov/2020026487

Padoskoks: A Jacob Neptune Murder Mystery is Volume 72 in the American Indian Literature and Critical Studies Series.

The paper in this book meets the guidelines for permanence and durability of the Committee on Production Guidelines for Book Longevity of the Council on Library Resources, Inc. ∞

PADOSKOKS

1

Rolling Thunder

Take time—
before time takes you

The water is deep here. Deeper than I could go without the aid of considerable apparatus—me not being a competitive free diver or a Japanese Ama. As I look below, I'm looking for something I hope is not there—though I am fairly certain, from the pricking of my thumbs, that something bigger and less friendly than a dolphin this way comes.

I'm too far out to make it to shore on my own in less than half an hour. The boat that I thought was supposed to be accompanying me is nowhere in sight. Sure, I'm capable of swimming that far. I could lay out into a convincingly fast Australian crawl, even though I lack the flipper feet of a Michael Phelps. But the image of a pike lure being reeled in fast enough to catch the attention of an overly dentured predator prevents me from engaging in any pursuit that will create ripples.

Pursuit. Not the best choice of words right now, seeing as how I'm feeling like the incipient pursuee.

Why the hell am I here? Was this a necessary part of my investigation? Why don't I remember anything before finding myself in the exact geographic middle of this far-too-wide bay?

As the sun is starting to set.

No need to panic. But then again, as I feel the old Greek demigod's hand clutching at my chest, I may not have a choice. But maybe, just maybe, I can go unnoticed as long as I stay like this, salt water holding me up, head leaning forward, snorkel in my mouth, not moving arms or legs, until someone comes along to rescue me. Relaxed in a perfect dead man's float.

3

Nice image, Jacob. Let it not be prophetic. And how about my not being overdramatic? There's nothing here to fear except fear itself.

Oh, aside from that very large, long-necked creature rising up out of the depths with its mouth gaping open . . .

I woke up to the sound of thunder. (Actually, by the time that rumble rolled, I'd already been extricated from my dead-end dream by the sound of certain night moves from the forest behind my cabin. But wasn't that lead-in sentence pretty cool?)

I've always loved thunderstorms.

When those rumbling sounds come rolling in through the Adirondack hills, they touch something deep inside me. They remind me of the old stories I heard from my Uncle John about the Pedongi, the Thunderers, when I was a kid. How they were up there riding the clouds, looking down for their enemies, the giant water snakes. How they'd soon be hurling down arrows of lightning at them. How those Thunder Beings sometimes befriended humans and would take them with them up into the sky.

What kid—at least what Indian kid, us not being as prone to a fear of heights as your average American—wouldn't want to be recruited into that war party? Who hung the iron for America's tallest buildings? You can bet your best buckskin jacket it was not members of Skull and Bones. (Though I have it on good authority that those Yalies do still have their sentimental connections to us first Americans, possessing in their crypt, courtesy of the grave-digging grandfather of our Bush-league chief executive, the skull of Geronimo. Go, Elis! Yet another reason why Dennis and I reveled in beating the crap out of their football team whenever we former Indians played them.)

So, as I lay in bed with the high window above it open, when I heard that deep rumbling approaching, like the sound of motorcycles coming up the dead-end road that leads to my cabin, I almost closed my eyes to dream that I was about to ascend with those powerful old ones up into the stratosphere. After all, the glowing number on my clock showed it was only 5:54, barely dawn yet. My lips were starting to shape the old words of greeting in Abenaki. Kwai, Ktsi Nidobak!

Until I realized it wasn't thunder at all. It actually was motorcycles, the echo of their engines off the rock walls that rose on either side of the little-used trail to my house making them sound deeper and louder. And I dang well did not close my eyes. As I rolled out of bed, "Hello, Great Friends" was the furthest thing from what I actually said. Which in polite company might be rendered as "I am in deep doo-doo!"

I realized a couple of other things while still in mid-roll. First was that, yet again, someone who'd pulled out the "I love him not" petal on his daisy had decided to recruit bikers to teach me a lesson. (When, dear Pete, when will they ever learn?)

Second was that an obviously imminent frontal assault such as I sensed (trust me on this, I have abnormally accurate senses about such things) being heralded by their 1200cc engines meant that a backal (so sue me for verbal inventiveness) attack was about to occur first. Those had not been unusually loud red squirrels I'd been hearing behind my cabin, approaching with intended stealth for the last quarter hour. After all, red squirrels do not now and then say "Shit!" when they trip on branches or whisper "Shhh!" to their clumsy companions.

So why had I simply stayed recumbent, mentally composing yet another summer-themed haiku?

> Distant thunder rolls
> Waking me up from my sleep
> Thunder Beings call

Why had I been musing on Thunder Beings and not that rare bird called the Get Out of Dodge Egress? Because I was prepared, waiting for something to happen soon.

Right now, in fact.

"WATCH OUUU . . . !" "SHIIII . . . !" "FUUUUU . . . !" accompanied by the sounds of at least two and possibly three bodies falling into the steep-walled Burmese tiger traps that my friend Dennis and I had labored over following my return from Abenaki Island signaled the arrival of those uninvited visitors. That we'd placed a half circle of those man-catchers had, as we'd planned, assured that my flank was not exposed. (That we had not affixed ordure-coated sharpened pungi sticks in the bottom of said deeply dug pits is a tribute to our humanitarian natures. Then again, my Uncle John, who'd served in Nam and taught us how to construct said structures, viewed those impaling additions as both over-kill and too much of a reminder of his sojourn in Southeast Asia.)

I did not stop to savor the moment but kept rolling. Once, twice more, and I had reached the trapdoor to the tunnel beneath my house. (Thank you again for your inspiration, Uncle John and Ho Chi Minh.) As I raised it and slid headfirst down the ramp I'd carefully installed, I heard other all too familiar sounds from the road in front of my cabin, where the roar of Born to Be Wild Harleys had ceased. Safeties being clicked off. Bullets being racked into chambers. And then, though muted by the earthen walls of my tunnel, the BRAP-BRAP-BRAPBRAP-BRAP of automatic weapons aimed in the direction of my recently vacated accommodations.

From the sound of those weapons, handguns, AK-47s, and deer rifles, I probably would have had little to worry about had I remained in the cabin. The walls of my home are solid, thick hemlock logs. Cut and trimmed from my woods. Nothing short of a .50-caliber heavy-duty M2 machine gun was going to penetrate more than a few inches. Admittedly, my kitchen shutters might let in a few rounds, but there was little there for them to damage. I've managed to curb the urge to collect crystal goblets or display Dresden china on my kitchen shelves. All my plates and drinking mugs are made of wood, and if they get damaged I can always carve more.

My cabin is located in the midst of a glacial moraine. A place where the advance of those mountains of ice my ancestors skated across ten thousand years ago—as they went back and forth visiting drinking buddies in Siberia—slowed down and retreated, depositing a sizable hill of sand. The local quarrymen were deeply disappointed when I demurred to selling them mining rights and placed all of my property in a conservation easement. That permeable substrate beneath my foundation meant that tunneling—as Dennis and I did one spring—was relatively easy. (Like the excavation of those ten-foot-deep man-traps out back.) At least until we came up against the Adirondack granite that cupped the sand like an immense hand. Which meant my tunnel ended at the base of an outcrop after only a hundred feet.

Plenty far enough, though. Especially since we'd made sure it angled up to come out—with a little root trimming—behind a large white pine. It had been a quick and easy crawl. Since my fellow mole man Dennis has the bulk of an adolescent rhino, my tunnel was large enough for me to scamper through barely bent over. Not crawling on my belly as Uncle John used to when playing tunnel-rat tag with Viet Cong soldiers near Khe Sanh. Soldiers he learned to respect for their dedication to defend a homeland they loved as much as our own Native people cared—and still care—for Ndakinna.

I lifted up one of the several things I kept stored in the chamber below the white pine—a hand-sized mirror, which I held out from behind the tree. It gave me a good view of the tableau below. I'd expected to see three or four Harleys, plus an equal complement of riders. But apparently I was better loved—or respected—than I thought. There were seven hogs, and the same number of porcine horsemen of the apocalypse fanned out on their bellies fifty feet from my front porch as they unleashed their futile storm of lead at my unperturbed ever-so-humble home. None of them seemed aware that I was no longer within.

During my odyssey on behalf of the Children of the Mountain, I'd displayed my lack of prejudice toward the leather-jacketed biker fraternity to which I once swore allegiance. After all, to paraphrase my favorite and now sadly little-known marsupial philosopher Pogo, quite often the enemy is us. Most bikers, whether "outlaws" or "in-laws," are okay people. As with pit bulls, it just depends on how they were house-trained.

But the guys I viewed below me had crossed a line . . . if not obliterated it. While it may be true, as Cat Stevens avers, that the first cut is the deepest, the first shot is seldom the one that ends the battle. Especially when someone else commands the higher ground.

I lifted the second thing I had brought up with me from my hideyhole. Using the bolt to rack a shell into the chamber, I took careful aim and pulled the trigger of my Remington 700 30-06.

Due to the racket they were making in attempting to ventilate my cabin, I am fairly sure that none of the non–Magnificent Seven heard my shot. But there's no doubt in my mind that they heard—and experienced—the result. It's amazing how much noise a Harley fuel tank makes when it explodes as a result of the faster-than-sound arrival of a superheated bullet. Nor, as I worked the bolt, aimed, and fired four more times in rapid succession, could they have failed to note the similar results on the four further bikes I was able to detonate. At which point I paused and slid back behind the pine for several reasons:

1. The ensuing smoke and flames were making it hard to aim.
2. Additional fire from me might have given away my position to those two or three men still holding firmly enough onto their weapons and their wits to start shooting somewhere other than at my innocent domicile. (None of them, I might add, sending any of their shots within fifty feet of me.)
3. Enough is enough.

I might also add that silence not only is golden, it can also be unnerving. After allowing several minutes of it to sink in, I ventured another peek, via the mirror, at my adversaries.

None of them, it seemed, had chosen to go down with the ship. All had abandoned their positions and were, depending on their degree of disability, either limping or running down the road away from my cabin, leaving their mangled iron steeds and, with the exception of three of the less cowed combatants, their weapons behind. Glenn Frey and his fellow avian musicians would have loved it. Their loads were loosened indeed.

It was at that point, just to make sure, that I engaged the other device—or rather devices—I had installed for just such an event. Multiple concealed speakers placed at intervals in the trees along the road.

They proved efficacious. The still-armed trio only discharged their weapons—inaccurately—at the first speaker when the words "Bye, bye, gentlemen" came out of it. The second speaker's message, perhaps a bit overly ironic, the recording of my favorite musician's rendition of "I Won't Back Down," prompted no further fire. And the third one's "Have a Nice Day!" was totally ignored as they disappeared as rapidly as they could around the bend.

Yes, I admit, I am a wise-ass.

But now I had a problem. Three, I assumed, from what I'd heard.

2

Catch and Release

Sometimes today is just yesterday
wearing new clothes

After reloading my rifle, I made my way along the slope until I had a good view of the back of my cabin. I detected no motion, but waited until I had counted silently to a thousand. Then I moved closer, stopping when I was still a stone's throw away from the formerly hidden hole—now clearly visible with its covering of thin branches and hemlock boughs caved in.

Did I detect a sound? I cupped my left hand behind my ear.

Hmmm.

A stone's throw away was the literal distance between me and the pit trap. And the stones piled near where I'd stopped would allow me to test that. I picked up a fist-sized rock and lofted it so that it fell straight down into the hole. I heard a soft thud as the stone hit something other than earth or stone, and a louder *"ow"* voiced a split second after that contact. Followed by a somewhat plaintive:

"Hey, man! We're in here!"

I refrained from pointing out that was stating the obvious. Instead, my reply was a somewhat smaller egg-shaped stone that followed the trajectory of its comrade. The result this time was a nearly perfect D major of a *bonk!* that suggested cranial contact, followed by a more plaintive plea.

"Stop! Please!"

Politeness does count for something. I dropped the third stone by my feet and advanced closer. But not close enough to be seen from the hole.

"You down there," I called. "How many are there of you?"

A moment of silence ensued, likely while thought was in process and the conclusion was reached that dissembling would provide no advantage.

"Three," a rough voice answered, a voice that sounded as if its owner had been gargling with antifreeze. "But Larry's out cold."

Which would make you either Shemp or Moe? I thought.

But my assumption was quickly disproved by his next words. "My name's Charley. I'm not bad hurt, but Phil here's got a broke arm. You gotta help us outta here, man."

It not being Biker Season, I had to admit that he had a point. It was either help them reenact the Emergence from Mother Earth myth so common to southwestern tribal traditions . . . or bring in a few dozen yards of fill and a bulldozer. The thought of having a white man grave-yard to close to my home was, however, disquieting. Though perhaps a plot element for some future novel I might write.

Help them out I would. Catch and release was my only realistic option.

But my momma did not raise no fools.

"Right," I said. "I'll get you guys out of there. But first I need something."

"Hey," Rough Voice said, "you want our promise we won't try nothin'? You got it. Man. I mean, we was just hired to scare you some."

Right. And if I believed that, did he also have a treaty on hand for me to sign?

"Lovely," I said. "But you also have to take apart whatever guns you've got with you, field strip them, and chuck them up here."

A moment of silence followed, broken by a flurry of whispered muttering back and forth between Rough Voice Charley, Broke Arm Phil, and Not Actually Comatose Larry. Had they been aware of my auditory acuity, they might have whispered more quietly, used sign language, or texted each other on their phones. I could hear the plan they were attempting to hatch. It was soft-boiled at best.

I picked up another stone and tossed it into the pit.

"*Ow!* You didn't need to do that, man!"

"Start chucking. Oh, and flip your phones up first. Or the next metamorphic reminder coming your way is going to be shotput size."

Two Nokias and a Blackberry came flying out of the hole. At which point, awkward me, I stepped on each of them. The constituent parts of a sawed-off semi-auto 12-gauge shotgun and an AK-47 took flight soon after. Followed by a pause.

"Fellas," I said, "there's three of you. How about one more long gun and then the peashooters I know you have to have brought along?"

The handful of gravel that I kicked into the hole stirred them to quick action in the form of a second disassembled AK-47, a .45 Colt, a jet-black 9mm Beretta, and a bargain-basement Luger.

Who knew, I thought, *that disarmament could be so easy?* I may have missed my calling as an arms negotiator. But, to paraphrase our former "Where's the rest of me?" commander in chief, trust without verification don't mean much. And guns were not the only weapon known to semi-primitive man.

"You know what, buddies?" I said. "This may be the start of a beautiful friendship. But I need one more thing."

"What, man? You got all our guns."

"Shanks, Charles. Pig-stickers, Ka-Bars, gravity knives, switchblades. I know you got 'em."

As I spoke those words, caution being my middle name (aside from Jesse), I backed up and moved four steps to the side. With good reason, as it turned out. The half-dozen blades that came spinning up in my former direction—including a Bowie knife—might have done me some damage.

"Buddy?" The hopeful tone in his voice left little doubt that those hurled hand weapons had been thrown with less than benevolent intent. I busied myself tidying things up, securing the various weapons in the specially built cage that keeps my garbage cans safe from raccoons and bears.

Meanwhile, the whispering from my fallen angels in the pit began again, the theme being how they might escape via a human pyramid now that I seemed to have been turned into a pincushion.

Kids these days.

"Charles," I said.

Silence, then a rather chastened "Yeah, buddy."

"Your shoes. Now."

That, of course, was just the start. Three coats, shirts, and pairs of jeans later (I allowed them to retain their undergarments, both in the interest of modesty and in the memory of what happened to the onlookers during Lady Godiva's bareback journey), I dropped a roll of duct tape into the hole.

"Wrists," I said, "wrapped together in front of your body."

When they came up the ladder I lowered, Charley first, followed by the other two, they noticed immediately that I was not only fifty feet away, I also had the drop on them with my Remington. Any plans of rushing me were rapidly reassessed.

"Happy to see," I said when all three were lined up, "that Phillip's arm appears healed and that Lawrence has awakened from his slumber. Now I have two questions for you. First, where did you park your bikes?"

Charley raised his duct-taped hands like a kindergarten kid with the answer to the sum of one plus one.

"About a mile back down the road. We circled through the woods."

"Excellent. And back down that road is where you will now be heading if you answer my next question correctly. Otherwise . . ." I worked the bolt to chamber a round, the sound of it convincingly threatening.

Their responses tumbled out in a nearly simultaneous chorus.

"Ask it."

"What is it?"

"We'll answer, man."

Music to my ears. I nodded approvingly.

"All right. Second question. A name? The name of who sent your crew?"

They might not have replied quite so rapidly had I not raised my rifle to my shoulder. But then again, if one (or three) is naked and afraid, there is some incentive to being honest when an armed man posits a query.

One word was all they said. In unison. It was more than enough and made perfect sense. It also made me wince, but only mentally.

"Full marks," I said. "You all pass. Now put on your shoes, pick up your clothes, and skedaddle."

"Huh?" Charley said.

"*Run!*"

Shoving on their footwear and grabbing nearly all of their garments, they did just that. Leaving me with that one word. A word I said out loud with some distaste when they were out of earshot.

"Malsum."

3

The Would-Be Wolf

The name you choose
may not choose you

Malsum. Wolf. In our oldest Penacook stories, that's the name of the four-legged one, and also of one of the faithful helpers of our culture hero, Gluskonba.

To be a wolf among all—as far as my experience goes—of our Native nations here on Turtle Island is an honorable thing. Call someone a wolf and you're complimenting them. Our wolves, human or otherwise, are devoid of unhealthy addictions to scarlet-robed adolescents. Despite all the lurid depictions in print and film. About the only one who got it right was Rudyard Kipling when he told his story of a brown-skinned boy being raised by a benevolent pack.

In the sign language that was used pretty much universally across the continent, before being co-opted by the Boy Scouts, the sign for a wolf was the same as that for a scout. (Got that, kimosabe?) One who ranges out looking for danger that might be approaching.

But what about the evil twin brother of Glooskap in Passamaquoddy stories? Wasn't he named Malsum? Yup, in that Iroquois story about the twin—a story that got grafted onto Wabanaki culture. However, as any Haudenosaunee folks who know anything about their own culture can tell you, in their original story those two boys were the Good Mind Twin and the Twisted Mind Twin. Flint and the Sprout. No werewolves need apply. Plus the three main Iroquois clans are Turtle, Bear, and Wolf.

Am I digressing from my narrative? Only a bit. For all that positive lobo lore was meant to serve as a contrast to the person fingered by his less than efficient minions as the one who let the hawgs out.

13

Malsum. The unearned and inaccurate name adopted by my old unfriend Mook Glossian, a man more amphibian than mammal.

Yes. Dennis and I exposed him as a traitor to our people and a poseur.

Indeedy-do, we did. Along with his ersatz Penacook cohort Ricco Carlotti, a.k.a. "Sammy Loron," who was just as Indian as all his spray-painted Italian role-playing predecessors in Hollywood films—such as Sal Mineo playing a noble Cheyenne warrior. (And, yes, they were actually spray-painted. I cherish the photo hanging over my desk of the movie tough-guy gangster Jimmy Cagney being prepared for an early bit-part role as a renegade savage by the application of a base coat of brown.)

Not that Mook was a phony Indian. No, alas, he was one of ours. Not a phony Native American—but a Native American phony betraying his own at the behest of the powers that be.

And in that last prepositional phrase lies the entire reason why Mook was not only walking around as a free man, but actually strutting in a position of power as a casino manager. Once again using the name he'd bestowed upon himself as both his own moniker and the name of his LLC: Malsum Gaming.

And who became his pit boss? Yup—free at last to claim his proud Mediterranean roots, it was Ricco, the former part-time Penacook. It's hard to keep a bad man down when he has friends in high places. A grateful government set them up, despite the fact that they failed in setting up my comrades among the Children of the Mountain. The only person who ended up being sent up the river was Packy Palehua, the Hawaiian former professional wrestler and part-time cannibal killer.

I suppose I should not have been surprised that Mook held a grudge against me. But it was now over a year and a half since the siege had happened and he was shown up as a turncoat. And he'd been in his job as the headman at Running Wolf Casino for a solid year. Why had it taken him so long to seek revenge?

Only one way to find out. Time to load my pockets with quarters and hop on the bingo bus.

But only after getting some backup. I took out my new Nokia 1110, flipped it open, and dialed.

4

Two Big Greenies

He who laughs last
probably didn't get the joke

Dennis picked up on the first ring.

"Keggy here," he said, in a nasal voice that was meant to imitate the sound of a talking beer barrel. It had been a running joke between us former Dartmouth Indians for the past two years, since a group of students had come up with the idea of using "Keggy the Keg" as a new mascot for the school. Keggy rapidly became a fan favorite at Big Green games, although some alumni would undoubtedly still prefer the racially insensitive Native American impersonator they used to cheer for. No matter how many times I'd heard it, my big buddy's Keggy impression always made me chuckle.

What I did not hear behind Dennis's voice were the familiar noises that formed the auditory landscape of the Mitchells' log home. Which was curious. Where were the whimpers, occasional barks, and sounds of happy scuffles from the dozen and a half rescued canine companions for whom that big two-story cabin was a doggy paradise? Nor did I hear any of the equally puppyish sounds from the smaller two-leggeds of the family.

Dennis and Patty Ann now had four children between them: the one-year-old whose DNA they had mutually contributed to, and the three from Patty Ann's previous marriage. Plus four foster kids. All equally loved and cared for. As a skilled workman and much-in-demand contractor, Dennis was using a good part of his income (and labor) to add on to their home (making it likely that it would one day rival Mervyn Peake's mythical castle of Gormenghast) to fit in further family members. That count included Patty Ann's sister, uncle, and two teenage cousins.

Dennis's place was, in short, the kind of typical Indian household that has been the norm among our people for countless generations—and would drive a census taker to distraction.

"Us Penacooks have always shared to survive," is how Uncle John Neptune always put it.

And as my years of experience among other nations in Indian Country have taught me, it wasn't just us Eastern tribes who lived—and still live—that way. I was out on the Pine Ridge Reservation a few years back to do a little job. Walter Wolf Jaw, the Pine Ridge School's senior bus driver, was given the job of showing me around—seeing as how no one knew the maze of back roads better. That turned out to be to my benefit in more ways than one. But that's a tale to tell at another time.

Our second day together, he slowed up as we drove past a neatly painted single-story house with a pair of truck-tire planters overflowing with wildflowers in the front yard, a water tank on its eastern wall, and a well-used swing set in the back.

"My place," Walter said, tilting his head in that direction. "Fourteen of us live there."

In a BIA pre-fab house of the style built in the '60s—designed to hold a family of four in its three small rooms.

"Fourteen," I said, nodding. "You've got a big family."

Walter shook his head. "Not really," he smiled. "Only four of 'em are from my wife and me. The others are all kids was on their own, living in wrecked trailers or in cardboard boxes or whatever. Parents dead or in jail or . . . you know." He lifted one hand from the wheel to mime tipping back a bottle. "But like our old people say, all children are our children." He smiled wider. "So I guess we do have a big family."

Then he told me the simple rules for the house, which were exactly the same as the ones Dennis and Patty Ann expected everyone under their roof to live by.

Be patient with each other and share all the chores.

That meant that Patty Ann was never overburdened and even had time to keep working toward the nursing degree that had been interrupted by her decision (emphasis on *her*) to rescue my big buddy from a life of bachelorhood. Big as Dennis was, he was nowhere near the force of nature that his self-assured, broad-shouldered spouse embodied. I'd never seen Patty Ann angry, but I'd been assured by Dennis that when she was *really* mad, naming a hurricane after her would be an understatement.

Hard to believe when I'd hear her voice, clear and strong as a bell, asking right after the phone was answered, "Who is it, darling? If it's Jacob, you tell him he owes us and his godchildren a visit."

But I didn't hear that. Dogs, kids, relatives, spouse, none of that.

The lack of that usual Mitchell homestead soundscape might have led me to think I'd somehow gotten a wrong number. Except for an unmistakable familiar background noise that made it clear my big buddy had pressed the button for the speaker on his phone to have his hands free. It was the nearly metronomic thwick, thwick, thwick of his favorite lock-blade knife as he carved a piece of wood into some shape from one of our old Penacook stories.

Would it look, I wondered, anything like what I'd just seen rising out of the depths of that last dream of mine?

I also wondered—worried, actually—whether Patty Ann might have finally discovered the secret that Dennis had been hiding from her and kicked him out with an ultimatum. That secret—that he had a life-threatening piece of shrapnel near his heart, which he'd refused to have surgically removed—was the reason he had secretly taken out a very large life insurance policy naming her as the beneficiary.

I could imagine her saying to him something along the lines of, "Get out, bozo! And do not come back without a note from your doctor scheduling that surgery!"

"Hey, Dennis," I said. "It's . . ." I would have said more, but those three words were the verbal equivalent of what would have happened if that mythic Little Dutch Boy had removed his finger from the hole in the dike—thereby releasing a flood.

"PODJO!" my oversized best buddy roared so loud that it almost knocked the phone out of my hand. "HOW! How you doing, nidoba? Whazzup? Tell me you need backup. Please!"

"Unh-hunh," I replied, figuring that attempting anything other than a fast affirmative would be drowned out by my large economy-size friend's enthusiastic response. Which it was.

"All right! So you want me to come get you? Your Explorer is still in the body shop, right?"

"Right," I said. Sadly, my now less than two-year-old ride had suffered the sort of problems that SUVs experience when one is forced to go off road and into the woods to avoid a welcoming party of well-armed

Sinaloans seeking payback for one's efforts in rescuing the kidnapped son of a much-more-honest-than-usual police chief.

"Pick you up at your place?" Dennis asked. "Right? And should I bring . . ."—he paused in the way someone pauses when they remember that cellular transmissions are even easier for certain three-letter acronymed parties to listen in on than land lines—". . . uh, you know?"

"Unh-hunh," I repeated. "We'll be visiting an old friend. At Toad Hall. So we should bring him . . . something, you know?"

"Yeah," Dennis growled, a tone of pure delight now in his voice. "Toad Hall. All right. Got it, Podjo. Us two Big Greenies will bring a smile to . . . our friend's face. See you soon."

True to his word as always, Dennis pulled up less than an hour later in his Jeep Renegade. As usual, his PENACOOK AND PROUD OF IT bumper sticker had pride of place on his front bumper.

What I had forgotten was that my triple-X buddy was currently on semi-leave from daddy duty. He was spending four days a week not far from me, in an old barn attached to an equally old farmhouse on the outskirts of nearby Greenwich. The remaining three days he was back at his home on Abenaki Island. It was because he'd volunteered to help another of our disabled veteran friends, an upstate New York Abenaki named Bill St. Francis. The wounds that put Bill in a wheelchair came from a Marine overseas summer-abroad program a generation before our own misadventures in uniform. We'd met Bill five years earlier at a VFW get-together for Native vets.

Bill's own son, who normally handled much of the work, was deployed till November somewhere near the Khyber Pass. His wife had passed the previous year, and Bill was on his own. So Dennis was helping Bill get ready for winter—making sure there was enough wood cut and stacked to heat the house and barn, repairing leaky roofs, and doing the other work needed around the property, including care and feeding of the animals: three cows, two horses, and a herd of sheep. Plus one bad-ass llama named Dolly. Who was as good at beating up any coyotes that dared threaten the flock as Dennis was at seeing to all of Bill's other needs.

Right now, with winter still a season away, the roofs repaired, and most of the firewood already cut, split, and stacked, Bill would be fine on his own—even if Dennis, while aiding me, should happen to be gone more than a few days.

Which I did not expect. After all, how long would it take to make it clear to our old acquaintance that, like the movie star Greta Garbo of old, all I vanted vas to be left alone?

Ah, great expectations. Me and Pip.

"Hop in," Dennis grinned, gesturing at the seat next to him, a seat that looked to have once been part of a newer, posher vehicle. A step up from the wooden bench he'd had bolted there the last time I rode shotgun. It even had a working seatbelt. Which was good, seeing as how, despite the new seat, Dennis had not gotten around to replacing the doors. As I hopped, per instructions, I noted another addition to Dennis's chariot. In place of the back seat was a very capacious, padlocked metal chest. Large enough, in fact, to hold half a dozen rocket launchers.

As he wiped his perennially smeared glasses with a none-too-clean handkerchief, Dennis nodded toward the road. His nonverbal way of asking, *Where to?*

"Kwanitewk," I replied, making the sinuous snake-like motion that means "river" with my right hand.

As we drove, I filled him in on my recent misadventure. Much of it through sign language, since the wind whipping through the open doors and the sound of his stereo playing the newest CD from Gary Farmer and the Troublemakers made normal conversation less than ideal. Mostly, though, we just drove. Enjoying each other's company. Talking is often overrated as a means of communication. Plus it might have interfered with Dennis's usual practice of reading while driving, a copy of the latest John Grisham thriller, *The Broker*, propped up on his steering wheel. As if going eighty miles an hour while turning pages was not suspense enough. At least for me.

It took three hours to reach the Long River State, where the Running Wolf Casino lurked at the foot of a bare hill. Recently bulldozed, it appeared. Probably prepped to add something just as lovely, garish, and greedy as the grim eyesore before us. Not the new Jerusalem—though it had plenty of pilgrims. More like Mordor reimagined in this once green and pleasant land. Lots of parking and handicap access, of course. How else would one drain the retirement accounts of elders such as those making their hesitant way off one of the buses Mook sent out on regular routes to ensnare septua and octogenarians, who were thrilled—if not hypnotized—by having bestowed upon them a delightful day trip, free food, and a twenty-dollar voucher each? "GET STARTED ON 12 HOURS OF EXCITEMENT!" proclaimed the slogan emblazoned in Day-Glo gold on the side of each of the numerous neon-blue air-conditioned night-mare buses parked in neat rows out front.

To say that in the casino lot we and our jeep stood out from the rest of the vehicles and occupants like bears at a bunny rabbit convention would be an understatement. And the sight of none other than Ricco Carlotti, the ersatz Sammy Loron, and two equally sunglassed retainers heading our way told us we had been spotted as soon as we arrived. But, to our surprise, all three of them raised their hands—empty of any expected weaponry—and grinned at us as they approached.

"Gentlemen," Ricco/Sammy gushed. "Welcome. Mr. Malsum is expecting you."

5

Now We're Talking

*The road does not go on
but you do*

The suite to which we were escorted held just as much subtle charm as the figure seated behind a desk only slightly smaller than the mixed martial arts ring we'd passed on our way to the elevator that took us—with the aid of the card Ricco slid into a slot—to the rarified air of the penthouse. A sybaritic man cave where everything that wasn't gilded or shining with silver was as plush and overdone as an orgy in a Fellini film.

"Nida-back!" Mook Glossian gushed, his mispronunciation of one of the simplest words in our language a perfect match for his insincerity. "My old friends! Great to see you both! Forgive me if I don't get up."

And why should he? Seeing as how his chair and desk were on a sort of dais that raised him four feet above us like a king on his throne.

"Nda," I said. Dennis nodded.

"Huh?" Mook replied, proving he was still as adept a conversationalist as he was a linguist.

"No—in simple English. No to everything and anything you are about to say."

We had been frisked on our way in. Bringing us in through the metal detector at the front door, which dinged convincingly when Ricco and his two bookends came in after us, had assured them we were the only souls in the room who were un-heeled. Polite ushers, still grinning like crocodiles, they'd followed two steps behind us.

Good for us. Not so good for them.

It's said that true masters of Pentjak silat, the martial art of Indonesia, can make themselves disappear. Whether or not that's so, I can't say. But it is certainly true that when you place your right foot behind you and then spin down onto your left knee, you vanish from the sight of anyone close behind you.

That move, accompanied by a straight strike to the solar plexus with your left fist, is so unexpected that the simple act of drawing a Sig Sauer from a shoulder holster is impossible. As is breathing when one's solar plexus has been impacted by said strike—as Ricco's was in the split second it took me to complete that move.

Not having studied the gentle art of that formerly Dutch archipelago, Dennis had taken a more direct approach to the two bruisers behind him. He'd simply raised both of his hands high toward the ceiling, stepped back between the men, and wrapped his twin pythons around them in such a way that their own arms were pinned to their sides.

Oh, and one more thing. As Ricco had dropped to the floor, I'd slipped my right hand into his jacket and removed his pistol. Which is how I knew it was a Sig Sauer. A P320, to be precise.

"Heyyyy," Mook said, holding up his hands, palms toward me. "No need for violence."

"Really?" I said. "So what was nonviolent about that attempt at turning my cabin into Swiss cheese?"

"Cheese?" Mook said, genuinely puzzled and clearly not at home with discussing any milk products other than the government commodity type. No whey, José. Not a Brie man at all.

"Holes made with bullets. Like the ones I'm tempted to put in you."

"Man," Mook said, shaking his head. "That was a major misunderstanding. A breakdown in communication. Those guys went way beyond what they were supposed to do. All they were supposed to do was, like, send you a message." Then he smiled, managing with that one forced facial expression to make himself look even shiftier than before. "But you're okay, right? And you're here, which is what I wanted all along."

"Ever hear of using a cell phone?" I asked, partially as a reminder of the fact that his own use of a cell phone was part of what had given him away when he was trying to thwart the Children of the Mountain.

"Would you have come if I'd called you?"

Good point.

"Unnnh," someone groaned to my right.

"Dennis," I said, "maybe a little less pressure on those guys you're bear-hugging."

Dennis opened his arms, allowing the two bodyguards to drop to their knees. Somehow he'd managed to slip his hands into their holsters, so that when he stepped back, he was holding his own twin versions of the P320 in my possession.

I looked back at Mook. "Okay," I said. "So I'm here. What do you want?"

Mook's grin got so much bigger, it looked as if his face was about to split. Not a pretty sight. He pulled back his hands and rubbed them together like a silent movie villain about to tie a damsel to the railroad tracks.

"Now we're talking," he said.

6

A Simple Task

The easy way
seldom takes you home

"Now, this is an offer . . . ," Mook began.

I held up my hand, the one that was approximately twenty-one ounces heavier due to the gun in it. "That I can't refuse," I said. "Stop doing a bad Brando in *The Godfather* and get to the point."

Mook looked displeased. Bad guys usually are when you interrupt their monologues. But he pressed on.

"Got a job for you," he said. "The kind of thing that you and Bluto there are good at."

"Rearranging the facial features of people who piss us off?" Dennis asked in the mildest of tones. He was now sitting in an easy chair in the corner of the room, which offered him both comfort and a clear field of fire. His feet were elevated on the backs of the two bodyguards, who had responded to his sign language command, using their confiscated pistols as pointers, that they were required to get down on all fours and serve as hassocks.

Mook ignored him, too dull to appreciate sparkling repartee.

"Our parent company's got a new Indian casino operation on the Northwest Coast. Deep Bluewater Resort. High-class place, even better than this. But there's been some, ah . . . problems. Like I said, the kind of thing you and, uh, . . . him are good at. You straighten it out, you get a good payday, and I get a job as casino manager there. Everybody's happy."

I always keep the back of my neck clean-shaven. But if I didn't, the hair there would have been standing up as soon as Mook said that

24

word—"problems." For a split second I was back in the deepwater dream that had woken me before my uninvited guests arrived. I was having one of my moments, the kind that made some of my ancestors gain a rep as mdawelak. Deep see-ers. What Siberian Buryats call shamans.

"How many?" I asked.

Mook looked puzzled. "How many what?"

"Dead," I replied.

Mook recovered quickly. "You saw it in the news? Far as I know, only the first two have been made public. Anyhow, it's four. Two regular workers, and the two kilt in the water—divers."

I have to admit, despite my deep-seated and richly deserved contempt for the person making me this offer, I was getting intrigued. It wasn't so much because of what he said as it was what I felt. A kind of calling. Like when you hear someone's voice and you know they are in distress, and your first instinct—for most people—is to head that way to see if you can help.

Mook picked up a letter opener shaped like a small samurai sword and began to clean his nails with it. Anyone who knows anything about reading body language would have understood what that meant. He was feeling in control, superior, almost contemptuous of Dennis and me.

"My people have brought in some experts—icky-ologists or whatever. Scientist types who know a lot about sharks, which might be what the problem is. But the locals—Natives like us . . ."

Mook paused, almost long enough for me to interject what I was thinking with regard to his use of that particular two-letter word. The punch line to that old joke where the Lone Ranger and Tonto find themselves facing a hundred Indians armed to the teeth and the masked man says, "Looks like they've got us surrounded." And Tonto replies, "What do you mean 'us,' kimosabe?" But I held my tongue because I wanted to see where the Mookster was going with this.

"They are saying it's some sort of water monster that's pissed about the work being done there. Right up your alley, I'm thinking. To say nothing of the fact that you two boys went through all that Navy Seal–type crap, right? So underwater stuff should be as easy as falling off a log, eh?"

Mook flicked something black out from under his right thumbnail. Luckily for him it did not fly off in my direction, or I would have made him eat it.

"So," he concluded, "that's why I figured you two would be perfect for this. And the pay will be good." He grinned, showing his teeth in a way that deepened his resemblance to a moray eel. "If you survive."

Yup, Mook's proposal was a win-win. If we succeeded, it would be a fair amount of moola for us and the gravy train for him. But if we failed, then he'd be rid of the two Penacooks whose geese he'd most like to see fricasseed.

I looked over at Dennis, who raised one eyebrow. I understood what that meant. Like me, he was getting interested. I was about to acquiesce to negotiations about our remuneration when Mook, who never knew when to quit while he was ahead, decided it was time to up the ante.

"Plus," he said, turning his computer around so that I could see the picture on it, "you do what I ask, and nothing happens to these two. Gah!"

That last exclamation had not been part of his planned speech. It was a reaction to what I did as soon as I saw whose images were on Mook's screen. Namely that I leaped over his desk, stripped the letter opener from his grasp, and spun it so that it pressed into the toad-like flab under his chin. Just hard enough to draw a drop of blood as I sat straddling his chest.

"What," I said, my voice a growling whisper, "have you done to them?"

The implicit threat that I was about to open his jugular like a piece of junk mail was not actually real. Killing people who upset me and threaten the lives of such friends of mine as Tim and his dog is not my first option in most cases.

Two of my beloved buddies, Tim and Pal. I'd assumed they were away, him at the Walter Reed hospital in D.C. for more surgery that just might make walking more than a pre-IED memory, and my favorite Lurp-dog, Pal, being cared for by his sister in Chevy Chase rather than bunking down with me. (The dog, not his female sibling, who was lovely but already hitched to an equally attractive airline pilot named Charlene.)

Mook's panic, however, was far from feigned. Both the look of terror on his face and the olfactory clue that he was going to have to change his knickers convinced me of that.

"Nothing," he managed to gasp. "I've done nothing to them. I was just trying to, you know, incentivize you."

I flipped the knife backhand so that it flew through the air and buried itself in the forehead of the picture Mook had pinned to the wall of the current resident of the White House. (And lest I be accused of being unpatriotic, let me assure you that the wall in general had been my target, and the impaling of any autographed photograph of Junior was purely fortuitous.)

I stood up and did a lazy cartwheel over the desk to land back in my chair. Yes, I am a showoff.

"In that case," I said, glancing at Dennis, who nodded at me as Mook struggled to right his chair and regain what little grain of dignity the Great Spirit had granted him, "we choose to accept the assignment."

7

Through the Dark

The more you need
the less you know

"We could've asked for more," Dennis said as he reclined his seat.

The fact that the person in the seat behind him neither complained nor let out a cry of anguish as his knees were crushed was not due to politeness on the part of that fellow traveler. It was, like the meal being served to us—an actual hot meal, not the typical compressed and overly processed airline food—simply a sign of our current status in first-class seats.

The amount of leg and elbow room afforded to our larger than average bods was a true luxury, especially with five more hours of flying time ahead of us on our red-eye. It meant we might actually be able to walk and not hobble down the jetway upon deplaning at dawn in misty Seattle.

It also helped mightily in reducing the flight anxiety, which was one of the things no end of hours of meditation had failed to banish from the reptilian part of my brain. The fact that I was not in an aircraft only slightly larger than a dragonfly with my knees pressed comfortably into my teeth also assisted in lessening my stress. But not removing it.

Still, despite the size of our current flying coffin, I found myself remembering what the anthropologist Robert Bruce told me happened back in 1990, not long after he boarded a plane in Mexico City with Chan Kin Viejo, the 110 (or more)-year-old patriarch of the Lacandon Mayan village of Naha, who he was taking to a gathering at Onondaga where indigenous elders from around the world came together to consider

28

the state of the world. I was at that gathering, too, having served as the chauffeur for the Missisquoi Abenaki chief, Homer St. Francis, and Mike Delaney, the tribal judge.

"You know what Chan Kin here did right after we took off on his first-ever plane ride?" Bruce asked me as we sat in a circle, me to his left and the self-possessed centenarian to his right. We were all waiting for the wampum belts to be brought out and explained by Lee Lyons.

"He peered out his window," Bruce continued, looking over at Chan Kin, who, with his long black hair and wearing rope sandals and a simple white toga-like chikal, seemed perfectly at home. "Then he said in Spanish, 'Ah, a long way down.'"

Bruce spread out his hands. "'Of course,' I agreed. Then he asked, 'If this place should fall, we would all die, yes?' And once again I had to agree."

Bruce chuckled. "You know what he said then? He said, 'Net soi, that is good. It is good we should all die together.'"

"We could've asked for more. Right?" Dennis repeated, drawing me back from my recollections of things past.

"True," I replied. "We might have demanded more. Such as a uniformed driver waiting with a stretch limo on our arrival."

"Uh, we did ask for that."

"Oops, forgot. But we might have insisted on double overtime hazard pay. After all, agreeing to do what we're about to do might involve us in a scenario worthy of Peter Benchley's darkest subaquatic fantasies."

"BUM-BUM-BUM-BUM, BUM-BUM-BUM-BUM," Dennis intoned in a baritone reminiscent of the ominous soundtrack for the film that wreaked havoc on Cape Cod's beach economy for a few years.

"But," I continued, "what good does more money do you when you're finding out firsthand how Jonah felt when he turned out to be the fish course? And after all, this is our kind of thing, isn't it?"

Dennis nodded and held up a large paw for me to high-five. "Yup, Podjo," he said. "And who else would be foolish enough?"

"Who, indeed," I replied. Then I turned back to the ocean-oriented book I'd been reading, one that might have some bearing on the hot water we'd soon be diving into. Better well-read than dead being one of my mottoes.

The densely written tome dealt with communications between humans and the delightful species whose Latin name is *Tursiops truncatus*. I'd learned that in a class I took at Dartmouth when I was toying with the idea of becoming a marine biologist—before dropping out to become an actual Marine. The gentle, playful bottlenose dolphin.

Or so you'd think if you've ever watched *Flipper*. Or seen that famous ancient Greek image of the boy riding the porpoise. Or heard any of the stories—most, admittedly, true—about porpoises deliberately saving drowning people.

But, as Dennis and I had learned, there's another side to the dolphin story, one you need to know if you want a real sense of porpoise.

Killer dolphins. Fellow combatants by the sides of us frogmen. And, on occasion, swimming suicide bombers. I won't say more than has already reached the public ear about dolphins being trained to act as spies on enemy shipping and even deliver magnetically attachable charges to the hulls of the boats of bad guys. Or say if the rumor is true that they can even be taught to kill targeted enemy scuba divers by ramming them in the belly with their snouts, rupturing a host of vital organs. Doing pretty much what they've done for millennia to sharks—which usually give schools of dolphins a very wide berth.

But I will say that I was always very careful to stay on the good side of this one male dolphin we worked with, who we all called Tough Guy. He had seven white crosses marked on the harness he always wore. They were way more than mere decoration. You did not want to piss off that porpoise.

I looked over at Dennis. Like me, he'd been eschewing headsets for either the sound channels or the movie showing on the drop-down screen. He'd been reading, and the book he held was one I'd lent him. The collected works of my favorite poet, William Stafford.

It was dark outside and I closed my eyes. No dreams this time, but when I opened my eyes again, I saw by my Mickey Mouse watch that half an hour had passed. Next to me, Dennis still had the book open to the same place. He was looking at it as if he'd been hypnotized, his thick glasses all the way on the end of his nose.

I peered over my buddy's massive shoulder to see what page it was he'd been staring at for the last half hour. Maybe make a joke about how well that speed-reading course he'd taken was working out. But when I saw it was the poem called "Traveling through the Dark," I deep-sixed that sort of flippancy. Half an hour was hardly enough for that one. I'll never lose the image of Stafford pushing that pregnant doe killed by a car off the edge of the late-night road.

I closed my eyes again and dove into the deep waters of memory.

Back when I was young, and aspiring to write, I actually paid a visit to that good gray poet. Way out in Lake Sunnydale, Oregon. It was summer break at Dartmouth—six months before Dennis and I decided to skip out of school, join the Armed Forces, travel, and meet interesting people who were trying to kill us.

I'd been corresponding with Bill—as all his friends called him, and as he'd been signing his letters—for months. He was a generous letter writer and, I'd learn, always treated everyone with the same unequivocal Quaker kindness. He read the poems I sent him and encouraged me to write more, even though some of them were pretty weak. The one that interested him most was called "Walking the Creek." It went:

It's dry, that old creek.
The white houses built
Upstream from our rez
Killed off everything
All the clear water
Where swam the brook trout
My buddy and I
Used to catch each spring
How many houses
Will they have to build
Before their own hearts
Go dry as our creek?

Yup, syllabics. Five per line. So shoot me. All I can say to defend myself is that's what my creative writing teacher was into back then.

Thinking back on it, I guess part of the reason he was so responsive to me was that I was Indian. William Stafford was part Indian himself, or at least he believed that. A tribe somewhere in the Northeast called the Crowfoot Indians is what he said.

I didn't hold it against him. At least he hadn't claimed to be descended from a Cherokee princess. I've run into so many would-be descendants of Red Royalty over the years (half of whom seem to think proving that genealogical link will guarantee their kids a free education or give them some kind of cash stipend from a government whose benefits provided to our various Native nations have historically included such generous gifts as plagues, removal from our homelands, and the kind of medical care from the Indian Health Service that ensures you'll never have any kids) that as my buddy Dennis put it once, "Those Cherokee princesses had to have been popping out little mixed-blood babies by the dozen."

"Come and visit us. We have a spare room."

That's how he ended the letter that sent me on my way the morning after I got it, knapsack on my back. I was supposed to report to football camp that week to get ready for the 1991 season, when Dennis and I would be freshmen. But knocking over tackling dummies and pushing sleds while coaches were barking like rabid dogs into my ear about putting my back into it, goddamn it, took a distant second place to being in the presence of a real poet. Since he walked on in 1993 at the age of seventy-nine, Stafford would have been about seventy-seven then.

So I thumbed my way across the map of Manifest Destiny they call the United States. Hiking the last two miles uphill from Portland to reach Bill's place in his Lake Sunnydale suburb, I saw the top part of a distant broken peak rising above the trees before the moss-covered roof of his house came into view. It had to be Mount St. Helens, who had blown her stack in 1980. Loo-wit, the fire-keeper. No longer looking like the perfect cone she'd been eleven years before.

As I was walking toward the door of the poet's house, a high voice came floating from the sky.

"Up here!"

I turned my gaze heavenward. There, at the top of a very tall evergreen to the left of the house, was William Stafford, balanced on the highest rung of the longest extension ladder I'd ever seen.

"Just trimming out some dead limbs," he called. "Be with you in a minute."

Was I impressed? Was I hoping I was not about to witness the unfortunate fatal fall of my favorite poet? Yup and yup.

Of course he made it down okay, chipper as a scrub jay and eager to introduce me to his home, where his wife had made dinner for us.

"Just in time to eat," he said as he ushered me in.

A decade older and supposedly wiser, I found myself wondering in retrospect if he had set things up for me. Brought out that ladder and scaled it just to be able to provide a little shock and awe to the fanboy. After all, I had called from town both to see if his invitation still stood and to let him know I had arrived and would be at his home in an hour or so. But it doesn't matter. His welcome was warm and sincere, and the spare bed he gave me turned out to be in his study just off the dining room. The same study where, after rising early every morning, he famously looked out the window and then wrote whatever came into his head.

"This is great, Mr. Stafford," I said.

"Call me Bill," he smiled. "If you want, you can use my typewriter." Then he gestured toward the old Smith Corona on the table by the window. (By the way, remember the typewriter? That mechanical thingy with no backlit screen or memory? Google the word if you're under the age of eighteen.)

Wow, I thought. *Tomorrow I am gonna get up, look out the window, and write a poem just like William Stafford does.*

I could hardly sleep. Words were running like deer through my head. When the first light came through the window, I jumped out of bed, scrolled a piece of paper into the typewriter, lifted my hands over the keys . . . and heard a familiar klack-klack-klack-klack sound from the next room. It was Bill Stafford writing his second poem of the morning on his spare typewriter.

I opened my eyes again, a smile on my face.

Dennis was looking at me. "Whatcha thinkin' about, Podjo? That tough little Iroquois gal of yours, Ruth?"

I shook my head. Dennis was not totally inaccurate, though, since Ruth had been on my mind an hour earlier. The relationship we'd developed after my stint with the Children of the Mountain was a pretty good one. Lots of mutual respect—both vertical and horizontal. Her third-degree black belt in Northern Shaolin made her a great match for my own eclectic Wu Su. Sparring with her was almost as much fun as the further physical activity we inevitably engaged in when left alone together for more than a few hours. And I shall refrain from describing that any further (because I am a gentleman), other than to say it always left me remembering my favorite song from the late, great Buddy Holly: "Oh Boy!"

I admired Ruth's activism for Native causes—of which there were always too many. Right then she was working on their rez to develop a combination substance abuse center and shelter for abused women. Plus, their community being nicely bisected by that invisible curse white folks call an international border, she was also deep into work regarding First Nations issues in Canada, such as its plans to develop the Athabaska oil sands in northern Alberta.

As a result of that, plus my own work and my reluctance to relocate closer to her neck of the woods, we had both, as the sainted Rosemary Clooney put it, become "aware that our love affair was too hot not to cool down" and agreed—maybe Ruth more than me—to part as friends.

"Him," I said, pointing my lips toward the book Dennis was holding in his catcher's mitt–sized fist, still open to the same poem.

"Oh," he said. He tapped the page delicately with the little finger of his right hand. "I been thinking about this poem."

"Which explains why I could smell feathers burning."

Dennis grinned. "It's a good one. Gave me a lot to think about. But, you know what?"

"What?" I said.

"I mean, if he didn't have a knife or the time to field dress it, why didn't he just load it into his trunk and take it home? I mean, that's a lot of venison he let go to waste."

I just nodded. Dennis, the practical Indian romantic. What could I say?

8

Final Destination

*Should the hand always want
what the eye sees?*

O ur flight arrived forty-five minutes early. Sort of an unexpected surprise. I actually was able to walk off the plane without my legs shaking. Another surprise, which I chalked up to
my fond memories of those two old men who'd each inspired me. Followed by the equally pleasant recollections of the time Ruth and I had
spent together. Gone, perhaps, but not forgotten. Ah, yes, Mr. Proust,
things past.

But yet another surprise was waiting for us when we arrived at the
baggage claim area at Sea-Tac Airport.

We were not there because we had any baggage to pick up. It was just
where our toad wolf unfriend had told us that the Deep Bluewater driver
would meet us. Dennis and I always traveled light whenever we flew—
the sort of heavy ordinance we packed when driving anywhere being
frowned on up in the friendly skies. Mook had assured us we would be
re-heeled with weaponry of our choice as soon as we reached our final
destination.

(He made those words "final destination" sound even more ominous
than George Carlin always does in his rap about air travel. Carlin's had
his struggles in recent years, but he's still got a keener intellect than
almost any other comedian.)

Having nothing other than hand luggage had not prevented Dennis
from engaging in the sort of joking that might have ended up with us
being escorted to a private room for an extended chat.

35

"Hey," he said as he put his backpack and shoulder bag on the conveyor belt. "It says you are only allowed two, but I've got three dead raccoons in here."

He winked at the security guard, who looked vastly unamused. "Carrion," he said. "Get it?" Then he grinned at the blonde woman studying the x-ray machine and trying not to smile. "Can I have her for the strip search?"

For some reason, they let him through. I was the one who was taken aside to be wanded and patted down. Go figure.

Dennis had been entranced by the bronze statue of a Seattle Seahawk, then the Dungeness Bay Seafood House (luckily not yet open) and the various other eateries that we passed. I managed to keep him going, feeling like the owner of a bird dog trying to lead his retriever past a duck farm. But I was still in the lead when we reached the escalator. As a result, it was moi who observed the first surprise awaiting us.

There, holding up a sign with our hand-printed names almost spelled correctly on it, was our driver. Not a bored, black-capped, professionally suited male chauffeur, but a tall, broad-shouldered young woman with long black hair and abalone shell earrings. She looked like a winner of that Miss Indian World contest they hold every year at the Gathering of Nations in Albuquerque. Short blue jean jacket with beaded bird shapes on it. Skinny jeans with strategically placed holes in the knees and thighs.

Yup, she was good-looking, but as I was thinking while the escalator brought us closer, she also had that "I know who I am and you will not mess with me, bozo" look about her, which is way more attractive than the "do with me what you will" appearance of those Miss America girls that Donald Trump so enjoys groping.

"Raven Tillamook," she said in a firm voice, holding her hand out toward me as I tripped on the final stair of the escalator.

Suavely recovering, I took the proffered hand, barely managing to prevent myself from dropping to one knee. "Uh, I'm Jacob . . ."

"But you can call him a cab," Dennis boomed, pushing me aside to shake Raven's hand. "And I'm his bodyguard, Dennis."

He grinned back at me, ignoring the daggers in my return stare.

"So," Dennis said, "the first question is where can we get something to eat? I ate all my carrion on the plane."

"Luggage?" Raven asked, looking over her shoulder toward the door in what seemed, strangely enough, to be a furtive manner.

"No," I said in a firm voice, re-establishing my role as the leader of our team as I glowered at my overly verbose buddy.

"Good," Raven said, turning toward the farthest door and breaking into a walk so fast that it was almost a sprint. "Follow me."

Six words. That was all she'd spoken thus far in a voice that was, though clipped, decidedly melodic.

Only six words. But enough to make the limbic system of my brain start playing that old Elvis hit: "I can't help falling in love with you."

Ah, the good old limbic system. That place in the temporal lobe where such emotions as fear and love are located, where the always yearning amygdala is constantly receiving input from such brain functions as memory and attention.

And I was getting boring. But running through that scientific explanation of what was happening to me as I followed was my way of coping with the runaway train that hit me as I looked into Raven's dark eyes.

"Hey, Podjo," Dennis said, "I bet she knows a good place to get fresh salmon. They cook it on a plank out here, you know. Salmon for breakfast. Although what with the time change, it's like lunchtime back home, right?"

I looked back toward him, but said nothing. I let him babble on. Hunger always does that to Dennis, turns him into a motor-mouth until he can stuff his maw.

Suddenly I was no longer feeling love-struck. Why? Because what I had seen over Dennis's shoulder had sobered me up like a pail of ice water poured over my head.

A few feet ahead of us, Raven was holding the door open and gesturing for us to follow. Which we did. Dennis thinking about brunch, and me about what I had just seen entering the main door of the terminal a hundred yards behind us.

A bored, black-capped, professionally suited male chauffeur, bearing a large sign with the words DEEP BLUEWATER emblazoned across the top and bearing our names, properly spelled, in black block letters.

Maybe we'd reached our final destination after all.

9

Let's Go

The last one to know
may be the first one to decide

There's this character in one of our Penacook stories. She's called Woman Who Walks Alone. You might say she is the embodiment of the sort of female independence all our people used to take for granted back before anyone on this continent had to worry about women's liberation.

As we followed Raven toward her illegally parked vehicle, that is who she was now reminding me of. It's said that Woman Who Walks Alone runs with the wolves and sleeps with the bears in their dens. Her voice is so sweet that she teaches the birds their songs. No mother or aunt is there to tell her what to do as she braids wildflowers into her hair. If she sees a man she likes, she may just call to him and he'll follow her. Together they will lie down on a bed of mosses high on the mountainside. But when the morning comes, she will rise and leave him behind.

And in some darker versions of that tale, he will not rise ever again, and his bones will bleach white on the mountain.

"On the other hand," Dennis was saying, "steak and eggs wouldn't be bad, eh? Diner food's just fine in a pinch."

I dropped back next to him. "Dennis," I whispered. "She's not who . . ."

Dennis put his fingertips on my arm. "It's cool," he said in an equally soft voice. "I saw the real driver, too. Wanna just see how this plays out?"

"Come on," Raven called to us from her vehicle fifty feet away. "Let's get going."

Five whole words. Spoken in a decidedly nervous voice.

Enough, I thought. *Forget about playing it out. We're the visiting team on a strange field.*

"One question," I said, not stepping any closer to the car—a markedly un-limo-like old Jeep Cherokee with the back door missing on the driver's side. A true soulmate to Dennis's buggy. His eyes had lit up as it came into view, and he was stroking its right front fender the way another man might pet a beloved dog.

"Yes," she said, her eyes briefly meeting mine before quickly looking off to the side. The kind of "tell" about doing something dishonest that only an amateur would allow herself to show.

"How dumb do you think we are?"

She looked back at me, clearly trying to make the look on her face an innocent one. But not doing that good a job of it. Try that sometime; even the most accomplished liars find that a hard task to accomplish, continuing to look guilt-free when someone has caught on to their game.

I looked back over my shoulder toward the distant driver standing at the foot of the same escalator on which Dennis and I had so recently descended.

But when I returned my gaze to Raven, to my surprise her feigned look of innocence had been replaced by something else: a broad smile that had a tinge of mischief in it.

"Dumb enough?" she asked, raising her eyebrows, holding her hands out palm up, and gesturing with her chin back toward the jeep.

Don't ask me why, but for some reason I decided right then and there to trust this woman we'd never met before. Part of it was that unspoken voice that I sometimes hear deep in my brain, telling me what to do or not do in situations where normal reasoning might lead me in the opposite direction. And part of it, to be totally honest, was that smile of hers.

"Podjo?"

Dennis was standing by the open back doorway of the Cherokee. During our brief dialogue, he'd taken it upon himself to do something typically practical—namely scope out potential problems with that proposed ride, by leaning into the unlockable vehicle and checking out its contents.

"Clean," he said. "At least weapon-wise." Then he tossed his backpack onto the seat and climbed into the back.

"Okay," Raven said, pulling from her skinny jeans a set of keys connected to a large beaded fob in the shape of a black bird and turning toward the jeep. "Let's go."

I sighed, thinking again of that not-so-old story about the idiots who chose to follow Woman Who Walks Alone.

Then I tossed my bag in next to Dennis and hopped into the front seat.

"Okay," I said. "Let's go. Just don't talk my ear off."

10

The Same Old Song

The road does not go anywhere
It just stays where it is

I had vowed to myself that I would not be the first to break the silence. At least conversationally. Between the wind whipping in through the opening where that back door used to be, some hopefully superfluous part of the vehicle rattling beneath us, and Dennis tunelessly attempting to hum what I think was a Hootie and the Blowfish song, it was far from quiet inside the Cherokee. "Only Wanna Be with You" from *Cracked Rear View*?

We were now on the 99 heading north toward Seattle only thirteen miles away from us, the traffic light that early in the morning. Our dark-haired driver saying nothing, concentrating on the road and now and then checking the rear-view above her windshield—the place on her door where the driver's-side mirror had been now displaying nothing other than a few sheared and rusting bolts. A match for the extra bolt left over from some previous repair that was rolling around by my feet.

So I sat there amusing myself with my own thoughts, which at that moment were to attempt to mentally enumerate all the various products of Detroit crossing the continent bearing the stolen names of dispossessed, slandered indigenous nations and murdered leaders. Apache, Cherokee, Comanche, Dakota, Navajo, Pontiac, Renegade, Seneca, Winnebago. I was pondering just how to fit in the Thunderbird when the bird woman at the wheel cleared her throat.

"Yes?"

"Don't you guys want to know where I'm taking you?"

Hallelujah, the conversational dam had burst. Ten words. Almost as many as the total of everything she'd uttered before entering her car.

"Yes," I said. Mr. Monosyllable.

"Our chief," she said. "He wants to see you."

In the back seat, Dennis the off-key jukebox had transitioned to his own version of "Mammas Don't Let Your Babies Grow Up to Be Cowboys," in which the word "cowboys" was replaced by "Indians," and new lines such as "Don't let 'em build tipis, sweat lodges, and such, let 'em grow up to be BIA crooks" were inserted.

"Chief?" I asked.

She nodded. "That's why I hijacked you guys. So you can hear our side of the story before you get hit with all the Deep Bluewater propaganda."

"Okay," I said, thinking why stop now with my one-word prompts that seemed to be priming her verbal pump?

"You know," she said, "they took it all away from us in the fifties."

I did know. Outside of Indian Country, there aren't many who know just how dark those years of the mid-fifties were for our tribal nations. Termination.

The federal government's idea was once again to "help" the Indians. Like the Dawes Allotment Act, which chopped up the Oklahoma reservations and opened what had been meant to be Indian Territory forever to the Oklahoma land rush, in which thousands of white settlers flooded in to grab their 160 acres full of sunshine. Or the Indian Reorganization Act, or the blight of the Indian boarding schools that stole our kids from their homes for the better part of a century. All in the name of bringing us such blessings of civilization as poverty, welfare, and alcohol and drug dependency, and making us more a part of the fabric of a nation that was still not acknowledging its past treachery or accepting us for who we were.

"I tremble for my country when I reflect that God is just." Words spoken on his deathbed by none other than President Thomas Jefferson, that good old slave-owning Founding Father.

Termination meant just that, ending the reservations. Raven's last name, Tillamook, was the name of one of the tribal nations that had suffered from that process. After the so-called "Rogue River Wars," in which various tribal nations of what became southern Oregon and northern California tried to resist the taking of their lands and the murder of their people during the gold rush of the early nineteenth century, no less than twenty-seven different tribes were herded together onto something called the Siletz Reservations. Originally a coastal strip of about a million acres, it was whittled away by brutal federal policies until Congress passed the Western Oregon Termination Act, ending the government-to-government relationship with the Siletz Tribes. And paying each tribal member a whopping $250 to compensate them.

The Confederated Tribes of Siletz Indians was one of the first tribal groups to successfully lobby Congress to repeal the Termination Act as it applied to them. They got back federal recognition in 1977. But not that million acres.

It's the same old song.

While I was recollecting all of that happy history, Raven was talking as she drove. Not slowing down either her vehicle or her monologue as she took one screeching turn and then another. My method of giving her space to talk had not just opened the floodgates, it had breached all the levees. And what spilled out proved that my initial comparison of her to Miss Indian World had been spot-on. According to the competition's rules, the title should go to someone "who demonstrates a deep understanding of her culture, traditions, people and history." She was explaining in great detail the parallel history of the government's betrayal of her people farther to the north of the Siletz, me nodding while Dennis kept serenading us from the back seat—this time with what I barely recognized as "Money for Nothing."

The first thing, I thought, *that I am going to do whenever we get anywhere near an Army-Navy store is pick up a nice lock-blade knife for Dennis and hand it to him with a chunk of wood.*

When he's whittling, he doesn't attempt (emphasis on that last word) to sing anything.

"They're after us!" Raven said, her voice becoming even more intense.

"Unh-hunh," I agreed, using the good old Penacook word for yes that is used today by every American. Then, figuring I owed her at least a few more words, I added, "Washington always is."

"No!" Raven said, adjusting her rear-view mirror. "Not D.C., dummy. Those guys!"

I turned around to look behind us. Two cars were following us closely, black Buicks with tinted windshields.

"You sure?" I said.

"Didn't you see when I got off the highway, turned right, then turned right again to get back on? They stayed behind us the whole way."

Oh.

No, lost in the dark mists of past governmental infamy, I had not. Shame on me.

"She's right," Dennis said. I also had not noticed that he'd stopped murdering a medley of melodies. "They're following us for sure."

Bad guys in pursuit? Great.

Déjà vu all over again.

11

Getting Gas

When in doubt
stop doubting

When you've seen a lot of movies—like pretty much everyone in America over the age of four—you know how a car chase goes. Pursuer and pursuee with their pedals to the metal. Lots of dodging in and out of traffic, sideswiping the occasional car, bus, and tractor-trailer. Bad guys leaning out their windows with the required ordinance: pistols, AK-47s, even the occasional rocket launcher. Much screaming, crunching of metal, explosions, fire, all that jazz. And, of course, the requisite shocking turn of events when there's an abrupt crossing of lanes and they're suddenly going the wrong way, dodging traffic.

Not so shocking, of course, since it is now decades since William Friedkin—whose movie *The French Connection* has been the standard for car chases since 1971—woke up from a nightmare about driving the wrong way on the L.A. Freeway and said to himself, "I gotta get this into a movie." The result of which was William Petersen doing just that in *To Live and Die in L.A.* in 1985.

Anyhow, what we were doing was not that. Unless we were in slow motion. Perhaps because, even with Raven flooring the gas pedal, we were not going faster than a sedate—by car-chase standards—sixty miles an hour. Even being passed by impatient drivers giving us the friendly "You're number one!" hand signal.

"Please," I said, turning around and shaking my head at Dennis, who had just broken into (or maybe thrown a brick through the window of) Guy Clark's classic "L.A. Freeway." "Not now."

Dennis smiled and made the zipping-my-lip sign with his thumb and index finger.

"Oh no," Raven said.

"Don't worry, he's not going to start singing again."

"What is wrong with you two?'

"Nothing a little chicken soup and an understanding shoulder to cry on can't fix," I said.

"*Look!*" she said, tapping the dashboard display. The arrow on the gas gauge had just buried itself below the E—standing for "Eeek!" at that particular moment in time. "I was going to fill up on our way from the airport," she said. "There wasn't time enough on my way there if I was going to make it in time to . . ."

"Kidnap us?" I asked. "No problem. There's a sign for gas. Just take the next exit."

She jerked her chin over her shoulder.

"They will, too," she said.

"Indeedy-do," I replied, picking up the bolt that I'd pinned down with my right foot. "I'm counting on it."

Still proceeding at slow-motion car-chase speed, Raven stuck her arm out her window to signal a right turn.

"Really?" I asked. "Your turn signal is broken, too?"

She just shrugged.

As we pulled into the lot of the Kwiky-Stop gas station, I stepped out of the still-moving car before we were halfway to the pump, then turned to stand in the middle of the road with my arms spread out, a benefi-cent look on my face. Sort of like a crucified martyr. Which meant that the lead car of the two black pursuit vehicles found itself having to either stop or run me over. With the second Buick close behind it, there was no way it could back up.

That simple move I'd learned in Pentjak—stepping deeply behind my right leg with my left as I dropped down—made me disappear from the vehicle's field of vision for a moment to pop up next to the door on the driver's side.

"This is one way," my old pendetta had explained as he taught it to me, "that we earned the reputation of being magicians back in Sumatra. Being able to disappear from our opponent's view to reappear as if from nowhere." Then he had smiled. "One way. But there are other ways as well."

Which I will not discuss just now.

I then tapped gently on the driver's window to get his attention. Well, not all that gently. And since I did my tapping with that bolt I'd picked up from the floor of Raven's jeep, the result was that the plexiglass shattered into a shower of popcorn-sized pieces.

"Ooops," I said, shrugging regretfully at the driver, who was decorated like a Christmas tree with shiny plexiglass shards. "Don't you just hate it when that happens?"

The bulge under the right side of his coat meant several things. First, that he was right-handed. Second, to paraphrase Mae West, that it probably was a pistol in his pocket, and not that he was glad to see me. Third, because it remained there, that either his anger management classes were working or he was under orders not to damage my merchandise. After all, he was the same driver I'd last seen waiting in vain for us at the bottom of the stairs in the airport. I knew that from my keen talents of observation—and the sign with the names of Dennis and myself on the seat next to him.

The sound of a window being rolled down behind me turned my attention away from the driver, who was sitting stoically like a statue. Admirable self-control, that.

"Hey, brother," a voice from the back seat said. "No need for that."

I peered inside the car at the large middle-aged man who'd just uttered those conciliatory words. His long black hair and buffalo-nickel features, along with the abundance of silver turquoise in his finger rings, bolo tie, concho necklace, and hatband, made him as obviously Native—in a sort of modern stereotyped way—as Tonto with his buckskins and feathers was in the old *Lone Ranger* TV series. If he stood up, I had no doubt I'd see a huge silver and turquoise belt buckle and tribally decorated Tony Lama boots. Probably equipped with a briefcase covered with beadwork like the one I saw Russell Means lugging through Chicago O'Hare on his way to his first-class seat to Los Angeles.

Indian, yup. I didn't doubt that. But that internal voice my elders had taught me to trust was also telling me that there was something about him—behind the Hollywood tribal leader facade—that was just plain wrong.

A tanned hand was thrust in my direction.

"You must be Jacob Neptune, right? I'm Chief Sea Antelope, CEO of Deep Bluewater."

I nodded.

Chief Sea Antelope. Right. And who gave him that name? Unless it was himself? Which was why he could say it with a straight face.

He thrust his hand farther in my direction, lifting himself up off the seat as he did so.

I suspected that if I took that offered hand, the result would be some sort of nowadays Injun handshake, involving various hand positions, wrist grasps, and the like—showing membership in the Real Red Brothers Club. So I just brushed his fingertips with mine.

"Uh, all right," Chief S.A. said, his enthusiasm a bit more feigned than formerly. Then he waited for my reply.

I stayed silent. True silence, if not golden, is usually at least turquoise. One of the best ways to get people to talk is to say nothing. It's an old interrogation tactic that is a lot more effective than torture. Forget waterboarding; just keep your lip zipped and wait.

It had the desired result.

"So, Jake, why didn't you wait for your ride? Carlo here was hurt when he found out you'd already left."

First of all, nobody calls me Jake. Second, from the lemon-sucking expression on Carlo's face, the only hurt applicable to him would be the hurt he was aching to put on me.

"But no harm, no foul. Just you and your friend hop in. Okay. Plenty of room back here. Even a minibar if you want some firewater. Ho ho."

Ho ho, indeed. My face impassive, I looked at him. Actually at his forehead. With the kind of look you use when someone has a spider crawling across his noggin. He lifted a nervous hand to run it back across his hair, just to make sure there was nothing there.

"Well," he said.

I almost replied "pump," but somehow guessed that he wasn't playing a word-association game. Time to break the silence, I supposed.

"We're okay," I said, as I felt a hand placed gently on my shoulder. Raven and Dennis had just come up behind me, and it was her hand. "My friend here decided to meet us, and when your man Carlo here didn't show up, we accepted her offer of a ride and a little sightseeing. She'll get us to Deep Bluewater in plenty of time for"—I looked back at Raven, who was now squeezing my shoulder just about hard enough to bruise it—"dinner?" I said.

She nodded.

Chief Sea Antelope looked at the three of us, deciding what to do next—short of the bodily violence that he realized would have to be employed to change our plans.

Then he smiled. "Righht, righht," he said. "You young folks go ahead. I'll see the *two*—and he did emphasize that word—"of you in our wonderful World of Water Restaurant at seven."

He held his smile in place for almost as long as it took for that tinted power window to roll back up. But not quite long enough to keep me from getting a glimpse of that smile morphing into a teeth-bared grimace, like a great white shark about to bite a seal in half.

As the two black vehicles pulled away, Dennis looked at me.

"Sea Antelope?" he said. "Are you kidding me?"

"Sherman," Raven said. "Sherman Washington. That's what his birth certificate said before he got in with the casino people. He never had a real Indian name until then. Nor did anyone in his whole family after his great-grandparents met at Carlisle."

"Chief?" I asked.

Raven looked for a minute as if someone was asking her to swallow a bug. Then she nodded. "By two votes in the last tribal election. On the 'Prosperity for All' ticket."

Ah, the wonders of majority rule in twentieth-century tribal politics. In the old days, before so-called democracy was forced on our tribal nations by the benevolent U.S. government (cue the Thoreau quote), most of our communities made their decisions by consensus—even if it took days or weeks for everyone to talk it over before coming to an agreement. Then along came the Indian Reorganization Act of 1934.

Some of our nations have managed to live with it, but in far too many cases, what was introduced was not just the idea of "one man, one vote" but also the Tammany Hall vote-buying, one-party-domination kind of corruption that went with it. And, yes, Tammany Hall was named after the Lenape leader Tamanend, the one who famously stated around 1683 that his people and the English would "live in peace as long as the waters run in the rivers and creeks and as long as the stars and moon endure."

Oh yeah!

We walked back to Raven's jeep parked by the pump, where an attendant—oblivious to the power play we'd just experienced—was screwing the gas cap back on.

"I got it," I said, handing the gas jockey two twenties. "We're on an expense account."

"Plus five of these," Dennis said, holding up the buffalo jerky he'd just liberated from the rack in front of the store.

Soon we were back in the rattletrap jeep, Dennis in the back seat managing to hum "We're off to see the wizard" despite the dried buffalo meat he'd stuffed into his mouth.

"So," I said, as I knotted together the two loose ends of my broken seatbelt, "who is it we're going to see now?"

"Our real chief," Raven said, thrusting her foot down hard on the accelerator. "My grandfather."

12

Totems

Never take a long walk
on a short dock

Where Raven took us was far from an elegant casino. It was a
downtown coffee shop, near Pioneer Square. Although the
square had been cleaned up a bit over the last decade—
which meant moving out any so-called "drifters" hanging around it—it
still had an air of faded colonial elegance about it.

As we alighted from the jeep—whose passenger door almost came
off in my hand as I opened it—I paused to take in the sights of the
square: the Iron Pergola, the old brick buildings, the bearded guy who
obviously knew nothing about the banks in the city since his sign read
ONLY JESUS SAVES, and then that totem pole. As if its name was not bad
enough for my aboriginal sensitivity, Pioneer Square was dominated by
a tall totem pole facing north up First Avenue. Various birds and animals playing piggyback all the way up to what looked to be our local
guide-slash-abductor's namesake at the very top.

All joking aside, it looked both stately and sad standing there.

Respect, I thought. *I give you respect.*

I felt ready to drop to one knee in front of it.

Raven saw me looking at it. "Grampop will tell you a story about
that," she said. Then she grinned, a really nice wide smile that made
her look as if the sun was shining from her face. (Be still, my heart!)
"He always does."

The coffee shop—with the words OUR COFFEE, YOUR COFFEE HOUR
hand-lettered on its quaint front window—was not a Starbucks, which
would not be remarkable anywhere other than this historic district of

51

the city. Seattle is, after all, the place where the Starry Dollars brand was pioneered before it set out to take over the majority of America's caffeine addicts. Irrelevant facts tend to lodge themselves in my brain after I read them somewhere, and the opening of the first Starbucks in this moss-covered Northwest metropolis was one of those trivia-quiz tidbits tucked away somewhere in the recesses of my brain.

The tall, silver-haired man wearing rimless eyeglasses who put down his cell phone and stood up from a corner table as we entered was even more remarkable. Unlike the first self-proclaimed chief we'd just met, he was not a "name brand" stereotype. His long hair, pulled back into a ponytail that made his high, wide forehead more prominent, was held in place by a rawhide string. Aside from a bolo tie with a clasp in the shape of a raven with outspread wings—which looked to have been carved from the same red cedar as most totem poles—he wasn't wearing any jewelry. None of those pounds of turquoise and silver that added so much weight to Sea Antelope that the casino CEO probably would have sunk like a lump of lead to the bottom of the bay if he'd ever fallen into the water.

"Luther George," Raven's grandfather said, looking over the top of his glasses at me and touching his chest with his right palm. His voice was deep, but gentle. Just hearing him speak his name made me want to hear more of that voice, which reverberated in me like a drumbeat.

But instead of saying anything further, he just extended his right hand.

I took it without hesitation. It was a working man's hand, strong, long-fingered, callused, and smooth with age. His grasp was gentle, though. He let go to take Dennis's hand, who was standing there looking as mesmerized as I was by this man's presence. My guess was that my best bud was also half a second away from dropping to one knee and saying, "I'm not worthy." Some elders are like that; there's a sort of aura around them that you feel. Not like a force field. More like an embrace. The first time I experienced that was when I went to an AIM meeting where Phillip Deere, the Muskogee medicine man, was speaking. It was a year or two before he walked on to the spirit world in '85. After his talk—about how the majority can often be wrong—there was a sort of meet-and-greet. I'll never forget how, when he came to me, he put his left hand on my shoulder, looked at me, and then started to smile and shake his head. He didn't say a word, but it was like we were sharing a joke that no one else was hearing. Then he moved on.

Now, don't get me wrong. I am not saying this is just an Indian thing. The first time I met the Dalai Lama—who had glasses just like the ones

Luther George wore—I knew I was in that same sort of presence. I'd walked the last twenty miles to Dharamshala in India. If it had been possible, I would have walked the whole way from where Dennis and I had been stationed in Afghanistan. There was a lot I had to be cleansed of back then. When I bowed my head and he put that scarf around my neck, it felt as if electricity was coursing though my body. Then he leaned close to whisper in my ear, "Young man, you know I am just a humble monk."

Luther George let go of Dennis's hand. He looked up at us over the top of his glasses and made a circling motion with his hand before letting it fall like a leaf to rest palm down on the table.

The three of us pulled out chairs and took our places. Luther George took one final look at his cell phone, which had some sort of game on its screen, then turned it off and dropped it into his shirt pocket.

Then we all sat there, no one saying anything.

I took the opportunity—force of habit—to scope out the room. One main room, ten tables with four chairs each, and ours the only occupied one. A counter to the far left of the room, where a glass case displayed pastries, and a variety of items related to the making of various non-alcoholic beverages were arranged on shelves. A tall young man, the single server behind said counter, who had nodded at us as we entered, was the only other person there. To the far right of the room, past several photos on the wall that depicted various aspects of tribal life, most connected with the ocean, were two signs reading RESTROOMS and EMERGENCY EXIT, with arrows that pointed to an unseen area around the corner.

"See that pole out there?" Luther George finally said, pushing back his glasses and looking toward the square.

Sitting by her grandfather's side, Raven raised one eyebrow at me. *Here we go.*

Both Dennis and I nodded.

"There's stories about that pole and how it got here. Some, nice sweet little stories, are in them printed guides to Seattle, and some, which are not quite so nice and sweet, are told by our people. But the one thing they all agree on is that it's a Tlingit pole from Alaska. Kooteeyaa is what those Tlingits call them cylindrical chiseled ones. Not totems. Totem, now that there is a word from way back east where you boys come from. Right?"

Dennis and I nodded again in perfect unison. Whatever he had to say, we just wanted Luther George to keep talking in that deep storyteller's voice of his. We'd both been suckers for tales told by elders ever since we were little kids on Abenaki Island listening to my Uncle John.

We also nodded because Raven's grandfather had been dead-on about the word "totem." It's a real Native word, but as foreign to the indigenous nations of the Northwest as the English word "guitar" (with its roots in the Greek word "kithara") would have been to a kora-playing West African. Odoodema is how our Anishinabe cousins said it—the kinship group to which you belong.

"So," Luther George said, leaning back in the old wooden chair he occupied like a throne, "the nice story about it is that it came from a village in Alaska, back in the gold rush days when this was the jumping-off place for prospectors hoping to strike it rich." He chuckled. "Didn't have any Indian casinos back then. Anyhow, back in 1897, a group of prominent citizens who were members of the Chamber of Commerce— the Committee of Fifteen, they called themselves—bought the pole on a trip to Alaska, brought it back, and presented it to the city. Which had it set up"—he paused and then continued, using a cultured voice like you'd hear in a documentary film—"to commemorate Seattle's part in the development of Alaska."

He took a sip from the coffee cup on the table before dropping back into his normal voice.

"But here's where the plot sickens," he continued. "In 1938 someone poured kerosene on the base of the pole and set it on fire. Nobody ever found out who. The powers that be had gotten real attached to that pole as a symbol of their city, so they sent what was left of it up to the village in southeast Alaska where it had come from, and then"—he returned to the documentarian tone—"Tlingit craftsmen graciously carved a reproduction, which was erected and dedicated with tribal blessings."

He paused, took another sip of coffee, and looked out the window. "Like I said, nice, sweet story, eh? But that's not how we tell it. What happened is that those fifteen prominent citizens were on a trip to Alaska, and the ship they were on stopped at a place called Fort Tongass, where there was a Tlingit village. From the boat they saw that big pole set up in front of one of the houses and liked it real well. So they sent three sailors ashore to get it. They chopped it down like a tree, sawed it in half, rolled it down to the beach, rowed it out, and hoisted it onboard. Seems everyone in that village was away fishing, so there was no one to stop them. Those sailors were paid a whopping two dollars and fifty cents for their efforts, and Seattle ended up with a stolen totem pole as a symbol of their fair city.

"Tlingits tried to get it back. It belonged to the Raven Clan, the kind of kooteeyaa called a commemorative pole. It had been put up in honor of a woman who drowned. When the city refused to return it to them, they asked to at least be compensated what it was worth—about twenty thousand dollars. But that never did happen. So that pole stood there for four decades, Raven on top of it looking out on First Avenue. Then it got burned."

Another sip of coffee and a longer pause. Luther George held up his cup. "You boys want to order something? On me. Anything you want— except Tazo tea. I can call the server over."

Much as we wanted to hear the rest of the story—which we knew was coming, like the punch line in a joke—we nodded. When an elder offers you food or drink, you can't refuse. He waved his hand at the big blond kid behind the counter, who grinned and waved back, exposing the tribal tattoo circling his forearm.

"Be right with you, Chief," he called, putting down the blender he'd been washing.

"My great-nephew," Luther George said. "Billy. Best tight end on any local high school squad. His mom owns this place. Family business here."

"Chief?" I said.

"I suppose so," he said. "Get whatever you want. Pastries, too."

We ordered—iced tea for me, black coffee for Dennis, along with a plate of those pastries. Chief George waited for the order to arrive before saying anything further.

"Go ahead," he said.

Then he waited as I drank my tea and Dennis demolished half a dozen donuts, wiping his mouth with one paper napkin and neatly folding half a dozen more to place them in his hip pocket.

"Never know when you'll need one a' these," he said. "And these sure are nice thick ones."

Chief George nodded.

Then we waited some more.

Neither Dennis nor I said anything, even though the amount of time we were kept in suspense would have made the average white person start squirming in their seat. Or ask him to continue. Or maybe just get up in exasperation and leave.

We were being tested.

"Sooo," Chief George said a good five minutes later, adjusting his glasses again, "the city fathers wanted a totem pole just like it, and like

I said before, they turned to the place it came from. 'How much would it cost to make us another one just like this?' they asked the elders' council in that village at Fort Tongass.

"'Well,' the elders' council told them, 'that pole would cost twenty thousand dollars. Cash. Paid in advance.'

"The city fathers of Seattle figured that was a fair price. So they got the money together and handed it over to the Tlingits.

"'Thank you very much for paying us for that pole you took back in 1897,' the elders said. 'Now, if you'd like us to make you one to replace it, that'll be another twenty thousand dollars.'"

Chief George nodded toward the forty-foot-tall pole outside, visible through the coffee shop's front window. "And there it stands," he said.

Dennis and I both nodded. And waited.

Chief George slowly finished his coffee. Then he sat there for a while, looking into the cup like a fortune-teller reading tea leaves. Finally, he rubbed his hands together.

"Sooo," he said. "Want to know why we kidnapped you?"

"I don't know if I'd call it that," I said.

"I would," Raven interjected. And that was a very good sign. When a woman starts teasing you, at least in Indian Country, that's a good indication that she's interested.

Chief George looked fondly at her. "My granddaughter is a lot like my late wife. She's got a way of making sure things go the way she wants them to. It was her idea to shanghai you boys, you know."

I didn't doubt it.

"Soo," Chief George said, "want to answer a question for me before I go any further? How did you two get roped into this thing with their casino?"

Their casino. A meaningful choice of a possessive. "Their," not "our."

Dennis nodded at me. "You're the storyteller, Podjo. Go ahead."

I sighed and then did just that, starting with how my interest was piqued by the two-wheeled, well-armed visitors and their ballistic attempts to provide better air-conditioning for my cabin, and ending with our visit to see my old frenemy the toad wolf. Plus a little background about how my relationship with Mook went back decades and had been renewed through his nefarious involvement with the Children of the Mountain.

And then I paused for breath.

"Children of the Mountain, eh?" Chief George said. "Heard some about it. So that was you two?"

"Yup," Dennis said, jumping in before I could come up with an appropriately modest reply. "Mostly him."

"Hmm," Chief George said, picking up his spoon and studying his reflection in it. "So why did you agree to work for this moke named Mook? Money?"

Nice, I thought. *Mook the moke. Nuke the mook. Spook the mook.* Then I shook my head to both clear away the cobwebs of free association and deny any pecuniary motive on our parts.

"He tried blackmail first, threatening a couple of my friends if I didn't go along."

"And how did that work out for him?" Raven asked, a small smile on her face.

Dennis chuckled. "Not so good. Seeing as how Podjo informed him he'd be walking on crutches if he took that approach."

"So what convinced you?"

"What usually gets Dennis and me into things like this. The same thing that killed the cat."

"Curiosity?" the chief said.

"Yup."

"About what?"

"About what's been killing those people. And about whether or not we could do something to help. Not help the casino, even though they paid our way here and they think they hired us. We came here because we might be able to prevent more folks from getting hurt."

Chief George kept looking at me, waiting for something.

I paused then and took another deep breath. Might as well say it.

"I just had this . . . *feeling* . . . that we might be the right people for the job."

"Seeing as how," Dennis chimed in, "we have had some relevant experience and welcome the opportunity to employ our unique skill set."

Chief George ignored Dennis's remark. "A *feeling*," he said. He took off his glasses, leaned over the table toward me, and looked me straight in the eye. Not as if he was looking *at* me. More as if he was looking *into* me.

Then he chuckled, a chuckle that was downright musical, leaned back, and restored his glasses to the bridge of his nose.

"Like your Great-Great-Aunt Sophie," he said to Raven.

"Thought so," she said.

"Okay," Chief George said. "I guess it's time to tell you about the Water Monster."

13

The Water Monster

*The story remembers
what the mind forgets*

The Water Monster. When most people think of a water monster, they get an image of that lake in Scotland made famous by doctored twentieth-century photos and brief, blurry movie footage of families of otters humping their way across the loch. Or if they live in the Northeast, they may think of the Green Mountain State's own entry in the cryptozoological sweepstakes, in what white folks labeled Lake Champlain on their maps. (You call it corn, we call it maize. You call it Champlain, we call it Petonbowk—the Waters Between.)

Nessie and Champ aside, there's no debating the fact that stories of sightings of strange creatures in lakes are all over the map. And not just on the North American continent. Try the heart of Africa, where the Congo is supposedly home to something like an aquatic dinosaur.

And if you turn to our traditional tales, there's more than just sightings.

One of my favorite stories that my Aunt Mali told us when we were kids was the one about Gluskonba and the Water Monster. That Water Monster was a very un-jolly green giant that built a huge dam to hold back the waters of the Connecticut River. (And, by the way, that is one name on modern maps that get it right. Kwanitewk means "Long River" in Abenaki.)

When their river went dry, people went upstream to see what had happened to the water that they needed to live. And there they found that huge creature, Aglebemu, floating in the lake he'd made behind the dam

58

and chanting in a big, scary voice: "AGLEBEM, AGLEBEM! I WILL GIVE THEM NONE."

They tried to fight him, but he just swatted away those people with one big hand. Those who survived ran back to their village and told what had happened.

"How can we fight a monster?" everyone said.

And that was when the one named Gluskonba walked into the village. We say that he was the first one shaped like a human, and that Ktsi Nwaskw, the Big Mystery, gave him great power.

"I will go talk to this Aglebemu," he said.

So Gluskonba walked upstream to that dam. And when that monster refused to share the water and threatened to destroy him, Gluskonba simply stomped his foot on the ground four times. Each time his foot thudded on the earth like a drum, Gluskonba got bigger and bigger till he was taller than the trees. He pulled up a huge dead pine tree, swung it like a war club, and broke open that dam.

Aglebemu jumped at Gluskonba, but Gluskonba just caught him in midair and squeezed so hard that the monster's eyes bulged out and his back got bent. Then Gluskonba began to pet that creature, and every time he did so, Aglebemu got smaller and smaller until he fit in Gluskonba's hand.

"Now," Gluskonba said, "you can no longer keep all the water for yourself. You're no longer a monster, you're just a bullfrog."

Then Gluskonba tossed him back into the river, where he still lives to this day in the water that is meant to be shared.

It's a story, I realize now, that Aunt Mali chose to tell us because we were sort of fighting over something—and it's not important what it was—that we should have been sharing. And, as I recall, though maybe we didn't get it consciously, that story's message got through, and nearly all of us realized we should stop being so selfish. Except for Mook Glossian, who, as soon as Aunt Mali finished the tale and most of us were sitting there still feeling like we were in that story, took the opportunity to grab that thing—a Michael Jordan basketball—and run off with it while Aunt Mali shook her head.

I guess Mook always was a frog.

"Did you just go somewhere?" someone said. Raven.

"He does that sometimes," Dennis said. "Always comes back, though. At least so far."

I shook my head. I was no longer on Abenaki Island, and the three of them—Chief George, Raven, and Dennis—were looking at me.

"Good story?" Chief George said, the kind of smile on his face that I used to see on Aunt Mali's when she caught me in one of those moments when I was so buried in the memory of a story that the rest of the world went away for a while.

I smiled back at him and nodded. It's funny how some people can seem to become part of your family almost as soon as you meet them. Without knowing anything much about him, I knew enough. Deep inside me, that voice was telling me Luther George was someone to trust and respect.

Chief George leaned back, put his left hand on the table—sort of like someone in court getting ready to swear on a Bible—and lifted his right hand.

"Got to confess," he said, "a lot of what I know I didn't get when I was young. I was a Catholic boarding school kid. And even though that place wasn't as bad as it had been when my own grandparents went there, it was plenty bad enough. Those nuns would beat the crap out of you if you did anything that didn't match up to their idea of what was Christian behavior. I still can't look at a straight ruler without remembering what it felt like to have it brought down across your palm so hard your hand was swelled up for days after."

He stopped, looked at his right hand, then dropped it down to rest on the tabletop next to his left hand.

"The best part of that education I got there was never in the classroom. It was when some of us kids could sneak off somewhere and talk Indian. We were all Salish, and even though our dialects were different, we could make ourselves understood to each other in Lutshootseed or whatever. And we'd tell stories—nowhere near as good as our elders might have told them, but just good enough for us to get away from that place in our minds. That was when I first heard about this one monster white folks call Ogopogo. One of the boys in my class, Eddie, he was Okanagan, from up in British Columbia. He'd ended up in our school in the States because his family had moved to Seattle. He shared with us what his grandma told him about N'ha-a-itk, their name for the being that lives in Lake Okanagan.

"'It's like a big snake,' Eddie said, 'with a head sort of like a cross between a horse and an alligator. We stayed away from the one part of the lake where it lived, off of Squally Point. It was sort of sacred. N'ha-a-itk, it never hurt anyone, just wanted to be left alone. It would dive down to the deepest part of that big lake whenever anyone tried to bother it.'

"Eddie frowned then and shook his head. 'Kind of like my people and the white men. We just wanted to be left alone. But we couldn't dive down to the bottom of no lake to get away from them.'"

Chief George lifted up his right hand, four fingers extended, and made a circling gesture with it.

"Right away, Uncle," Billy called from behind the counter. "Refills on the way!"

Once again, we waited until the drinks had been served. Waited until Raven's grandfather had taken his first sip of his coffee, leaned back, and nodded as I was glancing toward the clock on the wall, noting that an hour had now passed since we'd first arrived at OUR COFFEE.

"You got a name in your language for that thing?" Chief George said, pointing at the clock with his chin.

"We didn't," I answered. "But we made one up, seeing as how it seemed so important to those Jesuits who were teaching us how to be bad Christians back in the seventeenth century. Papeezokwazik is what we came up with. That thing that makes a lot of noise but does nothing useful."

Chief George let out another of his mellifluous chuckles. "We got a story here about Mink. He's the one stole the Sun so that the people could have light. When the white people came, he saw they had this thing they called Time that meant everything to them. So he stole Time. Carried it off. A big metal clock. But as soon as he took it, it turned out he couldn't get rid of it. He has to wear this big key around his neck, and every day he has to use it to wind up Time—which owns us all now, the way we used to own the Sun."

Dennis started humming 'Time Is on My Side," in a not at all Mick Jaggerish fashion. I made a throat-cutting gesture, and he ended his unmusical accompaniment with a "Hmmpf." I was either going to have to find him a knife and a slab of softwood soon or risk being convicted of friend-icide.

Raven leaned over and put her hand on her grandfather's right arm.

"Grampop," she said. "You can see they're okay now, right?"

"Saw that as soon as they walked in. Just been a while since I've had a captive audience that hasn't heard any of my favorite stories."

"So tell them why I brought them here."

Chief George rested his left hand on top of Raven's.

"Young folks," he said. "Always in a hurry. Back in the old days, it took four days just to get settled in before you even started to talk about serious things. But my favorite granddaughter's right. The time has come. Sooo, let me cut to the chase. Okay?"

I nodded, and despite Dennis's urge—which I sensed, knowing my big buddy's mental playlist all too well—to start humming "Time Has Come Today," he kept his trap shut and nodded along with me.

Chief George lifted up both hands, index fingers pointing toward the sky.

"Some say there's two sides to every story. Others say there's one right and one wrong. But what's going on out here now has got more sides than a sea urchin's got spines."

He tapped the table with a long index finger. "First, there's the casino folks in our tribe who brought you here to figure out what's killing people and holding up their pet project. Led, more or less, by Sherman Washington, the new chief. You met him, right? The progressives, they call themselves. Who progressed to where they are with some old-fashioned election fraud. Which we have lawyers looking into, even though ballot stuffing is an old Native tradition, ever since Indian Reorganization back in '34 gave us what the D.C. boys call 'representative democracy.'"

Dennis and I both nodded. The Wheeler-Howard Act was the centerpiece of the Indian New Deal. Intended to slow assimilation and strengthen our tribes by giving them an official voice in their own affairs through home rule and elections, it had its good points—and its bad. The worst was the imposition of social and political ideas that were not our own. In a lot of our communities, it drove a wedge between those who preferred the old ways and those who adopted European ways (and usually won the elections). Half a loaf may be better than none, but when it comes to U.S. Indian policy, that loaf is usually stale.

Chief George had paused, his thoughts probably going where ours were. Then he tapped the tabletop a second time.

"Next, there's those of us you might call the traditionals. That's two. Matter of fact, should have mentioned us first. We'd rather not see that project done—even though there's no way most of us would want anyone to get hurt. Me, I'm sort of the head of that side. I wasn't elected chief like Slick Sherm—Sea Antelope as he calls himself now. But I come from a family that's always served our people, and that's how I came by the title. From those of us who got de-Indianed, half of our people cut off of the tribal rolls by Sherm and his new council members."

Chief George took a sip of his coffee and drew a line with his finger through the ring of moisture the cup had left on the tabletop.

As he did that, I slid my own hands under the table—and found what my sixth sense had told me I was likely to find there.

"Now," Raven's grandfather continued, "I'm not asking you to come over to our side. I just want you to know who we are," he said. "And we're not against the casino itself. Far as we're concerned, it can stay where it is. We don't want it; they can have it, for all the good it's going to do them. Which is not that much—except for what Shermie and his cronies can rake off—seeing as how the sea lion's share goes to the off-shore investors who came up with the money to build the damn thing. But what we don't want is for them to build that new project in a place we've always held sacred. And why is it sacred?"

He drew a second line through the circle, making a shape like a Maltese cross.

"Now, this is where it gets more interesting. Because that place, that particular headland where they want to build their big new casino hotel with a quarter-mile-long pier thrust out into the bay, that's where the Big One has always lived."

"Padoskoks," I said—before I even realized I was about to say anything.

"Really Big Snake," Dennis added before the chief or Raven could request a translation.

That was when I heeded the prickling of the hairs on the back of my neck and rolled said neck as if trying to get rid of a crick in it. It enabled me to turn my head just enough for me to get a quick glimpse out the window at the ivy-draped brick building across the street. And an all-too-familiar glint of sun reflecting from the glass of a telescopic sight on its rooftop.

14

Up on the Roof

Actions aren't always louder than words
but they can end a conversation

I stood up, my broad back to the window.

"I need to go to the restroom," I said to Chief George. "All that air travel."

I held my hands in front of me where they could not be seen through the front window and made the signs for "gun" and "outside" to him. Why, me being from the Northeast and him being a northwestern native, did I assume he'd understand?

Indian sign language is an interesting thing. In Alaska and the Pacific Northwest, I've heard it referred to as the old "trade language," a way of communicating between indigenous people where more than a dozen very different languages might be spoken within a few hundred miles of each other. When Lewis and Clark crossed half the continent, traveling from the Mississippi River to the Columbia, George Drouillard, the half-French, half-Shawnee man who was their sign language speaker, found that every tribal nation understood the unspoken things he was communicating to them with his hands.

I also signed for Dennis to come and take my place, facing Chief George and screening him from the view of anyone outside.

Why didn't I just say it out loud? Because as we'd sat at the table—the favorite one Raven's grandfather always chose—my hands had found stuck under the tabletop the telltale shape of a microphone.

Chief George reached into his shirt pocket, pulled out his phone, and turned it on.

"Take your time," he said, clicking on the games icon. "I got plenty here to keep me busy."

I walked away from the table quickly, like someone in need of a rest-room respite, turned the corner, went past the portals marked M and F, and pushed open the exit door. The alley behind the building was empty of anything save a dumpster, though I did peer inside it just to make sure. I ran the full length of the block and crossed to the other side, screened from sight of that rooftop by the Iron Pergola, for which the square is almost as well known as the totem pole. Then I made my way around the back of the building facing OUR COFFEE.

Yes, Seattle, thank you for your safety codes. There was a new fire-escape ladder. And although my chosen sport in college was football, the basketball coach at Dartmouth had tried to recruit me for his team because I could outjump almost anyone on his varsity squad. If there'd been a parkour team, I could have been its captain. Thus it was no stretch for me to take off at a run, then bounce off the side of the build-ing to reach said ladder with one vertical leap. I grabbed it with both hands. Luck was on my side, because as my weight extended it down, it neither creaked nor made a screeching metal sound like some of the ladders I've used in other cities to access a rooftop when necessity demanded.

When I was near the top, I paused. No point in putting a full stop to my narrative by getting my head blown off while vaulting over the par-apet onto the roof. But I did, not having shown enough foresight to bring a periscope, have to take a look. I did so by bobbing up and then down again, as fast as a prairie dog checking to see if that hungry coyote is still lurking around its burrow.

That split second allowed me to garner two useful pieces of informa-tion. Well, actually three. No one ever expects the Spanish Inquisition. Item number one was that I'd been correct in assuming that glint was from something potentially lethal. Namely the scoped long gun held by the bad guy dressed all in black from his ski hat to his soft-soled shoes—black, how clichéd—who had the window of OUR COFFEE in his sights. The second important item was that his attention was riveted on that window, and he had not registered my presence. Third was that the roughly fifty feet of rooftop between me and him looked smooth. No crunchy gravel or potentially noisy debris to traverse.

There's a simple way to walk quietly that's taught in Pentjak. But it isn't solely used by Indonesian martial artists. My friend John Stokes—who runs something called the Tracking Project down in New Mexico—teaches that same technique. You move slightly crouched, one careful step at a time. You don't come down on your heels but sort of roll each foot, instep first, front to back, with your hands held down in front of you. You can do it as slow as a heron stalking up on a fish, or speed it up some if your quarry is not looking your way. About thirty seconds is what it took me to get close enough to the man in black, who was definitely not Tommy Lee Jones.

I suppose I could have just clubbed him, but where's the fun in that? Plus it might have resulted in a twitch of that finger on the trigger of the sniper rifle. A Barrett M82, which I easily recognized—it being the U.S. Army's weapon of choice for taking out the trash. Less than nine thousand dollars each on the military market. Pretty much the best of its kind for range, accuracy, and reliability. Plus its ammo—same as that for a Browning M2 machine gun—can penetrate brick and concrete. And, from less than a hundred yards away, pretty much overkill.

But underkill was what I wanted right now. So I dropped to one knee and leaned closer to his left ear.

"Whazzup?" I whispered.

Hard not to be startled in such a circumstance. Harder not to turn around in a panic.

Making it easier for me to twist the gun out of his grasp and step back as he tried to rise, which is not that easy after you've been in a sniper's stance for too long, legs cramping up and all.

"Don't you just hate it when that happens?" I said.

Apparently my black-suited new dance partner was not as good as moi at verbal repartee. For his only response was a growl, accompanied by an attempt to reach inside his vest.

I doubted he was searching for either a cigar or his gun permit. That is why my even faster response was a roundhouse kick delivered COD to his chin. Which ended our tête-à-tête with a pied-à-tête.

After removing the ten-shot magazine and clearing the chamber, I placed the rifle ten feet away and rolled him over. Limp, but still breathing, his hand still thrust, Napoleon-like, into his vest. (Did anyone ever find a cure for that little French general's persistent itch?) Moving his hand aside, I found what he'd wanted to employ in lieu of conversation: a straight-edge, fixed-blade USMC model Ka-Bar. Just like one I had back home.

I fastened the sheath to my belt and then put my new Arkansas toothpick to good use. The cloth strips I cut from his jeans—making them much more fashionable—worked just fine for tying his hands behind his back. Then I searched him. His face had looked sort of Russian to me—from long experience—and the driver's license in his cash-stuffed wallet almost bore that out. Except that the name Kassan Maskhadov sounded Chechen to me.

Not wanting to deal with all the hassle of adopting an exotic new pet—house-training, proper feeding, and the like—I left him there. From that long experience I just mentioned with a certain kind of combatant from greater Eurasia, I doubted that I'd get much out of him through interrogation. Enhanced or otherwise. Plus I had his cell phone.

I toyed with the idea of dropping his wallet down a nearby chimney, but abandoned that at the thought of clogging up some innocent establishment's furnace, and just dropped the wallet—cash still in it—next to him. I did, however, keep the gun, which I took with me down the fire escape and shoved under the back seat of Raven's jeep before reentering OUR COFFEE.

I put the one cartridge I'd ejected from the gun on the tabletop.

"Time to find another venue," I said.

15

Lots of Folks

"Close but no cigar"
doesn't mean as much to a nonsmoker

It turned out that Chief George's wife had dropped him off to go
shopping, intending to pick him up later. So after he called her on
his cell phone to explain the change in his plans, all four of us
ended up in Raven's rattletrap chariot of doom.

"How's come you haven't shot this thing yet?" her grandfather asked
her as he refashioned the bungee cord used to hold the right back door
shut. Then he tapped the M82 under the seat with his foot and put his
hand to his chin. "Maybe too soon for that kind of joking, eh?"

"No problem," I said from the front seat, where I was turned around
to face him. "The best time for gallows humor is after a stay of
execution."

"Staa-a-ay-a-ay, jes a little bit longer," Dennis began to hum. No
more than half a dozen notes off-key.

"Can you pull over for a minute?" I asked Raven.

I hopped out, ran down to the beach we had just been passing, grabbed
the two-foot-long piece of driftwood I'd seen, and brought it back to
the car.

"Here," I said to Dennis, dropping it in his lap and giving him the
Ka-Bar. "Will this pull the plug on your jukebox?"

"Unh-hunh. You bet! Podjo, thank you so much."

"Nda kagwi," I replied, which means "Don't mention it" in Abenaki. "Our sanity thanks your silence."

With the blessed sound of whittling as our background soundscape,
we continued on up the road.

"Soo," Chief George said, as he took a clean tissue from his shirt pocket and used it to clean his glasses, "think the plan was to punch my ticket?"

I cocked my head to listen. Nope. The mangled melody humming of "Ticket to Ride" was not emanating from my best bud's piehole. The knife and that piece of driftwood was working. Excellent.

"Maybe," I said, answering the chief's question. "Or maybe cancel mine. But then again," I added, "maybe it was meant to be a near miss, to just give us a scare so we'd back off."

"Would that work on you?" Chief George replied, tapping his chin.

"Not hardly."

"Me neither. After being on Okinawa, there's not much scares me anymore. My fear-of-death tank got overfilled for life."

Okinawa. From what my uncles—who both semper-fied their way across the Pacific from '43 to '45—told me, that was the bloodiest fighting in the whole war. Some 38,000 American dead. Over 100,000 Japanese soldiers and another 100,000 Okinawan civilian deaths.

I peered a little more closely at Luther George. He barely looked like a man in his mid-sixties.

"Ninety-one," he said, "this past May. It's those Indian genes of mine." He paused. "Or maybe it's my dress pants."

"Grampop!" Raven groaned, as my own already considerable admiration of her grandpa went up a few more notches. Not just for being a more elder elder than I'd realized, but also for being able to come up with such a terrible pun after a possible attempt on his life had been thwarted.

Dennis surfaced for a moment from the deep waters of wood carving. "So where are we headed now?" he asked.

"Thirty miles north. Peaceful Bay," Raven replied.

Peaceful Bay. Five miles farther north from the main casino that we had passed. It was easy to see how it got its name. From the headland where we parked, we had a clear view of its calm waters edged by tall trees—except for the one spot near the tip of land on its northern edge where a considerable clearing had been made, a large foundation and construction equipment—even from our distance of four miles away—clearly visible. As was the start of a pier that would thrust like a dagger out into those calm waters.

We were not on the main access road to the project, a half-finished highway that was going to be four lanes when completed. We'd taken a series of smaller roads to come out on a rise of land across from it. Puget Sound widening out toward Vancouver Island to our west.

The four of us stood on the bluff, quietly looking out. Even Dennis. However, as he silently scanned the scenic vista below, his hands were still engaged in bringing a shape out of that piece of red cedar.

"Over there," Raven finally said. "Off that point is where She lives."

"She?" I said.

"The Big One. You-know-who. We don't say Her name when we're near the water."

That made me nod. It's the same for us. Whenever we're on the shores of Petonbowk, we never utter the name of Padoskoks, our own Really Big Snake.

Chief George was digging something out of one of his shirt pockets. Not the cell phone this time—a Bic lighter. He flicked it and held the flame to the dry cedar and sage bundle he'd already extricated from his pants pocket. It lit quickly. Then, when he shook it, the flame disappeared, but smoke kept coming.

He nodded at Raven, who leaned forward to cup some of the smoke with her hands and draw it back over her head. She stepped back to make room for me, and I did the same, followed by Dennis, who handed me the knife and the piece of cedar that was already beginning to resolve itself into something recognizable. When he'd alighted from the jeep, Dennis had gathered up a good-sized mound of whittled-off curls of wood and placed those shavings gently at the base of one of the small, wind-twisted junipers by the parking area.

Leaving the smudge bundle still burning on top of a flat stone, Raven's grandfather sat down, his legs dangling over the edge of the cliff that dropped off a hundred feet straight down, and nodded for us to join him.

We sat, me on his left, Raven on his right. Dennis, who'd left the knife and the piece of wood on the same stone as the smudge bundle, plopped down on my other side.

"Us Penacooks," he said to Raven and Chief George, looking down between his knees, "we are not afraid of falling." Then he leaned back and grinned. "On the other hand, landing can be sort of scary."

Chief George opened both hands and spread them out wide. "All this, this has been ours to take care of for more years than can be counted. This land, these waters, they know us. We fought to keep it, then we fought more battles in the courts to get it back. But now our new chief and his tribal council are selling out. All that over there will be cleared to build million-dollar condos to be bought by outsiders. And that point there, that was so sacred we only went there for ceremony. And we didn't fish close to there, either. It wasn't that we were afraid of Her, just giving respect. And it wasn't just stories. We used to see Her out there." He shook his head. "I sure wish some of my own elders hadn't been so eager to please the anthros who got them to tell our oldest stories, including the ones about . . ."

"You-know-who," Raven said.

Chief George sighed. "Remember I was saying there's more than one side here. I only got as far as mentioning the progressives and the traditionals. But there's others lined up here. Those old stories about Her, the Big One, have drawn a few different—really different—folks here. All with the blessing of the Super Chief."

He held up his left hand and began counting them off with his right.

"There's this cryptozoologist who wants to prove She exists. Hobbyist with a lot of money to spend. Got his own boat with sonar, a mini-sub, the works," he said, lifting up his little finger.

"Then," his ring finger raised up, "there's a film crew from one of those cable stations. A show called *Creature Catchers*, where they have this guy going out to fish for undersea giants. They've even used a helicopter to film things from the air."

Dropping the first two fingers back into his fist, he lifted his middle finger. "Third," he said, "is maybe the craziest one of the group. See that big white boat out there?"

I shaded my eyes with my hand and was just able to make out what had to be a very large yacht out past the mouth of the bay.

"That's owned by a Chinese billionaire from Hong Kong. Word is that he's one of the silent investors in the new casino project, so Old Sherm put out the welcome mat for him. No one has ever seen him. Never leaves that yacht of his, which is like a floating city. But we know quite a bit about him, seeing as how my granddaughter did some research on him on the Internet."

Raven put her hand on her grandfather's shoulder. It was such a sweet gesture of support that it made me want to say "Ahhh." Or maybe that "Ahhh" would also have been an expression of my appreciation of Raven in general.

"Seems," Chief George continued, "he wants to add our big friend to his personal collection, which already includes whales, dolphins, and a dozen different varieties of big sharks. I don't know if it's true, but there's this rumor going around that he doesn't just collect 'em to keep in his giant aquariums. After he's had 'em and looked at 'em long enough, he has 'em butchered and served to his guests at private dinner parties." He held up his middle finger higher and swung it in the direction of the distant aircraft carrier–sized yacht.

"Fourth," his index finger lifted now to join the middle finger, "that's our other casino investors building that stuff. The long pier they've got planned will also have underwater viewing areas—so visitors can look out into the ocean and maybe get a glimpse of Her. A tourist attraction. And did I mention that the money for all that, from those primary offshore investors, is coming from Russian oligarchs and Asian billionaires like that fish eater out there?"

He cocked his two fingers as if raising a pistol to sight down its barrel.

"We've been researching that group of investors—the ones who paid your ticket to get here," Raven said. "Looks like much of the Indonesians' wealth comes from hardwood lumber, which is worth a fortune now. They're the ones wiping out the rainforests on the islands of Borneo and New Guinea. They also have investments in gold mines in various places where there are no regulations preventing them from poisoning the rivers with the cyanide used to leach out the gold from open pit mines. The Russians, they're all oil and natural gas. They have this big-time influence peddler named Jack Abramoff working for them in D.C., making sure everything has the blessing of the BIA and the appropriate Senate committees."

Chief George was nodding his head and looking out over the bay.

"Grampop," Raven said.

"Ki, little bird?"

"There's still your thumb."

Chief George looked at his left hand, then lifted the final of his five fingers. "Last one is a wildcard," he said, pointing that thumb down like a Roman emperor deciding the fate of a losing gladiator. "Sorta ties into what happened back in town. Seems those major investors have some rivals in the casino business. Not Donald Trump. He's too busy losing the money his daddy left him and hating on the Pequots. What I'm talking about is the Italian mob."

Dennis began humming again. This time I didn't try to stop the music. Not only was he almost in tune, I had to agree with his choice of background music for the moment.

"Which side are you on?"

16

More than Mere Myth

*In the land of the blind
there are no one-eyed people*

"*Myths and legends abound throughout all the primitive tribal Indian nations of North America regarding monstrous aquatic serpents. While some might write off such tales as mere superstition, the credulous beliefs of preliterate tribes, one must also take into account the fact that similarities exist from one side of the American continent to the next in these rough oral traditions and, more importantly, that such reptilian mega-fauna have been observed throughout the centuries by European explorers, colonizers, priests, military personnel, and upstanding members of various communities—all men of some education. Thus, such crudely told aboriginal stories might serve as a starting point for truly scientific study.*"

That was the first paragraph in the dog-eared pamphlet Chief George had pulled from his back pocket and handed to me. Its title—*More than Mere Myth*—and the cover illustration of something resembling a plesiosaur with a canoe grasped in its impressively dentured jaws had somewhat prepared me for that piece of purple prose by someone named Dr. Malcolm Grattington, Ph.D. But not totally. Talk about a colonial mindset! I looked at the copyright notice, hoping it might have been in the nineteenth century. Nope. 1995.

"What do you think?" Chief George said, a sort of chuckle in his deep voice.

"He had me at 'myths and legends,'" I said. "Our 'crudely told aboriginal stories,' that is."

Chief George nodded. "Yup. And primitive me with a degree in Comparative Liter-ture from USC."

"Grampop was on the faculty for twenty years at Portland State," Raven interjected.

Chief George retrieved the pamphlet from me and studied the cover. "Dr. and Ph.D. is sort of overkill, don't you think?"

I nodded. "Unh-hunh. Taking a look at that cover illustration, seems like a scantily clad Indian maiden is the only thing mything."

Raven groaned. "Not you, too?"

"Indian Myth America . . . and a myth is as good as a mile," Chief George added. "Looked up the good Ph.D. doctor's credentials, by the way. Only degree on record is from Bob Jones College, an evangelical school down south—which does not have any doctoral programs."

He looked out toward the bay, where we could see a distant wake from a boat. From where we were, it looked no larger than an insect.

"Anyhow, seeing as how he's a published author, he is the official technical advisor to that cryptozoologist scooting around in his rubber whaleboat looking for our friend."

He pushed his glasses back up onto his nose. "Any given day, you might see three different crews out there with their boats. Two of 'em loaded up with enough camera and recording equipment to make James Cameron jealous. And the third one carrying nets and harpoons. And maybe a sushi chef. Makes you wish they'd just run into each other and sink to the bottom of the bay. But all of 'em have the written permission of the Super Chief, who knows how to talk about defending tribal rights while holding his hand behind his back to take bribes."

"Tribal elections," Raven said, "are coming up in two months. Grampop can't run—having had his name taken off the tribal roll—but he could still win. We have a slate of candidates running for the council who are honest men and women, but have kept quiet about what they plan to do if elected—which is restore tribal citizenship to all those of us . . ."

"All hunnerd and twelve," Chief George said.

"Who got kicked out." Raven cracked the first real smile I'd seen on her face. "And bring back real tribal leadership." She nodded at her grandfather. "Plus we have a good Indian lawyer still looking into the results of that last stolen election. So there's two ways we might come out on top. Then there'll be some big changes."

Another reason, I thought, *for the Russians, the Chinese, or Old Sherm himself to bring in Chechen assassins.*

"What can we do?" I asked.

"Just what you were hired for," Chief George replied. "Find out what killed those people and keep more from getting hurt."

"And while we're doing that?" Dennis asked.

"Just do what feels right," Chief George said. "Having met you boys, it seems to me that's what you naturally tend to do."

17

Deep Bluewater

When some people shake your hand,
count your fingers afterward

Raven dropped us off in front of the main casino, two miles from the new project on the bay. A slightly hesitant blond bellboy came up to us. I could understand his uncertainty. Few big tippers climb out of a car that looks as if it's held together with duct tape.

"Uh," he said, as Raven rattled off, leaving a plume of smoke behind her, "welcome to Deep Bluewater. Help with your . . . uh."

"I think the word you're looking for is luggage," said Dennis, the always helpful one. "Of which we've got next to none," he added, indicating our minimalist backpacks and his shoulder bag with a jerk of his head.

Had we not decided to leave our new M82 in Raven's care, at least for now, we might have had more to carry inside. But since we were trying to not draw undue attention by entering heavily armed, Dennis had summed things up succinctly.

I pulled a ten out of my shirt pocket and handed it to the blond kid, prompting a surprised grin. Not a huge tip, but a heck of a lot more than our appearance had promised.

"We got it, Kevin," I said, initiating an air of intimacy while proving that I was literate enough to read the name tag pinned on his chest. "Just point us to the check-in counter."

"You bet," he said, leading us to the ornate front door and opening it. "Check-in's straight ahead, past the all-day buffet. Enjoy your stay."

"Of execution?" Dennis quipped, a remark that Kevin wisely chose to ignore as we passed him and entered into the air-conditioned nightmare of your typical Indian casino, where the slots are advertised as loose and the first drinks are free—along with enough secondhand cigarette fumes to give anyone without an oxygen mask lung cancer.

One of the benefits, you see, of tribal sovereignty is that Indian establishments do not have to abide by such namby-pamby rules as no smoking in public places.

We were only halfway to the check-in desk when our progress was impeded by a large gorilla in a man suit who stepped in front of us.

"Vere you tink you go?" he asked, in an almost human voice with a distinctly Eastern European accent.

I looked up at him. Yes, he was that tall.

"Check-in," I said. Single-syllable words work best with hostile simians.

I also held up my left hand as I spoke—a signal to Dennis, who I sensed was ready to interpose his nearly as tall and somewhat wider body between me and King Kong's kid brother, that his assistance was not yet needed.

This was all clearly a misunderstanding, a result of our apparel and accompanying luggage not matching the standards of their usual clientele. It also suggested to me that we were victims of mistaken identity, and further, that some sort of prior experience with well-muscled and less-than-well-dressed visitors had resulted in a beefing up of casino security.

It was at that point when a line was crossed. Not by Dennis or me but by Slobodan—whose name and Slavic origins I had cleverly deduced by reading *his* name tag—who thudded his large left hand into my chest.

I do not like getting pushed. Call it a post-traumatic stress reaction engendered by a childhood of being bullied before I—as we say in the North Country of New York—got my growth.

As a result of that—and two decades of training—I reacted immediately. Having seen said Serbian hand coming, I'd stepped back with my right leg, lowering my center of gravity into a firm tai chi stance. I then trapped that thrusting paw by pressing it against my sternum with my right hand as I cupped his elbow with my left. All it took then to give my new gigantopithecan playmate the choice of either suffering a broken wrist or dropping to his knees was for me to bow forward.

Which I did.

"*Aggh!*" Slobodan exclaimed as he rapidly knelt on the casino tiles. Which were, I noticed for the first time, nicely decorated with images of leaping dolphins.

Just as I was in the process of the quick shift of holds that would have ended with his arm behind his back and his face planted between the happy porpoises, a familiar oily voice called out from the direction of the progressive poker machines.

"Hold on! These guys are our guests."

None other, of course, than Chief Sea Antelope, who was hurrying forward, his lasso of turquoise and silver glittering around his neck.

I offered a hand to Slobodan. To his credit, he took it and allowed me to help him back up. To his further credit, he was smiling.

"Nice move," he said. "Maybe you teach me it?"

I only had time to nod before the Super Chief was upon us and Slobodan was turning in his direction.

"What's the matter with you?" the overly bejeweled casino owner said. "Didn't you get my directive to be looking for my new employees? Don't they teach you bozos to read back in Belgrade?"

He poked the huge man in his belly with a finger that I would have dislocated had it been thrust into my stomach that way. Slobodan, though, acted more like a whipped puppy than the Sasquatch he'd resembled as he came rumbling our way.

"Sorry, boss, I sorry. Just came on duty. No see directive. Sorry, sorry."

"Hey," Dennis said. "Ease up on the man. If I was doing security here and saw two bozos like me and Podjo here come in, I might react the same."

The casino chief turned his baleful gaze to Dennis—who failed to wilt before it as had the huge Serb. But that glare lasted only a split second, morphing into an insincere smile as he remembered that we were not his usual lackeys.

"Righht," Sea Antelope said. He waved a hand dismissively, and Slobodan swiftly departed our presence—though not without an almost unnoticeable grateful nod to Dennis. Who might have made a new friend.

"Thought you'd be here by seven. Took you boys a little longer than I expected," Sea Antelope said.

Not that long, I thought, *seeing as how neutralizing snipers is a fairly time-consuming task.*

Sea Antelope looked expectant. Waiting for me to explain our later-than-planned arrival.

But I just nodded.

No need for him to know more. Especially considering the fact that said potential assassin might just have been sent by our genial host to eliminate his tribal rival.

"So let me show you around. You want drinks, some chips so you can play? Here, let me comp you a couple hundred each."

As one, Dennis and I shook our heads.

"Just the tour," Dennis said. "Then dinner. Still serving, right?"

"Righht, righht. Absolutely. The all-day buffet just closed, but the main dining facility is open." He took a breath and then intoned, "Fine dining till ten every night in our world-class World of Water Restaurant."

Sea Antelope's voice had sounded as canned as a second-rate TV commercial. I hoped the food would be better.

"Okay," Dennis said, speaking for both of us. "And after that we wanna just go to our rooms. It's been a long day, and we gotta start early tomorrow."

"Righht, righht," Sea Antelope said. "Now follow me. Over here we've got . . ."

We followed along behind him, his running monologue nothing we had not heard before. Indian casinos are all pretty much the same, including the fact that a large proportion of the clientele of this palace near the Pacific consisted of retirees blowing their Social Security checks on the snowball's chance in Hades of a big payoff. Bussed in from local retirement centers. Many of them well stocked with enough adult diapers to sit all day pulling down the lever of a one-armed bandit.

("Grama, why is your right arm as big as Hulk Hogan's?")

Gambling is nothing new for us Indians. Here in the Northwest, our Pacific Coast cousins were playing all sorts of games long before any potential Italian restaurant founders and their Basque navigators blundered their way across the Atlantic. Stick games, for example. But it was gambling of a different sort. Not done to accumulate more material wealth than any single human—including Donald Trump—could possibly need in a hundred lifetimes. Plus, though it was banned for generations by both the Canadian and United States governments, there's the now-revived tradition of the Potlatch, where those who accumulate the greatest wealth ceremonially give it all away.

Where I come from, we used to play—and still play—a gambling game called snow snake. In the winter you make a long trough in the snow—maybe a quarter mile long—ice it down, and then slide long spear-like sticks—snow snakes—down it. The one whose snake goes the farthest wins all the snow snakes used in the game. And what does that winner do then? Sell them off? Ransom them back to the original owners? Keep them in a snow snake trophy room?

Nope. The winner chooses one to keep and then throws all the rest up into the air, and everybody who played is allowed to grab a snow snake to take home.

Not exactly capitalism.

But how did Indian casinos come to be such a big thing? Becoming, as I think Russell Means may have said, "the new buffalo"? (Russell said a lot of things.) Casinos: the new source of livelihood for tribal nations who used to live off the bounty of nature, but now may sustain themselves by using every part of the slot machine and the roulette wheel? Well, not exactly.

True, Indian gaming has become a multi-billion-dollar industry. But their take is still less than 10 percent of what's taken by non-Native United States casinos. The Florida Seminoles opened the first high-stakes bingo parlor in 1979, and twenty-six years later there are now about four hundred Indian gaming establishments. That's a lot. Four hundred casinos and some five hundred federally recognized tribes. But not all of them are doing well. I've been told that by next year maybe 10 percent of them will go out of business. The only ones really raking it in—and not just breaking even—are all located near big urban areas. Like Seattle. No way would a casino be successful at Pine Ridge.

The money to build those casinos, you see, came not from the pockets of Native Americans on typically impoverished reservations. Investors were needed—largely casino corporations, some offshore from as far away as . . . ta-da . . . Indonesia. Often, the share of Indian casino proceeds taken by non-Indians is way huge.

It started in the early eighties, when big prizes began to be offered in the bingo palaces of the Florida Seminoles, larger than those allowed by state law. When the Sunshine State tried to stop them, the Seminoles sued and won in the federal courts. The rule that Indian tribes had the right to conduct gambling on their own lands blew the lid off Pandora's box. That led to the 1988 Indian Gaming Regulatory Act, which authorized casino gambling on reservations. The fact that the new law stipulated that such gaming was to be for the promotion of tribal economic development, tribal self-sufficiency, and strong tribal government meant that a lot of good things resulted for those tribes with sizable casino revenues. New schools, retirement centers, and industries sprang up, and so did self-esteem.

As a friend of mine on the Oneida Reservation in Wisconsin put it to me a few years ago, "Our kids used to go to school wearing secondhand clothes. Now they go wearing brand-new jeans and Michael Jordan sneakers."

However, that much money earned by the prosperous casinos engendered something else in addition to tribal pride: corruption. Sort of the way a piece of honey-coated fry bread left out in the sun ends up being covered with yellow jackets. Some of those lethal insects in human form left Las Vegas—whose development from a sleepy desert city into a gamblers' mecca was aided and abetted in 1946 by the notorious mobsters Bugsy Siegel and Meyer Lansky—to try their hand in our former buffalo pastures.

Then there were the men with supposedly clean hands—white lobbyists, getting paid big bucks to grease the wheels in Congress for Native American tribes attempting to get into the gaming business and needing government approval. Such as the aforementioned Jack Abramoff and his fellow hyenas.

Despite the fact that Dennis and I had agreed to come to the den of iniquity we were currently touring, our sympathies were much more with the traditionals on various reservations who stood against casino gambling. My uncle had been behind the barricades with his traditional Mohawk friends at Akwesasne back in 1991 when a mini–civil war was fought over a casino that was being run largely for the benefit of a few individuals. The pro-gaming side was armed with AK-47s by casino investors looking to make a killing—and not caring who got killed as a result. Thankfully, that conflict ended without innocents getting murdered, and there's been a lot of healing on that rez since then.

It's a simple equation. Casinos × Big Money = Trouble.

But, as I pointed out earlier, we'd taken this job not to protect any casino interests, but for our own usual reasons. That we might actually do some good, maybe solve a murder or two in the process. And that my own unique talents had given me the "feeling" that this was the right thing to do. A feeling that had been borne out by our meeting with Raven and Chief George.

All that history had been running through my head as Sea Antelope gushed over one aspect after another of Deep Bluewater, frequently adding the codicil "But this is nothing compared to what we're gonna have on the bay."

Finally, thankfully, the tour ended back at the check-in desk, where Dennis and I were issued our room keys—each with a large plastic fluorescent porpoise attached.

"Here," Sea Antelope said, winking as he shoved a thick envelope into my hand, "some walking-around money for you boys. You know." Followed by a second, even more overly dramatic wink.

I accepted the envelope silently, briefly took the hand he extended for me to shake, then walked away feeling as if both my palm and the wad of dough I'd shoved into my backpack needed to be laundered.

The World of Water was easy enough to find—unless you needed a seeing-eye dog. Its entrance was marked by a ten-foot-tall tuxedo-wearing neon dolphin holding a sign in its teeth with the restaurant's name strobing on it rapidly enough to induce epileptic seizures.

I shuddered at the thought of what we might find within. But when we entered the still crowded dining venue and were met and guided to our table by a stressed-looking waitress wearing a uniform meant to look like a deerskin dress, it turned out to be worse than I'd expected. Not because it was decked out in the finest garish fashion by an interior decorator whose taste was confined to his or her mouth. Dennis and I had expected that. What was unexpected—and disturbing—was the back wall of the place. Like the much larger satellite casino being built a mile away on Peaceful Bay, Deep Bluewater I had been sited next to the water. I'd thought, seeing that the restaurant was at the back of the building, that we might be granted an ocean view. What we saw instead was the aquatic equivalent of a torture chamber. The entire back wall was that of an aquarium. Although large by some standards, it was far too small for what was being displayed there: a half-grown killer whale.

As it swam listlessly back and forth, I noticed that its dorsal fin was bent over. That happens to all captive male orcas. Their dorsal fin collapses; no one is sure why. The most common explanations are either that there's not enough space for them to swim and get the right amount of exercise, or that the diet they're fed of dead fish, frozen and then thawed out, results in their getting inadequate nutrition.

Depression is my explanation. The intelligence of an orca is at least that of a dolphin. I've always looked at cetaceans as self-aware beings (no, I will not say they have a sense of porpoise), and I believe they're at least the equal of humans in terms of intellect. And much smarter in that they never destroy their own environment and that of the other living things around them.

As that lonely orca swam, it was vocalizing at a subsonic level that most humans would not register. I could hear it, though. Another of those gifts I've been either blessed or cursed with. And what it was saying, even though it was not in human words, was breaking my heart. All it wanted was to rejoin the family from which it had been kidnapped. Somewhere out there in the Pacific. Though not in Puget Sound. In recent years the capturing of orcas off the Washington coast had been outlawed.

I was standing now with my hands on the glass. I had no memory of walking over to it. The captive orca had swum over and was sort of standing on its head in the water, bumping its nose again the glass between my palms.

The waitress who'd been showing us to our table was standing next to me.

"They call him Happy," she said in a soft voice that carried the same local Indian accent as the voices of Raven and Chief George.

I looked over at her. She bore a resemblance to one of my younger aunts. About the same height and build. Her profile much like that of Aunt Lisa.

JAN was what her nametag read. Her black hair was pulled back into a ponytail and held in place with a beaded hairpin that was more authentic than anything else in the joint.

"Happy," I said.

"Anything but," Jan replied. "I'd like to put *them* in there instead."

Then, as if realizing she might have said something that could get her into trouble, she looked quickly at me.

"I could not agree more," I said.

I stood there for another minute, Dennis next to us now. We watched as un-Happy turned, swam up to the surface, where a sort of ramp led into the water and there appeared to be a half-submerged gate of some kind, and then floated back down to look at us hopefully.

It should have spoiled my appetite, I suppose. But it didn't. After taking our seats, we ordered the best the menu promised. Two salmon. And three extra-large buffalo steaks. For Dennis. Plus one of each for me. After our plates were cleaned, the main course was followed by several slices of blueberry pie, which proved that, if no one else here did, their chef had excellent taste.

Our repast past, Dennis and I made as much like Elvis as we could—leaving the room even if we could not leave the building. (But only after giving Jan a cash tip that was equal to the cost of both our meals.)

I was silent as we walked to the elevator.

Dennis nudged me. "Bet I know what you got on your mind, Podjo. I can smell the feathers burning."

I raised an eyebrow in his direction.

"Oh?" I said. "Aside from dropping the chief back there into a tank of electric eels?"

Dennis let out a deep baritone chuckle. Then he grinned and lifted up his left hand. "Two words," he said.

"Say 'em."

"Free Willy."

We'd requested separate adjoining accommodations. Not that we couldn't have bunked together or were uncomfortable in each other's company. After all, when you've spent weeks sweltering together in some hole in the desert where the barrel of your gun gets hot enough to burn you even when you're not firing round after round in response to largely unseen enemies, or been hip to hip in a rocky crevice on a mountain slope in the Hindu Kush thankful that each other's body heat is slightly minimizing the chance of frostbite, sharing a room in a hotel is no big deal.

Except that when there's little possibility of anything lethal heading your way in the night, such as Taliban infiltrators creeping up on you in the dark or hand grenades being tossed into your bunker, the fact that your best buddy snores louder than a chainsaw can make you grateful for a wall between your ears and his adenoids.

Also, to be honest, Dennis himself might not be that safe with me that close to him when a certain sort of dream—if you can call it that—tiptoes into my sleep. That's when—like the guy who dreamt he was eating the world's biggest marshmallow and woke up to find half his pillow gone—my wrestling in my sleep with an unseen adversary ends up with yours truly's hands around the neck of anyone luckless enough to be bunking with me.

Needless to say, even though I can blame it on PTSD and not any evil intent of my own, it's made lasting intimate relationships with women rather unlikely. (Though I have to admit, the short time I spent with Ruth after the Children of the Mountain was unmarred by any after-midnight assaults—uh, of the violent kind, that is.)

And there was a third reason why I welcomed my own room. Dennis was, to put it mildly, wound up. When not snoring, he would be motor-mouthing. I would be listening to an extended recounting of our day's experiences mixed in with his speculations about what the morrow might bring, all punctuated by the snick, snick, snick of his new knife as he continued to shape that piece of wood.

The last thing I needed was a whittling monologue after the eighteen-hour day we'd just gone through. What I needed was to have my raveled sleeve of care quietly knitted back together. So after Dennis and I had looked both of our rooms over and he had retired to his own abode, I kicked off my shoes and tossed my backpack onto a chair, pulled off my shirt, extricated my toiletry bag and spread my few things out on the sink shelf, flossed (like a good little dental patient), brushed my teeth, used the loo, and then, after washing my hands (soap up, scrub well, then rinse while humming the ABC song), walked back into the bedroom to fall, half-clothed, face down on the pillow-top mattress and go right to sleep.

But not for long.

18

A Late Night Knock

Few things are more expensive
than a free ride in an enemy's car

Tap-tap. Tap-tap. I slid off the bed and went to the door. Well, not exactly to it. Next to it. Experience had taught me that certain large-caliber guns can be mortally effective when fired through a door—especially one like the door of my room, which I'd assessed as hollow-core wood.

I also did not look out through the peephole. Where one's final view might be down the barrel of a gun held up to it.

Further, while next to said door, I did not stand upright but dropped to one knee, just in case something propelled by gunpowder might perforate both the portal and its adjoining wall.

Paranoia, as the great sage Charles Manson so memorably put it, is the highest form of love. Love, I might add, for one's ability to continue breathing.

Once again, the somewhat furtive knocking on my door that had roused me from slumber was repeated.

"Hello," a high, melodic voice called from the other side. "Hell-ooo?"

I did not answer, though my curiosity had been piqued to the point where I needed to take a peek. But not by opening *my* door.

I stood back up and silent-walked to the door that led into Dennis's adjoining room. By mutual agreement and past practice, we'd kept both sides unlocked. I opened it to find Dennis sitting at the end of his bed, naked save for a rather inadequate towel, legs crossed Indian style—subcontinent Indian, that is. Resembling nothing more than an overly muscled Buddha. He raised an eyebrow at me and looked toward the hallway. He'd heard that knocking, too.

I tapped my chest. *Let me check it out.*

Dennis nodded.

I slid to the door. And this time I did venture a quick glance through the peephole. What it partially showed me—off to the side in front of my room—was interesting.

I quietly slipped off the security chain—which would have been about as useful as a charm bracelet if anyone large was really committed to making an impressive entry—turned the lock, then opened the door to observe the approximately six-foot-tall young woman in stiletto heels who was once again knocking and repeating that somewhat hushed "Hello."

Although she was a bit taller, she looked so much like Raven that she might have been a cousin. Her waist-length hair was equally jet-black, and her features were similar—although it looked as if they'd been loaded down with half of pound of makeup. Her clothing, though not totally immodest, was minimal enough for me to be fairly certain that she was not carrying a weapon—at least not in any place she could get to it quickly. Everything about her, including her muscle tone (minimal clothing, remember?) and her erect posture, screamed showgirl. It was easy to picture her onstage with a good deal less attire and a thirty-pound headpiece rising several feet above her lovely brows.

I leaned a bit farther out.

"Hello?" I said.

To her credit, she was only slightly startled.

"Oh," she said, turning my way, "I was just . . ." She gestured toward my door. "I was . . . ah . . ."

"Knocking on my door," I said, placing my palm on my chest. "Jake Neptune."

A smile came to her face. "Yes," she said, covering the distance between us with three confident and admittedly attractive strides. She lifted a well-manicured hand as if to place it on my arm. "The Chief sent me to ask if you needed . . ."

"Needed what?" Dennis said as he came up to look over my shoulder. Then he chuckled as he rested his arm around my neck. "You think we need something?"

The smile on her face was replaced by a look of uncertainty that was, to be honest, pretty amusing, as she took in our two unclothed torsos. If we had started singing "YMCA," she would not have been surprised.

"Oh," she said, taking half a step back. "You, uh, I mean I . . ."

At that moment, I saw something in her face that touched me more than her physical attractiveness, something of the child she'd been not that many years ago. She was, I realized, younger than Raven.

"It's okay," I said. "I never let him get past first base."

"Yup," Dennis said. "We just cuddle."

That familiar typical Native teasing restored a smile—a sincere one this time—to her face. "Okay, you two," she said, with even more of the kid she'd been in the tone of her voice, the three of us on familiar ground now. Skin to Skin, so to speak.

I should pause a moment here to explain something, lest I be suspected of homophobia. As far as I am concerned—and this is truly traditional—any other person's sex life is their own business. A recognition of gender fluidity, variety, whatever you want to call it, is part of our Penacook culture. Just as long as you don't hurt anyone, what you choose to do with another adult is up to you. During our time in combat, Dennis and I had more than one close friend who was gay. Everyone in our unit knew those guys and trusted them to watch their backs, just like any other soldier. And lest you think I protest too much, let me tell you what one of the men in our unit—who was a South Pacific Islander—had to say about how American culture was just beginning to accept the fact that people could be not just male or female, but also gay or bisexual.

"Man," he said, "what is wrong with you people? All you have is straight or gay or bi? In Tahiti we've got at least seven sexes."

I removed my big buddy's arm, which was getting heavy, from around my shoulders.

"What's your name?" I asked my after-midnight visitor.

"Charmaine," she said, then paused. "But my friends call me Charlie."

"Okay, Charlie," I said. "I'm going to put on a shirt. Then I'm going to open my door and let you come on in if you want. So we can talk. And I mean talk."

I was, I must admit, slightly chagrined when I saw a flicker of what looked like relief on her face. Maybe that manly physique of mine was not quite as much of a chick magnet as I assumed.

"Talk?" she said.

"Unh-hunh."

"I'd really like that."

"So," I said, after we'd all settled down sitting across from each other in the living room of the small suite, "do I need three guesses as to who sent you, or was it . . . ?"

"The Chief," Charlie said, tugging down the hem of her maximally mini little black dress. I handed her the small blanket that had been across the end of my bed, and she draped it over her knees.

"Thanks," she said. "I have to dress like this for . . . my job as a hostess. But I really like jeans better. And if we're not going to, you know . . . I feel sort of shy just talking."

I nodded. I was liking her more and more. While a part of me was feeling angrier and angrier. I've seen so many girls like her in the U.S. and Canada, lovely young Native women who get off the rez and come to the city with the idea of getting a job, making money to send back home, maybe breaking into modeling or even TV and the movies, or just finding the right guy who can give them a life. And they usually end up being used—at best.

But, I thought, at least Charlie did have some kind of a job here in the casino. And she wasn't among the missing. The disappeared. Not yet, at least. It's one of this continent's dirty little secrets. How many Native girls leave the bleak prospects of their reserve or reservation and then are just . . . gone? Dozens—maybe hundreds—every year. Law enforcement people look for them only halfheartedly, if they look for them at all. And many of their bodies are never found. In Canada, in Mexico, and, yes, here in the States. I don't know the statistics, but it's far too many. Year after year.

I'd had the good fortune of finding a few of them before it was totally too late—employed by their families to locate a beloved daughter or grandchild. And then I'd brought them back home, most of them wounded one way or another—but still more in one piece than the ones who had objected to my intervention—and strong enough to heal. But only a few. Plus there are always some young women who don't want to be found or rescued.

It made my head and my heart both ache to think about the whole mess.

"Mr. Neptune?" a female voice said. "Mr. Neptune?"

"Don't mind him," Dennis said. "He just goes on vacation inside his head at times."

I looked up. She'd called me Mr. Neptune. Old Uncle Jake.

Feeling as if I was only one step away in her eyes from being fitted for a walker, there was only one thing I could think of that would help in an awkward situation like this.

"You hungry?" I asked Charlie.

"Yes," she said. A little quicker than she'd intended, most likely.

"I could eat, too," Dennis added.

"Or three or four," I said. "But seeing as how the Chief of the Oceans said we could still get room service after hours, let's see what they can do for us."

Rare buffalo burgers, fries, and milkshakes, it turned out. Which was just fine. I ordered three of each, which took care of Dennis. Then added two more for our guest and me.

Talking got easier after we had done our bit to contribute to the second extinction of the noble bison. If anything, Charlie was hungrier than we were, despite our being more than double her size. She even helped herself to most of Dennis's third portion of fries.

We learned that she was from the Spokane Reservation. "The same one Gloria Bird, the poet, is from," she added with a note of pride.

One of ten kids, the middle child, sending money home every month. And taking accounting at a local community college. Her day job was as a hostess and drinks server in the Under the Sea bar in the east wing of the casino. Her night job, now and then, was being asked to look after a special guest.

I was feeling more like taking on a server role myself, namely delivering a knuckle sandwich to Mr. Sea Antelope. But I knew I'd have to put off that pleasure for the near future while we tried to do what we'd come here for—which was not to protect her boss's investment.

"So," I said, "what were you supposed to find out about me?"

Charlie looked embarrassed again. "Whatever I could. You know how guys sometimes talk after . . ."

Another awkward silence ensued. To his everlasting credit, Dennis didn't start humming either "After the Ball Is Over" or "Save the Last Dance for Me."

"Hey," I said. "Want to help us?"

Charlie nodded. "I like you two. You're funny."

"So what have you heard about the trouble out on the bay?"

Charlie leaned forward and lowered her voice, as if to avoid being heard by any surveillance device that might have been placed in my room.

A somewhat paranoid thing to do—and not necessary. When Dennis and I had looked both our rooms over, we'd each found no less than a dozen of the little buggers in the phones, the clock radios, the lamps, under the bathroom sinks (but not, perish forbid, under the toilet seats), and beneath the beds. We had also—duct tape being something we both kept in our backpacks—covered the lenses of the tiny cameras placed in the walls, ceilings, and air-conditioning units. Some of those electronic eyes and ears were found through diligence and long experience, while the rest were pinpointed using a little handheld transistorized unit that we'd gotten from a former fellow jarhead who had been recruited into the agency where intelligence is centralized. Empty screens and static would be greeting the secret sharers who'd been tasked with spying upon us.

"People are freaking out," Charlie said. "Some of the people working on the bay just up and quit. Even after their salaries were doubled. Especially the divers—all of them left. And nobody who's an Indian from around here is working there anymore. They say that it's sort of cursed. Working there is breaking some kind of local taboo—which I don't know anything about, me being a Spokane and all. Except we've got our own stories about water monsters, too."

Charlie shook her head. "There are some seriously weird white guys staying here at the hotel. Ones who want to film—or maybe even catch—what they think is out there in the bay. Me?" She shivered and hugged her arms around herself. "I am just going to stay as far as I can away from the water."

"Thanks," I said.

"Hey," Charlie said, "is that popcorn on top of the microwave?"

"Yup," I said. "Want some?"

"If it's okay with you, Mr. Neptune."

I hobbled my aged bones over to the counter, shoved a package of Jiffy Pop into the machine, and pushed the button.

"Anything else I can do for you, granddaughter?" I asked.

Charlie giggled, taking at least three or four more years off her age. "You're funny. You're not *that* old." She looked at the big-screen TV. "Have you see *Sin City* yet? I haven't had a chance, but you can rent it here."

One hour and thirty-five action-packed minutes and four packages of exploded maize kernels later, Dennis and I were feeling way more weary than Charlie, who was eyeing the list of New and Available Now Hollywood Blockbusters, and clearly—adding insult to injury—considering *The 40-Year-Old Virgin*.

"Well, young lady," I said, still channeling old Uncle Jake, "I'd say its way past your bedtime."

Charlie stood up. "Right," she said. "Thank you." Then she paused, looking about as awkward as a three-legged greyhound watching a mechanical rabbit go down the track.

I got it.

"How much?" I asked, taking my wallet out of my backpack.

"No," she said. "You don't have to."

She didn't add the "but" to her sentence, so I did.

"But you'll get in trouble if you don't get paid, right?"

She looked down and nodded. "A hunnerd is the usual," she said in a voice that made her sound like a six-year-old.

I took five twenties out of the envelope I'd stuffed into my pack.

"How much do you get to keep?"

"Twenny," she said, her voice even softer.

I put the hundred dollars into her hand. "This is what I gave you," I said. Then I took out ten more twenties. "And this is what I didn't," I said, holding out the additional cash.

"I can't," she said.

"Not even if I tell you this is Chief Aqua Pony's wampum?"

A smile came to her face that really made it light up.

"Okay, then!" she said, taking the money and shoving it into her already crowded bra. Then she grabbed my shirt, pulled me close, and hugged me with one arm as she kissed me—on my cheek. "You are really cool. I wish I'd known you when you were younger."

I opened the door for her, wiggled my fingers to wave goodbye, and then shut it.

"I wish I'd known you when you weren't such an old geezer, too," Dennis said.

Exercising admirable self-control—and not wanting to break my elderly calcium-depleted knuckle bones—I satisfied myself with booting my best buddy in his butt with a low roundhouse kick that sent him laughing through the door to his bedroom, which I calmly slammed behind him.

"Good night, Mr. Neptune," he called in a high voice through the door.

"Shut it, Dennis."

"But Neo, you know kung fu now."

"Go to bed or I will kung fu you."

Then his voice returned to its normal tone. "Hey, Podjo," he said.

"Yeah."

"You are a good man, brother."

19

A Balkan Bruiser

The small fish in the deep water under you
might turn out to be a shark

I would not be telling the truth if I said I slept well that night. The dreams that visited me were not the kind that leave you feeling refreshed when you wake up the next morning. They all were the sort that leave you feeling unsettled. Like the dreams in which you can't find your keys. Or the ones where you are wandering down what should be a familiar street, but you can't remember where you live. And even though you know it's a dream, either you can't wake up or when you do, you fall right back into that same scenario.

In this case, it was me being in the water with this feeling that something big was bearing down on me. Even though I could not see it. And every time I started to turn around, I would wake up.

Give me a straightforward threatening man-eating beast anytime over that sort of post-midnight uncertainty.

It's like that scene in the eighties Val Kilmer spoof about secret agents in which he finds himself walking down the hallways of his old high school and some of his classmates come up to him and ask him if he's ready for the math test.

"A math test?" he screams. "Oh no! I haven't studied for it." Then he wakes up. It's the present day, and he is strapped to a table and about to be tortured by Nazis. "Thank God," he says, "it was just an awful dream."

Dennis and I walked silently down to breakfast. We sat again by the back wall. Our simpatico waitress from the night before did not seem to be on duty yet. But our wistful orca buddy was there, hovering over us and making soft sounds from inside his glassy prison.

Not yet, buddy, I thought to him. *We have to scope things out.*

Dennis looked up from his morning steak and eggs and nodded at me as I was thinking that. It wasn't telepathy. Just that as so often happens with us, we were on the same page without having to read it aloud.

We'd not yet finished our breakfasts when a familiar, but definitely not familial, voice interrupted us.

"All right, boys! They told me you were down here already. Bright and early risers, eh? Ready to go?"

I restrained myself from answering "Anywhere except with you" to Chief Sea Antelope, who was displaying all his dental work in a wide crocodilian grin.

Instead I let Dennis answer for us.

"Soon as we finish eating," he said, spooning a pound more of home fries onto his plate.

"Righht, righht," Sea Antelope said. "A car will be out front as soon as you're done."

"After we floss and brush our teeth," Dennis added, as he slowly and delicately buttered his tenth piece of toast.

Sea Antelope looked at the Rolex on his wrist.

"Okay, sure. See you in twenty minutes?"

Dennis shook his head.

"Thirty?"

My big buddy shook his head again as I managed to stifle a laugh by taking a slug of my fresh-squeezed orange juice. I could feel the Super Chief's temperature rising.

Sea Antelope paused, perhaps realizing that any further speculation about our time of departure would just keep raising the ante. And that a direct order would be even less effective.

"Okay," he said, backing away. "Just . . . take your time."

Looking slightly less than beet-red in the face, he turned and left the room. Proof once again that not agreeing with someone used to being surrounded by yes men is a great way to gain possession of their hollow-horned ruminant mammal of the genus *Capra.* Getting their goat, that is.

Yes, when I was a kid (baaa!), I used to memorize dictionary definitions.

Just to make sure that our new employer would not think us obstreperous, as soon as Sea Antelope exited stage right as if pursued by a bear, we got up and followed him. So silently that when he stalked outside and began to express himself about us in colorful language, we were able to startle him quite satisfactorily when I said, "We're ready" from two paces behind him. He jumped the proverbial mile.

If I had thought his previous grins were as forced as any smile could be, I was proven wrong by the grimace he displayed after regaining his poise and turning fully our way.

"All right, boys!" he said through clenched teeth.

He gestured like an overly dramatic magician. Our Slavic friend from the night before emerged from behind a pillar.

"Yah, boss. You vant me now?"

Sea Antelope waved an imperious hand, as if telling a puppy to sit and stay. Then he turned back to us.

"My man Slobodan here will accompany you, show you what equipment you've got. He's a trained diver. Me, I've got meetings all morning. High-level."

As Sea Antelope spoke, Slobodan, who was standing behind his boss's back, raised his eyes in "Lord, help me" fashion toward the heavens. He cracked the ghost of a smile at Dennis and me for a second before his lips silently shaped a word in English having to do with our host's ventral orifice.

This time it was Dennis who concealed his amusement from the self-important casino owner, covering it with a strategic fit of coughing.

Me, I was exercising admirable self-control. And liking the big Serb more every minute.

"Okay?" Sea Antelope said again.

I nodded eloquently. The Super Chief studied me.

"You don't say much, do you?"

I shook my head.

At a loss for words—perhaps because he'd used so many of them on us with so little effect—Sea Antelope shook his own head and marched back into his casino.

"Guys?" Slobodan said, opening the side door of the van. "Okay ve go now?"

"Sure thing," I replied, climbing in after Dennis, who had lowered the suspension six inches as he hopped into the back.

Slobodan closed the door and slid—more gracefully than expected for a man his size—in behind the wheel.

"Short trip," he said. "Only take ten minutes—unless ve run into rush-hour traffic."

We quickly realized he was making a joke. The road we took was not the one we'd been on the day before. It ran directly between the main casino and the one being built on the bay, and was as deserted as the highway in "Hotel California."

As he drove, Slobodan pointed out the improvements being made—places where the road had been widened, a new bridge, the site of a planned convenience store that would mostly be used by casino employees—his English getting better the farther we got from Deep Bluewater. Especially when he began talking about the training he'd gone through to become not just a certified professional diver, but an actual divemaster.

Interesting.

"So," I asked as we swung onto the access road to the end of the headland, "how do you like working for Chief Sea Antelope?"

"Aside from that," he replied, turning to look deadpan at us, "how did you like the play, Mrs. Lincoln?"

It was so unexpected, and delivered in such a spot-on imitation of an American accent, that Dennis and I both guffawed.

"Good one, Slobodan," I said.

"Call me Sam," he said. "Like the piano player in *Casablanca*."

"Where'd your Eastern European accent go?"

Slobodan Sam turned around again to flash us a quick smile.

"When you're from Serbia and built like me," he said, "people don't expect someone who speaks the American version of good English. So I play the part of the semiliterate Balkan bruiser. It's more likely to get me good-paying jobs than working as a teacher. I was on the pro wrestling circuit for a while till I messed up my knee. That was where Old Sherm back there first saw me. I did not want to burst his bubble when he talked to me like I was a mentally challenged kindergartener as he offered me a job as a bouncer. People like him do not hire people who are smarter."

"How much smarter?"

Sam shrugged, driving now with one hand, the other over the back of the seat. "Master's degree in zoology. First came here as a foreign exchange student, to a high school in Berkeley, California. Which was"—he flashed us the peace sign—"way cool. Rad, in fact."

He swerved deftly to avoid a pothole, even though he seemed to be giving all his attention to us and not the road. Great hand-eye coordination.

"So, what about the diving qualifications?"

A complicated expression came briefly to his craggy face, sort of like a cloud passing over the sun.

"Long story. Before my family emigrated here—when I was nineteen—we used to spend our summers on the Adriatic. We had money—until that damn war. And they paid for me to take lessons. Then, here in the States, one of my first jobs was at Sealand Northwest. Good pay. Cleaning out the tanks in a wet suit. Working with the porpoises and seals. But . . ."—he turned, spat out the window, and then sighed—"it got to the point where I just could not stand it any longer. The looks in their eyes? Like they wanted to be anywhere but there. You know?"

Dennis and I both nodded. We knew. Confining a sea animal meant to swim free in the wide ocean to live in a tank and do tricks for treats was the sort of thing that turned both our stomachs. It was like clipping an eagle's wings to keep it from flying. Or forcing entire nations of people to live within the confines of desolate reservations.

Sam turned his attention back toward the road. We were approaching a checkpoint where a guardhouse had been built, and a large metal gate blocked the way. It was matched by an equally imposing ten-foot-tall chain link fence stretching to either side. Two men with AK-47s over their shoulders were unslinging their weapons as they stepped forward, the skinny blond guy in front of them raising his right hand to order us to stop. Heavy security.

Interesting.

Skinny walked up to Sam's window.

"IDs," he said.

Sam leaned back and raised his long middle finger. "How 'bout this, Brucey-boy?" he said. "Forget already you owe me two hundred bucks from the last poker game?"

Brucey-boy, whose actual name was in all likelihood Bruce (unless his parents had been overly overjoyed at having a male heir), reddened. "Not you, Mr. Slobodan. Your . . . guests." He held out a hand toward us. "IDs."

Dennis and I handed him our tribal cards.

Bruce looked at them as if they were strange insects. "I need guv'mint IDs."

"Hey," Dennis said. "Those are guv'mint. Our Penacook government, which we figure has been here on this continent since about ten thousand years before your Yew Ess of A. Right?"

"This is an Indian casino, isn't it?" I added, flashing him my most winning smile.

Bruce bit his lip, then handed back our cards.

"Just doing my job," he said, his tone notably ungracious.

"Bite me, Bruce," Sam said.

Bruce took a breath, as if he was about to say something. But then he thought better of it, probably since in addition to owing Sam two hundred dollars, he was outweighed by a good two hundred pounds. He stepped back and waved a hand at the pair of equally blond security officers behind him. As one, they slung their guns back over their shoulders and pushed the two halves of the gate open. The kind of precise, disciplined movement you see in the military.

"Open sesame," Dennis intoned.

Thus far, aside from the wait staff and the chambermaids, we had not seen anyone employed by Deep Bluewater who looked to be Native. Perhaps Sea Antelope felt that his own over-the-top Indian-ness more than compensated for that lack of indigenous personnel.

Or maybe they didn't want to work for him.

"How's come no Injuns?" I asked.

"All the Native American workers here," Sam said, "quit after the accidents started happening. Even the ones who didn't have to go anywhere near the water."

Pretty much what we'd heard before from Chief George and Charlie.

But Sam's saying that piqued my curiosity. He was clearly one of the people Dennis and I would have to talk with further. Maybe he could answer some more specific questions about the "accidents" and the disappearances. But my big buddy and I had agreed that doing interviews would wait until after we got the lay of the land—or, more accurately, the Sound. Get our own idea of how things were around there before the opinions of others might muddy those sea waters.

We skirted the half-finished shell of the mammoth casino building and drove around to the back, where construction was being pushed out into Puget Sound. We stopped before we got to the place where a crew was working atop the skeleton of the pier.

Sam got out. Dennis and I followed to stand next to him where he was looking across the Sound toward the Strait of Juan de Fuca.

"I love it here," he said. "This. Not that." He jerked his thumb back toward the pier. "I hope it never gets finished. But," he said, the tone of his voice changing, "that is why you are here, isn't it? To help make it possible for them to finish building this?"

I shook my head. "Not exactly," I said.

"Then why?"

"It's complicated," Dennis said. "Let's just say that my buddy Podjo here felt called to this place—and not just by Old Sherm back there. And now that we've met a few other folks, I'd say we are aimed more on what you might call a double mission of protection and detection."

"Hmmm," Sam said. Then he lifted both hands and held them out toward the water—almost like the way we'd make the gesture for thanks in the sign language that was common from one side of the continent to the other.

"You know," he said, only the slightest trace of a Slavic accent in his voice, "the real headwaters of the Sound are out there. So much salt water from the ocean flows in here every day—about thirty times as much water as from all the rivers that empty into it."

He paused to let that sink in. "Deep water, too. Over nine hundred feet in some places. No telling what might be down there. Maybe a school of salmon, or a pod of orcas, or a sixty-foot-long whale shark—or something else."

We stood there for a while in silence, aside from the calls of the gulls being brought to us by the wind off the Sound. That same wind carried away the noise of the workers. With no powerboats or ferries crossing our line of sight at the moment, what we saw and heard might have been the same five hundred or five thousand years ago.

Until, with a deafening sound like the beating wings of a thunderbird, the Black Hawk helicopter came swooping in.

20

Investors

What doesn't kill you
might get you the next time around

The Black Hawk UH-60 is a perfect killing machine. Especially the way they were decked out in Iraq and Afghanistan. Four 12.7mm GAU-19 triple-barrel Gatling guns mounted on the stub wings, Lockheed Martin AGM-114 Hellfire anti-tank missiles, Hydra 70 unguided rockets in seven- or nineteen-shot pods. Overkill, at times.

Used for air assault, air cavalry, and aeromedical evacuation units, capable of carrying eleven combat-loaded air assault troops, those black-birds could fly into the light of a dark black night mucho pronto. As Dennis and I well knew from experience, their top speed of 222 miles per hour would have you in the red-hot heart of a combat zone in next to no time—especially since where we were, the combat zone usually started once we stepped out of our tent.

At about six to ten million bucks each, with a cost of about $1,700 per hour flying time, they were the sort of lethal toys the Pentagon loved to invest in. And now, as war surplus, being offered to stateside contractors. Stripped of their missiles and Gatling guns, but impressive nonetheless.

The one the three of us were watching circled once over the helipad I'd not noticed before—some fifty yards to our right near the construction site. Then it landed, blowing sand in all directions, the nearest workers wiping grit off their uniforms and out of their eyes.

"Vatch who get out," Sam said, hunching his shoulders slightly and in voice and carriage reverting to his Slobodan self. Like an actor getting back into character before the cameras roll.

100

Ve vatched.

My first thought as the two passengers set foot on the concrete—two of said feet in stiletto high heels—was, I am sorry to say, a bit stereotypical, if not judgmental.

Boris and Natasha.

No, the man was not short, mustached, and dressed in secret-agent black. Nor was the woman, though femme-fatale-ish, wearing an equally ebony long, slinky dress. It was just that my internal radar was screaming Russkies.

Now, as my uncle used to say, don't get me wrong. I bear no ill will toward Russians in general. They already have more than enough of that among themselves. I've met and liked a lot of them—though not the four disguised as Peshmerga who attempted to punch our tickets in Kurdistan. The average Russian, aside from relying a bit too much on vodka and nicotine, isn't that different from us. It's the new elites who rub me the wrong way—with heavy-grit sandpaper.

There is something about the way the privileged class of Russians walk and carry themselves in these days of Putin's attempts to restore the glory of the former USSR. Multi-billionaires and high-level gangsters have that way about them. Names that are not mutually exclusive and that apply aptly to the new class of oligarchs.

"Soviet investors," Slobodan Sam said. Much the way you might say slugs, or hornets, or slime molds. (My apologies to all three for the comparison.)

Investors, indeed. Were Shakespeare writing *Henry IV, Part 2* today, the words out of Dick the Butcher's mouth in scene 2 might be "The first thing we do, let's kill all the investors."

Oh, and how about adding crooked (an assumption on my part, admittedly) casino managers to that list, I thought, as the third passenger in the killer bird climbed down. None other than Ocean Pronghorn hisself.

The casino chief looked our way, as did Boris and Natasha. Even at a distance, something about the way they looked at me sent a shiver down my spine.

Yes, you are planning to see me again.

Then, as if suddenly waking up from a trance, Sea Antelope quickly turned to his VIP guests and ushered them toward the half-built structure. Which looked as much semi-demolished as partially built. The only part of it that was as impressive as I suppose the whole shebang was supposed to look was the two thirty-story arcing towers, a quarter mile apart and each shaped like the tall dorsal fin of an orca.

"Look on my works, ye mighty, and despair," I intoned. Though I might have been getting ahead of myself on that one. It not yet being a desert ruin.

"Percy Bysshe Shelley—1792 to 1822," Sam added.

I looked at him and he shrugged his massive shoulders. "Memorized when exchange student. Real oldie but goodie. Dive shack now?"

"It's now or never," Dennis sang tunelessly back at him.

Truly the worst Elvis impression ever. Where was a knife and a whittling stick when I needed them? Or a gag?

The dive shack was a lot more than a shack. It could have been better described as a scuba condo. Two stories tall with bathrooms on the side. Located at the water's edge behind it was a small wooden dock. Tied to it, equipped with 300 horsepower Evinrude outboard motors, were three Zodiac rubber boats. They ranged in size from a twelve-foot Cadet to one roomy enough to carry a dozen or more people.

Sam opened the door and held it as we went inside. As I had expected, within was a full-scale emporium of everything needed for a human being to enter the marine environment.

As well as some things that were not.

Such as the large bookcase against the north wall. I ambled over to peruse its offerings. It was stocked, it seemed, with every book ever written about cryptozoological beasties. From Yetis to Nessies.

"Your library?" I asked Sam.

His response was to cup his hands against his chest and turn his eyes toward the sky.

I pulled a thin volume from the shelf. *Much More than Mere Myth* was the title. By, of course, Malcolm Grattington, Ph.D. I leafed through it quickly. Despite it having double the pages of his earlier volume, the typeface was large and the additional content small. The fact that I was speed-reading by the time I was seven made it easy for me to quickly take it all in, even though there was not all that much to take.

I slid it back into its place between *Loch Ness Deciphered* and *Ogopogo Lives.*

"The boss, Mr. S.A., he likes to try to play all sides," Sam said. "So he insists these books be here. All junk."

Junk indeed, including those that purportedly relied on "indigenous informants."

"I feel like I need to get into the water," I said.

Sam opened a cabinet containing wet suits of various sizes on hangers. "Not without these," he said. "Unless you like hypothermia."

I nodded. The waters of Puget Sound, even though they don't go below forty-five degrees in the winter, are not that much warmer in summer. Fifty-three at the highest.

Sam pointed at the array of equipment used when teaching entry-level diving skills to beginners. "Tanks?"

I manfully refrained from saying "You're welcome." Instead I looked over at Dennis, who shook his head. I concurred.

Conventional open-circuit scuba equipment could come later.

"Just masks and snorkels this time," I said. "We want to get a feel of the water here."

As Dennis daintily removed his glasses to place them on an open shelf—for there is no way one can wear glasses under a scuba mask—Sam handed him a full-face snorkel mask.

"Try this one," he said. "Prescription lens. −5.0."

Dennis held it up to his face.

"All right!" he said. "Even better than my specs. I could wear this all the time."

Half an hour later, we were way out on said water—so far that the hulk of the half-done casino looked like a broken teacup. Ordinarily there might have been a problem finding a wet suit big enough for Dennis's quadruple-X frame, but one of Sam's extras fit just fine. The same went for flippers. Both he and our new Serbian comrade were size sixteen. A brightly colored buoy rose above the water fifty yards from us.

Sam gestured at it. "Red and white buoy. That shows the water is deep enough for a ship to pass on either side."

I looked over the edge of the Cadet.

"How deep here?"

"Pretty shallow," Sam said. "Only 450 feet."

"Want to go for the record?" Dennis said as he adjusted his mask.

"Not deep enough for that," I replied, only half joking.

Dennis was referring, of course, to free diving. It's an actual sport, in which you see how deep you can go—without a mask or snorkel or any breathing apparatus. Holding your breath as you plummet down. Dedicated free divers routinely go below 100 meters. Both Dennis and I did the kind of training free divers do, learning how to hold our breath underwater for five minutes or more while engaging in one activity or another. Which comes in handy for the sort of activities in which we engaged in the Persian Gulf. Which I still cannot talk about. Though I can say that when you are working with dolphins, they get really bored with you if you only can hang under the surface with them for a minute or two.

Although I don't know much about it, a lot of doing free diving, aside from deep breaths before you go down to put as much oxygen as possible into your system, is getting in the right state of mind.

As far as static free diving—just calmly staying in one spot—holding your breath for over ten minutes is a piece of cake for serious FDs, once you've learned how to relax and control the impulse to struggle to the surface and gulp in air. And the world record for depth gets deeper every year or two. Some say that six hundred feet is the max, but people tend to surprise you. And once someone does it—like clearing the once seemingly impossible seven feet in the high jump—more and more people equal or better it. (Oh, by the way, the current world record for that over-your-head leap is eight feet and a quarter inch, set in 1993 by Javier Sotomayor of Havana.)

That said, free diving is not exactly safe. About fifty competitive divers die every year while doing it.

"Ready?" Sam asked.

By now Dennis was already in the water, having gone ahead of me while I was musing about free diving and Cuban kangaroos. He was the only one carrying anything like a weapon. He'd commandeered a spear gun with a reel holding over a hundred feet of line.

"Might as well pick up dinner while we're at it. Eh, Podjo," he'd said.

"Okay?" Sam asked again.

My mask was over my face and my snorkel was in my mouth, so I just gave a thumbs-up and rolled backward off the Zodiac.

It seems that there are few things as exhilarating—aside from dreaming you're flying—as the way you feel when you're swimming underwater. You're as free of normal gravity as you'll ever be this side of space travel. You're in a whole new world, one in which up can seem down and every creature you encounter is far different from anything on land.

A medawelin, that sort of person I've mentioned before who might be called a shaman if he or she was a Buryat, is also described as a diver. One who can go far below the surface where most people walk, go deep and bring back knowledge hidden from most eyes. The fact that this word is so close to the one for loon—who's also a diver—is telling. Medawela, the loon, is connected to strong medicine, able to fly up into the sky world, walk on the land, and then dive deep into the waters.

I hovered about twenty feet deep, turning slowly, looking up and down to see in all directions around me. We were a mile away from the point where the being so many were looking for—Her, as Chief George said—was supposed to live. Dennis was nowhere to be seen, and the dive boat was at least a hundred yards away now. I was alone. Sort of.

21

The Horned Snake

The hard part of riding a tiger
comes when you try to get off its back

Aunt Mali told me the first story I ever heard about the Horned Serpent. It wasn't like some of the later stories I heard, in which it was a fearful creature, tipping over canoes and swallowing people whole.

I was six years old, and I'd caught a water snake one summer on Paradox Lake in the Adirondacks. We were visiting friends who lived up there—the Swift Eagle family, who were working at a tourist attraction called Frontier Town. They ran the Indian Village down the hill from Fort Custer. That day we'd all been invited to a cookout on the beach by some tourists renting a place on the lake. I'd taken a fishing pole and wandered away out onto a rocky point of land thrust like an arm into the lake. It was when the water snake tried to take the fish I'd just caught off my line that I grabbed it.

I was holding said snake by the neck so it couldn't get me. It wasn't poisonous. The only poisonous snakes in the Adirondacks are on a couple of the mountains around Lake George—rattlesnakes that sometimes swim out to the islands in the lake. Poisonous or not, that brown and yellow banded water snake sure wanted a piece of me. It kept hissing and twisting in my grasp. It was really strong for its size, over two feet long, and I had to hold on with both hands. A real warrior. I admired its courage.

Aunt Mali came up behind me as I held it. I heard her footsteps. I'd also felt her coming and knew who it was without even turning around. Even back then when I was little, I could do that. And other stuff.

"Look at this little tough guy," I said, as he gaped his mouth and hissed even louder.

Aunt Mali sat down on the rock next to me.

"He was about to grab my fish—but I grabbed him first."

"It would be a good idea to let him go," Aunt Mali said. "His grandfather Jodikwando would appreciate that."

Jodikwando?

I was about to let him go anyway. So I did what Aunt Mali suggested. I bent over, dipped him in the water, and let go of him, first his body and then his neck.

And quickly jumped back and scrambled up the cliff, because as soon as I released his neck, he didn't swim away like a fish would. Unh-unh! He whipped around and came at me, mouth open. He would have gotten me if the rock face there had not been so steep.

Aunt Mali laughed from behind me. She'd retreated back up the rocks as soon as she saw me leaning over to put that aggressive little snake back into the water.

"He's still upset with you, wasosis."

Wasosis is what she called me. I don't think I've mentioned that before. It means little bear.

"What can I do to make him not so angry?"

"Give him a fish sometime."

I nodded and sat down next to her, watching that water snake swimming back and forth in front of the cliff.

"So who's Jodikwando?"

"I guess you need to hear the story."

Long ago, she said, there was a young woman named Swaying Reed.

Swaying Reed lived in a village along the Mahicanitewk, the river of tides people now call the Hudson. She was good-looking and kind to everyone. Her kindness was extended to every being, from the plants that she thanked for providing food for the people, to the birds and animals. Everyone liked her except for one person, another girl named Pretty Face.

Although Pretty Face did, indeed, have a pretty face, the thoughts inside her head were not pretty. She was jealous of Swaying Reed. She resented all the attention that kind young woman got, the way the elders praised her and the way other people spoke so well of her.

If she was gone, Pretty Face thought, *everyone would pay more attention to me.*

So she made a plan. It was the time when the berries were ripe. Pretty Face went to Swaying Reed.

"My friend," Pretty Face said, "would you like to come with me and pick berries?"

Swaying Reed was pleased. Pretty Face had never spoken much to her before, and it had seemed as if she did not like her. But now she was behaving like a friend.

"I would like that," Swaying Reed said. "Thank you for asking me."

"They are on that island far, far out in the river where the currents are very swift. If anyone tries to swim there, they will drown. But I can take you in my canoe."

The two young women got into that canoe, and Pretty Face paddled them to that island. There were many berry bushes, just as Pretty Face had said. Swaying Reed started to pick them.

"Wait," Pretty Face said. "Those are small berries. The best ones are over this hill on the other side of the island. You go pick them while I gather these little berries here."

Swaying Reed was pleased that her new friend was being so generous.

"Thank you," she said. Then she climbed over the hill to the island's other side.

But when she got there, there were no berries to pick. There were lots of bushes, but all the berries on them were white. As everyone knew, white berries were poisonous to people. Only the birds could eat them.

My friend must have made a mistake, Swaying Reed thought. *She will be so disappointed.*

Swaying Reed climbed back over the hill to the place where Pretty Face had been picking berries. But her new friend was not there. She was in her canoe, far out on the river, heading back to the distant other shore. Swaying Reed called to her, but Pretty Face did not even look back.

That was when Swaying Reed understood that Pretty Face was not her friend at all—she had tricked her into coming out to the island to get rid of her.

It would soon be dark. Swaying Reed looked around for a place to take shelter. There, on the beach, was a big hollow log that had been washed up by the swift current. It was dry inside that log and, when she placed some dry grass in it for a bed, a comfortable place to spend the night. She curled up within the log and went to sleep.

In the middle of the night, something woke her. It was the sound of voices. But those voices were so strange that she stayed where she was and listened.

"That kind young woman is there inside that log," a deep, deep voice boomed.

"Which of us should help her?" a second voice asked, one that was high and reedy like a heron's call.

"I will do it," a third, rough voice said.

"No," the first voice said. "You will frighten her. I will help her."

"That is good," the second voice trilled. "Let it be Jodikwando who comes to her aid."

"Yes," said the rough-voiced one.

"Yes, yes, yes," said more of those strange voices, one after another.

There was a knothole in the side of the log. Swaying Reed put her eye to it to try and see the ones who had been speaking, especially the one called Jodikwando. But all she saw were flickering lights that drifted away and disappeared over the river.

The next morning, as soon as the first shaft of sunlight came in through that knothole, she crawled out of the log. She was eager to see if Jodikwando was there as he'd said he would be, as well as very curious about who he might turn out to be.

What she saw took her completely by surprise. There, at the water's edge, was a giant serpent. A single horn in the middle of his forehead, rainbow scales glittering in the light, he lifted himself high above her. Yet, huge as that creature was, Swaying Reed was not afraid, for the look in his eyes was calm and gentle.

"You are Jodikwando?" she asked.

"Yess," the Great Serpent replied. "And you are in need of help?"

"I am," Swaying Reed said. "Someone pretending to be a friend brought me here and then abandoned me. Will you assist me, please?"

Jodikwando lowered his head. "Climb onto my neck," he said. "Take hold of my horn with both of your hands."

Swaying Reed did as he said. As soon as she was settled in place, Jodikwando turned, entered the water, and began to swim.

"You must do one thing for me," he said.

"Tell me what to do," Swaying Reed replied.

"The Thunder Beings are my enemy. They will try to kill me with their arrows of lightning. You must let me know if you see any dark clouds approaching."

"I will do as you ask," Swaying Reed said. "Right now the sky is clear."

The Great Serpent swam swiftly, and soon the island was left far behind.

As they went along, Swaying Reed constantly kept watch on the sky. "Clouds are forming off to the west," she said.

"I must swim faster," Jodikwando said.

Now they were more than halfway across.

"The clouds are getting darker," Swaying Reed said. "They are moving toward us."

"Then I must swim even faster," Jodikwando said.

Swaying Reed could see the place on her side of the river where people launched their canoes. But when she looked up into the sky, what she saw alarmed her.

"The clouds are right overhead now."

"Then I must dive," Jodikwando said.

And that is what he did. Just as he dove, a lightning bolt struck the water where he had been, barely missing Swaying Reed. She struggled in the water, sure that she would drown. But when she put her feet down, they reached the shallow bottom. She was able to wade the rest of the way to shore.

As she climbed out, she found that she held something in her hand. It was the tip of Jodikwando's horn, a farewell gift he had left her.

She turned and faced the water. "Jodikwando," she called. "Thank you for helping me. I will never forget you. I will bring you fish and leave them on the bank of the river for you."

When Swaying Reed got back to her village, almost everyone was glad to see her.

"Daughter," her mother said, "your friend Pretty Face said that she loaned you her canoe. When it floated back here empty, everyone was afraid you had drowned."

"No," Swaying Reed said. "I was on that distant island and had no way to get home. But then someone helped me."

She told the story of how Jodikwando had saved her. As proof of her story, she showed everyone the piece of his horn.

"That is a special gift you have there," her grandmother said. "The horn of the Giant River Serpent is great medicine. It can be used to cure people who are sick."

Pretty Face had not been pleased to see Swaying Reed. She feared that Swaying Reed would tell how she had been deceived. But Swaying

Reed said nothing of how Pretty Face had left her on the island to die. Even so, instead of being grateful, Pretty Face became even more jealous.

"That medicine horn should have been mine," she said to herself. Then she made another plan. She waited until it was close to sunset, slipped away from the village, and went to the river. Climbing into her canoe, she paddled to the distant island and reached it just as night was falling. As soon as she got out of the canoe, she shoved it off and watched it being taken by the current.

"Oh no!" she said in a loud voice. "Now I am marooned here. I need help to get back home."

The hollow log was there on the beach. Pretty Face climbed in and waited impatiently. Finally, deep into the night, she heard voices.

"The one who brought herself here is there inside that log," a deep, deep voice said.

"What should we do about this girl who is hiding in the log?" a second voice asked, one that was high and reedy.

"Let me take care of her," a third, rough voice said.

"No," the first voice said. "I am the one she is looking for. I will do it."

"That is good," the second voice said. "Let it be Jodikwando who gets this one off our island."

"Yes, let him take care of her," said the rough-voiced one.

"Yes, yes, yes," said more strange voices, one after another.

Then they were gone. All night, without sleeping, Pretty Face waited for dawn so that she could get her own special gift.

The next morning, when Pretty Face climbed impatiently out of the log, Jodikwando, the Great Serpent, was there on the shore waiting.

"Lower your head so I can climb on your neck," Pretty Face said.

"I will do as you ask," Jodikwando said.

As soon as she was settled in place, Pretty Face began to kick the sides of Jodikwando's neck with her heels. "Let's go," she said. "Start swimming."

Jodikwando did just that. He swam out into the swift current. As he swam, Pretty Face took out a flint knife she had concealed in her clothing and began trying to cut off the tip of his horn.

"Do you see any clouds?" Jodikwando asked.

"Yes," Pretty Face said. "Swim faster. There are some clouds in the western sky."

"Ah," Jodikwando said, "then I must dive."

And just like that he dove deep, leaving Pretty Face, who was never seen again, there in that swift water.

When my Aunt Mali finished that story, I sat there for a while beside her. She didn't say anything further. She never explained the lessons in any of the stories she told me. But those lessons, even at the age of six, were always pretty darn clear.

I'd tossed my fishing pole up onto the rocks when I grabbed that water snake. I stood up, went over to the pole, and took the sunfish that was still attached to my line off the hook.

I no longer saw the water snake. But I knew what I had to do. I climbed down and hopped onto a big rock that was in the water.

"This is yours," I said as I dropped the sunfish into the water. Quick as lightning, the water snake swam out from under the rock, grabbed the fish, and was gone.

I mention that story because it was what came into my mind as I floated there ten feet down in Puget Sound. Maybe it came to me because of what I was feeling just then. Namely that I was not alone.

I looked down toward the distant bottom over four hundred feet below me. The water was clear, but all I could make out were the tops of kelp beds, swaying green plants rising up from the bottom as tall as giant sequoias.

Did I see anything way down there? Something really big moving among those plants? Maybe. Or maybe not; maybe it was just my imagination. I looked around. Still no sign of Dennis. So much for the buddy system.

I had been under for a while without an oxygen tank. Three minutes and twenty seconds, according to the waterproof watch on my wrist. I kicked my way to the surface. As I bobbed up, taking a deep breath, I looked around in the direction where the boat should have been. But there was no sign of Sam and the Zodiac where I expected them to be.

I felt as much as heard the deep thrum of an engine behind me. I turned and saw a very large boat that had come out of nowhere. It was headed straight at me, like an arrow aimed at a target, its prow lifted partway out of the water. Like the thing I had felt but not seen in my dream. Except all too real this time. And doing at least fifty knots.

Even if I tried to do a swift dive from the surface, there wasn't much chance I would escape its propellers. I was about to be turned into mincemeat.

22

Threats

*The worst thing about dreams
is that sometimes they come true*

As the yacht bore down on me, I took a deep breath. Then I tried to bend my body forward to do a surface dive, knowing it was probably fruitless, but not willing to just give up before being chopped into bits by the propellers. But then something suddenly grabbed hold of my ankle.

And I was yanked violently down and to the side.

Just far enough that the boat missed me. Its deadly churning blades passed no more than an arm's length from my face. I felt the pressure sucking me toward it, almost pulling the mask off my face, but that life-saving grip never let go, and ten seconds later the boat was gone.

I looked down and saw what I thought I would. My faithful bro Dennis was gripping my ankle in his right hand. His left hand held the spear gun, its taut line fastened to the red-and-white buoy I'd seen before we went into the water. That was all that had kept us both from being pulled into the propellers.

Dennis let go of the spear gun, the weight of the reel causing it to plummet down and out of sight as the two of us kicked our way to the surface.

The yacht that had almost cooked my goose was already far away from us and getting farther. Maybe it had not been deliberately steered my way.

Right. And maybe salmon don't swim upstream.

I slapped Dennis on the shoulder. "Mmmpphhher, aaank oooo," I said. Then I spat out the snorkel, which I'd bit down on so hard that it was just this side of a dental implant.

"Brother, thank you," I repeated.

"Hey, hey, hey," he said, holding up his hand to give me a fist bump. "Just my turn, Podjo." Then he raised his arm over his head to wave. "*Over here*," he yelled.

Sam in his Zodiac was heading our way from beyond the buoy.

"God damns! You all right?" he called, holding out a pole for us to grab as he killed the engines to drift close. "God damns! God damns!" His face was red, his voice choked with anger, and his English distinctively less correct due to his current emotional state. He was way more upset than Dennis and me. Maybe because he was not as used to having people attempt to punch his ticket as we were.

He was still livid as he helped pull us into the Cadet.

"Son bitch come right at me. Then he turn toward you. You all right? God damns! God damns!"

He shook his fist at the yacht, which was now just a distant blip on the horizon.

"You just wait!" he shouted. "I get you."

Dennis and I lay there, side by side, our flippered feet still in the water.

"Was that who I think it was?" Dennis asked.

"Yup," I said. "That had to be our Asian gourmet billionaire. More of our competition, you might say."

"Everybody wants ta get inta da act," Dennis said in a raspy voice, doing his best imitation of Jimmy Durante.

"Yup," I said, reciprocating with the legendary performer's standard sign-off line: "Good night, Mrs. Calabash, wherever you are."

Sam, who apparently was not as well versed in mid-twentieth-century popular culture as he was in zoology, turned to look quizzically at us. "You guys all right? You hit your heads or something?"

"Not recently," I said.

"No need to worry about brain damage," Dennis added. "We've already been there, done that."

Aside from muttered curses in Serbian, our trip back to shore was a largely silent one. It gave me more than enough time to ponder about what had just happened—both below and above the waves.

I found myself making mental lists of the sort I usually create partway through a case—if you could call what we were doing that, rather than merely a mission in which we were setting ourselves up as sitting ducks for more than one potentially lethal adversary. Foes who, one way or another, wanted us out of the picture. Ranging from scaring us off to actual erasure. Which threats I included in my first list—creatively titled in my fertile mind "Threats."

1. Chechen assassin
2. Chinese gourmet billionaire
3. Russian mafia members
4. Rival casino owners
5. Semi-legendary serpent

My second mental list was a more specific one: the names of those who (probably) did not want us out of the picture. I titled it "Allies."

1. Chief George and Raven
2. Chief Sea Antelope
3. Our new buddy Sam
4. Mook Glossian

Though on second thought, the only people in that particular list who we probably could count on were Chief George, Raven, and Sam. What we had done thus far had not exactly endeared us to our local casino manager. It was easy to imagine him putting in a call to that wealthy Beijing-based gourmet suggesting that he might want to steer his floating mansion our way. Thus ridding the Super Chief of a pair of troublesome investigators by "accidentally" turning the two of us into macerated fish food.

And as far as our old non-buddy the toad wolf went, sending us out to the Northwest might have been his way of getting us out of his hair for good—at a safe distance.

Further, on third thought, was I wise to include our Serbian scuba diver in that list of folks we could count on? After all, we had only his word that he'd been forced to move by that oncoming colossal aquatic condo. Maybe he'd been signaling to that big-ass boat, pointing out just where we were about to surface so that we could be deep-sixed?

Welcome, Excedrin headache number one.

We were still half a mile from shore. A familiar feeling began to come over me.

Okay.

I opened my eyes to look at Sam. No, not exactly at him. Into him.

It's not something I can always do. It kind of comes and goes. But when I felt it like I did right then, a sort of prickling at the base of my skull, I could recognize it and, in a way, control it. Or at least control myself enough to not let on about what I saw. Which is good, since it used to get me into a raft of trouble when I was a little kid and would—when I got that feeling—look at someone and then blurt out the most inappropriate truths about them that I had just "seen."

Like when I said to my principal when I was delivering some books to a packed teacher's lounge, "Mr. LaPierre, how come you are meeting Mrs. Newell at a motel tonight?"

Oooopsie!

The whupping I then got in his office was what taught me, at the tender age of eight, three truisms: Silence is golden. Don't talk about what you don't understand. And keeping your mouth shut makes it a whole lot easier to sit down without a pillow.

I might add that even though said principal had learned the supposed value of corporal punishment during his years in a government boarding school, my not being able to sit well did not sit well with my father—who was still alive back then and had not yet been sent off to Vietnam to earn a number of medals and a free trip home in a flag-draped coffin. Dad was raised another way—a way in which any adult who hit a kid for any reason was regarded as a coward. When he finally convinced me to tell him why I was limping, and after he saw the stripes on my butt and upper thighs from the half a fishing rod Mr. LaPierre kept in the corner of his office, he embarked upon a quick parent-teacher visit to that same motel I'd seen in my vision when I'd looked into the principal's eyes that morning. After being absent from school for a week, when Principal LaPierre finally returned to work, his right arm was still in a sling and his dark glasses barely concealed his two black eyes. I'd already taken note, as I'd walked past his office and looked through the window, that his half a rod was missing from the place where it always used to hang on the wall next to his framed picture of Giovanni Battista Enrico Antonio Maria Montini, Pope Paul VI.

"Hey, Sam," I said.

Our Serbian guide turned his head my way, and as my gaze held his for half a second, long enough for a little shiver to go down my back, I saw enough.

"What?" he said. "Can I help you?"

"Just want to say thanks. It's been an interesting morning so far."

One in which I now knew we had at least one more person who actually did want to be our friend.

"No problem," Sam said. "Don't mention it."

"I won't," I said.

Which earned me a chuckle from Dennis, who knows my early history about as well as I do. He looked at Sam's wide back and then raised an eyebrow.

I nodded my head toward the huge Serbian, touched my forehead with my little finger, and then gave my buddy a thumbs-up.

"Cool," Dennis said. "You know what they say, Podjo. Takes two to tango, but when there's three, you got one to watch your back while you're dancing."

23

Cause of Death

It's better to light a candle . . .
unless there's a gas leak

After changing out of our wet suits and taking quick showers in the dive shack's well-equipped bathroom, we put on our every-day duds to proceed to step two of our day: interviewing the foreman on the construction site.

There was no diving going on anymore. That part of the construc-tion of the big pier had been halted after the second death. As we'd heard earlier, all the divers had quit. All the stuff connected to subsurface work, though, was still there at the edge of the water.

I could see how up-to-date it was. All of the past diving we'd done—Dennis and me back in the Persian Gulf—had been with pretty ordinary scuba gear. In our wet work (if you could call it that) we never used suits with air lines—seeing as how we were not doing stationary construction diving, where you'd stay in one place to work underwater. But we'd learned surface-supplied diving. We knew all the equipment and could do it our-selves if the need ever arose . . . which I hoped right now would not be the case. I've felt, the few times I've gone down in training while connected to a breathing hose, like the shiny lure on the end of a fishing line.

The diving helmet on the platform was nothing like those old copper and brass helmets that used to be the standard—the ones with a round front face plate and two more circular ones on either side of the head. This hat—or bonnet, as it's sometimes called—was a bright yellow Kirby Morgan SuperLite-17. Built on a fiberglass shell with chrome-plated brass fittings. Complete with oral-nasal mask, a microphone, and a loudspeaker for the communications system.

Dennis leaned over to pick up the helmet, even though the foreman scowled at him as he did so.

"Come a long way since the Deane brothers, eh?"

I nodded. Dennis was referring to Charles and John Deane, the two British men who pioneered designing and using diving dress equipment. He knew about them because, like me, Dennis always researches the history of anything that becomes part of our work. Those diving pioneers started back in 1828. By 1834 they'd progressed far enough for Charles to use his suit—in which you had to stay bolt upright or water would flood into it—to salvage twenty-eight cannons from the wreck of the *Royal George*. In 1836, John Deane would recover guns, longbows, and shipwreck timbers from the *Mary Rose*, which went down in the sixteenth century. That same year, the two of them put out a book about their new profession: the world's first diving manual, *Method of Using Deane's Patent Diving Apparatus*.

Dennis carefully put the helmet back down without saying anything further. No wisecracks from either of us. He understood, as did I, why the foreman—who'd known the man who died wearing it—had glared at him that way. That bonnet was probably sitting right where it had been placed after they took it off the diver. Like a grave marker.

Whatever caused the death of Matt Barner, the man who'd been wearing it, had not done any visible damage to the bonnet. But despite how expensive it was, and that it seemed to be in perfect shape, no one was about to use that dive hat any time soon—if ever again.

I stepped over the umbilical—the air hose used to pump the breathable mixture down to the man working underwater—which was connected to the nearby gas compressor. That hose was what they'd used to pull him up after hearing a sudden heavy exhalation of his breath through their com link—and then nothing else. Umbilicals not only carry air and communication cables, they're also strong enough to support the diver's weight so they can be used by surface personnel to pull the diver out of the water. As they did with Matt Barner's limp body.

"Cause of death?" I asked the hard-hatted foreman, a West Indian man who stood about 5'8" and was built like a boxer.

At Sam's urging, he had introduced himself as George, a bit of what I guessed was a Jamaican lilt in his voice. The few months I'd spent there had left me with a real appreciation of reggae and the eloquence of the island patois. As well as the real warmth of Jamaican culture. Whatever you come to Jamaica for, they say, you will find someone who can give it to you. You want ganja, we give. You want man or woman, we give. You want reggae, we give. You want .45 automatics with muzzle suppressors? Despite the tough gun laws, they could (and did) give those, too.

But George was not in a giving mood. His brusque tone and his physical stance so clearly telegraphed his resentment of our presence that I had resisted saying something like "George Foreman, eh? So are all your kids named George?"

Instead I had just held out my hand—and then dropped it back to my side when he ignored it as he turned and said, "You come this way." Followed by, "Watch where you walk."

"Cause of death?" I asked again as we approached the end of the partially built pier. No reply.

I was thinking of repeating my question a third time, if for no other reason than to fill in the deafening silence that followed my asking it, when George the foreman raised both his hands, even more quickly dropped them, and then sighed.

"Raas," he said, more of the island coming into his voice. "Did they not tell you? Officially an accident. Like the time before. Blunt force to the abdomen caused by him getting pushed by a freak current against one of those beams down there. That is what they said." He spat into the nearest wave washing against the skeletal pier. "An accident. Just the same as the first one. That is how they wrote it up."

I took a chance and put my right hand on his arm. That helps sometimes. Maybe it's just the physical human contact. Or maybe it's like a way to a psychic connection, helping whatever gift I have touch something inside that other person. Something we all have in common. Something that makes them readier to trust me.

"I don't care about what they wrote up," I said. "I want to know what you think. Or what you saw."

The foreman looked at me. "Just between us?" he said, his voice somehow softer.

I nodded and put my left hand on my chest. "Between us."

"No accident. Nanny raas! None of it has been an accident. We saw what happened . . ."

He paused and I waited.

"The water wasn't all that clear, but he was only forty feet down. And we all saw something. Fast. Blow wow! Moving toward him before . . ." He shook his head. "That is all. But everyone who saw it knows that it was no accident. And as long as I am still foreman—and it might not be that much longer—no way in hell am I going to allow any of my men to go down into that water again." He shook his head and then again growled out that Jamaican patois word for which we have no English equivalent. It's sort of a combination of anger, regret, and disgust. "Raas!"

Then he leaned close to me. "Tomorrow," he said in his soft lilting voice, "tomorrow no man will be working here. We are walking out! You understand?"

I did.

He nodded and then walked me back to where Dennis and Sam were waiting. By the time we got to them, I'd learned that there was no one else for me to interview. None of the other men who'd seen, or almost seen, the so-called accident were still working on the site anymore, according to George. (Whose last name, he finally told me, was Brown. Only the most common surname on the island.) One of them had gone back to Kingston, while the other two, both like George from Jamaica's mountainous Cockpit Country, had headed back to families living on Florida's west coast.

That was okay. I didn't need to talk to them. I already—just based on what George Brown had told me he saw—had a pretty good idea of what had actually killed those two men. It was not accidental. And the thought of what it probably was left me feeling a mix of anger and regret, like a knot in my gut.

Raas, for sure.

24

Mountains

The name of the mountain
is not the mountain's name

If you knew
the name of the rain
would it answer you
or, like an unfaithful dog,
would it turn away?

I can't answer
a question like that.
I'm just looking
out the window

watching the rain
walking over the mountain
leaving me dry
in the desert of my imagination

I closed the notebook—the small one about the size of a pocket protector that I sometimes carry in my pocket along with a pencil stub. Just in case something comes to visit my imagination. That way, whether it's worthwhile or not, at least I can catch it and, reading it later, tell if it was a waste of graphite powder and clay. There's something I heard Allen Ginsberg say once at a poetry reading that has always stuck with me. I can't remember his exact words, but it was something like "Nothing escapes faster than a poem in the night." Which is why he always kept a notebook and a pen on his nightstand in case he was wakened by a poem.

Dennis looked over at me.

"Had an idea?"

I made the sign for no or nothing, an open hand, palm up, swung off to the side of my body.

I didn't bother to pull out my notebook again and read him what I'd just written. The only salient part of it was probably the last line about "the desert of my imagination."

We were back at the casino hotel, on the roof, to be exact. It was early afternoon and an amazingly clear day for the Puget Sound area, where the safest thing a weather forecaster can say is "Chance of fog tomorrow." We could see Mount Rainier, all 14,411 feet of it, as clear as a picture postcard. I've always loved mountains—but not to climb them. That whole conquering-the-highest-peaks bit is such a white guy thing. Uh, correction there. Unless like Adolf Hitler in World War II you've made the Nipponese honorary Aryans. I am remembering that insane Japanese dude who decided to ski down Mount Everest in 1970. Yuichiro Miura, who got two members of the film crew accompanying him killed. Just to shushboom 6,600 feet in two minutes and twenty seconds.

Everest. Another place I've been—though not to climb its peak. Where the frozen bodies of intrepid but unlucky mountaineers act as trail markers: turn left at the dead guy in the red parka. And there are not only literal traffic jams on top of the mountain, but also multiple tons of garbage from the base camp on up. My time in Nepal was purely business, not the pleasure of depriving my body of oxygen to the point of death.

"Climb Every Mountain" is not my theme song.

It's not that high places bother me.

But respect for mountains runs deep among our Abenakis and most other Native people. If you are going to climb a mountain, you have to have a better reason than just "because it's there." It could be to show reverence. I have a Wintu friend, Frank LaPena in California, who used to climb Mount Shasta every year with his children to put prayer flags up there. Or it could be, to be honest, to earn a living the way the Sherpas do in Nepal. In the Adirondacks where I live, no nineteenth-century guide was more famous than Mitchell Sabattis. Descendants of his still live around Long Lake. He knew all the mountains and the lakes and the trails. Then, in New Hampshire, there's Agiocochook, the Place of the Great Spirit or the Place of the Concealed One. Another name for it is Kodaak wadjo, the Mountain Whose Top Is Hidden. Some also call it Waumbik, the White Place. It's the tallest peak in New England. Less than half the height of Rainier, but impressive nonetheless. And possessed of some of the most extreme swings of temperature anywhere on the planet. Try minus forty degrees Fahrenheit and two-hundred-mile-an-hour winds on for size. People die climbing it.

Of course, it's now named Mount Washington—for the president the Iroquois called the Town Destroyer. According to the historical record, it was first climbed by a guy named Darby Field around 1632 with . . . wait for it . . . two Abenaki guides.

Aunt Mali told me one of our stories about Agiocochook.

Long ago, she said, the rain started falling. It did not stop. The water rose high and overflowed all the rivers and lakes, and still the rain continued to fall. There was heavy fog everywhere, and no one knew which way to go.

"Surely we will all drown," the people said.

But that is when Great Hare came one night to a certain man and woman. Those two had always shown great respect to the animal people, never hunting more than was needed and always giving thanks to the spirits of the animals they killed.

"I will show you how to survive," Great Hare said. "Follow me tomorrow."

When the sun rose the next morning, that man and woman told the people of their village what Great Hare had said.

"Come with us," they said to the people. "Pack as much food as you can carry. We have been told by Great Hare that he will lead us to a safe place."

Some did not listen. They refused to follow, and when the waters rose even higher, all those people drowned.

But that man and woman found the tracks of a hare at the edge of their village. They followed those tracks, and the people who had listened to them stayed close behind them. Those tracks led uphill through the fog, higher and higher. It was a long, hard climb.

Finally they found themselves on top of a tall, tall mountain. Agiocochook. The fog began to clear around them, and as the man and woman and the people with them looked out, all they could see was water. They stayed there on that mountain for many days until the waters finally went down.

They were the only people left in the world, and all the other human beings on earth came from them.

And somehow, perhaps through Great Hare's magic, the animal people and the plants and all the other life on the earth survived that flood. The only ones who drowned were the foolish people who did not listen to that man and woman.

That is why, ever since then, we have honored Great Hare for helping us humans survive. We incised pictures of him into the birch bark of our canoes and wigwams to help us remember what he did and that we should always treat the animal people with great respect. We never know when we will need their help.

That was the story as Aunt Mali told it to me.

Why was I musing on mountains rather than mysterious maritime deaths—or murders? Maybe because that's the way my mind works, taking the roundabout way to a conclusion. Looking up to the Pacific Northwest's highest peak when I should, by all accounts, be considering not heights but depths. Or maybe it was because the mountain was telling me something, reminding me of something. Something that we might be able to do sooner than we'd planned.

That very night, in fact. Which we had free.

We'd originally been slated to meet with Sea Antelope that evening for what he called a working dinner. But when we got back to the hotel, the desk clerk, a thin Native kid with shoulder-length hair and a nervous look on his face as he checked his phone, suddenly noticed us just as Dennis and I were reaching the elevators.

"*Sir!*" he shouted, waving a piece of paper in his left hand like a semaphore flag as he pointed at it with his other hand. "*Sir?*"

I raised an eyebrow at Dennis, who was pressing the elevator button.

He pointed his lips at the front desk clerk and then toward the ceiling.

"Got it," I said. "See you upstairs."

"Roger that," Dennis replied.

"Over and out."

I strolled over to the over-excited desk clerk, who appeared relieved that I had understood the subtle hint that he had something for me.

"Sir," he said in a slightly less stressed voice, his free hand reaching up to adjust the bolo tie around his neck, which was secured with a clasp in the carved shape of a killer whale. It quite nicely complemented the classic gray business suit, which I'd observed was the uniform for the hotel's male employees in the hospitality areas.

"Either call me Galahad or call me a cab," I said, which caused a look of either appreciation at my clever Arthurian reference or total consternation. Probably the latter, considering the dismal lack of literary history currently being offered in our institutions of higher learning. Neither *Le Morte d'Arthur* nor *Idylls of the King* can be found on their reading lists.

So I tried another approach at getting him to crack his pursed lips into a smile.

"Is that a gun in your pocket, or are you just glad to see me?"

Alas, he looked even more perplexed. Poor Mae West. The world has forgotten you.

"This," he said, offering me the sheet of paper as if it were a sacred scroll, "is an urgent message for you. From THE CHIEF."

Having spoken those last two words in capital letters made the poor lad's current state of anxiety more understandable. Little men in big jobs often like to make their underlings feel like whale crap on the bottom of the bay.

"So, Morris," I said, looking at his name tag and then briefly into his rapidly blinking eyes, "what did he say? Threaten to can you if you didn't get this to me?"

Morris swallowed and then nodded. "He said it was my last warning. That I was on my phone too much when I was behind the desk." He grabbed the offending instrument of communication and shoved it into his pocket. "But I have to keep it handy because of my grandma, who's been sick, and I'm sort of all she's got to help her since my sis went off to school, and what with the diabetes and all . . ."

Morris bit his lip, realizing his conversational dam had not just broken but was threatening to flood the valley.

I reached up to pat his shoulder. "I'll put in a good word for you tomorrow," I said. I took the note from his hand and replaced it with one of the twenty-dollar bills from the wad of "walking-around money" the good chief had given me.

"Thank you so much," he said. He started to reach out to shake my hand and then stopped halfway, wondering if what he was doing was a breach of decorum. I cupped his elbow with my left palm and pulled his arm forward so that I could take his hand.

"You're doing great, Morris," I said as I shook his hand and stepped back. "And by the way, you are really rocking that bolo."

He started to reach his hands up to take it off, proving he was more imbued with Pan-Indian culture than I'd first thought. But I held my hand up and shook my head.

"No, no, I did not say I liked it. So you do not have to give it to me."

Morris laughed. It was like the sun coming up over a cloud. "Okay," he said. "It's our clan. Made it myself. Killer whale."

"Mine's bear," I said.

Morris leaned both elbows on the desk. "Sir," he said.

"Jake."

"Jake, stop by the desk tomorrow morning, okay? I'm going to leave something for you."

"Okay," I said.

"And if there's anything I can do for you, will you let me know?"

"For sure."

As I walked to the elevator, I unfolded the note, likely printed hastily by the Super Chief and not dictated to Morris, whose handwriting would, I'm sure, have been more grammatical, better spelled, and less messily aggressive.

DINNUR MEET OFF

BUZY

WE MEET TOMOROW

NOON

REPRT

I nodded at that, surmising that his two copter-borne Soviet VIPS were going to be monopolizing his time.

Sea Antelope was still expecting a progress report—or at least our reading of the situation after our trip to the construction site. But as I looked out over the water, I thought how fortunate it was that anything having to do with our ostensible boss could wait till noon tomorrow. In other words, we had more than twenty hours to be on our own.

What's that saying about idle hands? I had a good idea about how we were going to fill ours—and it was not going to be pulling levers or rolling dice . . . or engaging in any other vice.

Reading my mind, Dennis took a final sip of the extra-large Shirley Temple the waiter from the rooftop bar had brought him. And if you think that is a sissified drink, may I point out that one does not tell that to a 300-plus-pound former member of the Special Forces. And that, like me, Dennis had not been someone you would have wanted to be around before he became a teetotaler. Imagine spending time with an inebriated gorilla, and you may see what I mean. Between us we wrecked a few bars in our day, waking up the next morning with bruised knuckles and little memory of exactly how many bikers/foreign mercs/employees of Blackwater (choose one or all three) had failed rather dismally to teach us a lesson.

Then my big buddy turned to me and said, "Interesting view, eh," as he looked down toward the much too small tank ten stories below where a certain orca, its dorsal fin flopped over, was swimming in desultory circles.

"Tonight?" I said and then smiled, even though the version he began humming of that song from *West Side Story* might have made the late Leonard Bernstein do a pirouette in his burial plot.

"Oh yeah!" Dennis said as he finished two reprehensible bars of the tune. "Free Willy."

25

Sam's Story

Two's company
Three's a little more company

It being spring in the Northwest, we had to wait till after 8 P.M. for things to be dark enough. It being a color that was in style in any season, all three of us were fashionably dressed in black—from our watchman beanies to our soft-soled shoes. Three of us. Our third recruit was our new friend Slobodan Sam.

On the ride back to the main casino, I'd asked Sam about what his duties entailed there, other than casino bouncer-cum-diving instructor. Although I doubted it to be true, there was the possibility that, considering his size and the way he'd greeted our disreputable arrival at the hotel, his jobs might include a little leg breaking on the side. What little I'd seen of the casino chief had left no doubt in my mind that using folks with Sam's physical attributes in less than legal roles was something that Sea Antelope would not hesitate to do.

Sam had turned and looked at me in a way that made me raise my estimate of his intelligence a few points higher. He'd understood exactly what I meant.

"You mean?" he said, lifting both hands briefly off the wheel so that he could grind his huge right fist into the palm of his left hand. Then, before I could say anything, he shook his head. "I got offered, but I said no. Twice. Second time I refused. If I was not so qualified at scuba, I think he would have fired me then."

He looked ahead at the road for perhaps half a mile. Then, in a softer voice, "I don't like to hurt people for someone else's reasons. Not since . . ."

He didn't end that sentence, but both Dennis and I knew what he was talking about. What had happened between the Serbs and Croats in Bosnia between '92 and '95 was still fresh in our memories even a decade later.

More silence for another half mile.

"Before here," he said, "not long after I came to America, because of my diving experience, I got that pretty good job. The one I mentioned with Sealand Northwest. First underwater maintenance, then, because they saw I was good with animals, work with seals and porpoises. Three years there. Turns out that was another reason I got hired here. At first I thought it was just to be a dive instructor. Also some work as a bouncer at the hotel when the dive business is slack. But now Chief S.A., he plans to build out their little show—like the one out back of the hotel—when the new facility is done. Gods damn!

"The orca they have here, the one they call Happy? He has been trained some already and will be part of their show. You can hold on to his dorsal fin and ride him, you know."

There was almost a smile on Sam's face.

"You've done that?" I asked.

Sam nodded. "I think he likes the company." Then his face got serious again. "They plan for him to have plenty of that. The big tanks will be a million gallons each. They have made arrangements to have four orcas shipped across from Japan, since it is illegal now to capture them here. Big tanks will be visible through the wall of the new casino—which will be all glass. Half underwater. People can gamble and watch while trainers put seals and porpoises and . . . killer whales through tricks. Big fun for gamblers." His hands gripped the wheel tighter. "But not for seals and porpoises and whales. Look there!"

We'd been driving along a rise near the ocean, and now, as he slowed the car, he was pointing toward the part of the Sound that stretched out below us just as we were coming to a scenic-view rest stop.

"Let's pull over here for a minute," I said.

Sam turned the wheel and stopped. The three of us climbed out to watch what Sam had spotted before either Dennis or me.

We stood there, loving what we were seeing.

"They are back now," Sam said, his deep voice more hushed than usual. "From May to October they return here for the herring run."

Their backs lifting up and falling like dark waves come to life, their erect dorsal fins rising like proud black sails, a pod of at least twenty killer whales was passing by—no more than fifty yards from the shore.

As we watched, first one, then another leaped high and fell, sending white sprays of water above the deep blue of the Salish Sea.

"There was a time," Sam said, "back fifty years ago, when fishermen hunted orcas. They ate salmon, so everyone blamed the decline in the salmon harvest on the whales. Forget about the dams that kept the fish from getting upriver to spawn."

"Or all the pollution washing down the Columbia," I added.

"The only ones who complained were the tribes here. I heard from one elder that they say the orcas are their relatives. Maybe even ancestors come back as killer whales, no?"

"Yes," I said.

Sam let out a breath. "Smart people," he said.

I was thinking about a story I'd heard when I was in Juneau, from Nora Dauenhauer, a Tlingit poet and playwright. Killer Whale, she said, was the custodian of the sea and a benefactor to her people. If someone is drowning and a killer whale is nearby, it will come and rescue that person. And those humans who do drown too far away to be saved, they just go to live with the killer whales in their villages under the ocean. But it's not just us North American Natives. I once met an Ainu elder on Hokkaido, the northernmost island of Japan. His name was Aterui, after the leader of the first recorded rebellion—in 780—of those indigenous people against the southerners who were taking their land. He told me they call the orca Repun Kamuy, the god of the sea. If a killer whale's body drifts up on their shores, they have a funeral for it.

"Killer whales," I said, "are special."

A bit of a smile came to Sam's craggy face. "Da. And as ideas change, the whales start coming back. Now they are always here. But not as many as a hundred years ago. Still, their numbers you see increase here at the herring time. Like my friends out there. I see them almost every day when I come here after work."

We stood in silence. Dennis had picked up a piece of wood and was turning it in his hands. I knew what he was thinking. Perfect to carve, maybe find the shape of one of those leaping orcas in the grain.

He tucked the piece of wood under his arm and nodded toward the ocean, where the whales were still playing. Or maybe not. It just might have been that there was a school of herring out there, and what they were doing was an intricate bit of teamwork, herding their prey together. Either way, all the animals in that pod were clearly having a blast. I could feel their joy like a warm wave pushing all the way up the beach and up this slope to wash over us.

"They sure look happy," Dennis said.

"Yes," Sam nodded. "Not like our poor Happy."

Hmm, I thought. *Interesting observation.*

"You know," Sam said, "the first killer whale in captivity was from near here. Harpooned and brought in. They named her Moby Doll. Everyone thought she might attack people, but she was friendly to everyone. That started the capture of orcas for display. Between 1964 and 1976, fifty were captured here in the Northwest. In the wild they never attack humans. There's no record of a killer whale in the wild ever killing a human. But they could if they wanted to. Some whale pods prefer bigger game than fish. They eat seals, walrus, even great white sharks. A pack of them will hunt big whales like wolves hunting moose. But humans—they seem to like us. The more people began to learn, they even fell in love with them. Before long, scientists studying them realized they were animals with complex and stable vocal and behavioral cultures."

We both were looking at Sam now, our mouths slightly open.

"How'd you learn all this?" Dennis asked, taking the words out of my impressed mouth.

"Studied orcas a long time. I took marine biology courses the first time I was in America," Sam said. "My plan when I got back to Serbia was to get my degree, do oceanography. Then go study at Bergen in Sweden. There's a very good marine biology program there. But then . . ." he brushed his hands together as if wiping off the dust of impossible dreams.

"The war?" I said.

Sam nodded, then wiped his hands again and gestured down toward the ground. "Anyhow, I am here now. But not for long. I have had it up to here with Mr. S.A." He held his palm at eye level, then, on second thought, lifted it over his head. "Next week, I quit. A friend in Malibu says I can get a dive instructor job there."

I looked at Dennis, who nodded at me.

Okay.

"Sam," I said, "allow us to make you an offer you can't refuse."

And so it was three of us arrayed in the hue of midnight who set out on our little mission of liberation.

With an inside man by our side, I thought, *how could anything go wrong?*

I would soon find out the answer to that question—when it suddenly became nonrhetorical.

26

Back in Black

All cats are black at night
but some are blacker than others

Dennis leaned close to whisper in my ear.

"Back in black . . . ops, that is. Eh, Podjo?"

I didn't whisper back. One bad joke was enough, especially since we were in the company of someone who not only was not a Native speaker of English (like us two Skins) but also was unlikely to be as likely as us to crack jokes while breaking in somewhere.

Not that we had to break in. Since deciding that he would be terminating his employment sooner rather than later, Sam had thoughtfully provided us with the necessary keys and keypad codes to arrive where we were with a minimum of effort.

And where were we?

Deep Bluewater's entire miniature version of Sealand consisted of three connected tanks. The smallest, where we now were, was the unlit nighttime holding tank, which was not accessible to the public. It connected to the intermediate tank, which had the viewing window in the restaurant, and then the largest of the three seaquariums, where the shows featuring Happy, an equally unhappy porpoise named Flippy, and two seals were put on. A small set of bleachers had been built for spectators next to that biggest of the tanks.

The seawater that kept the three tanks full came in through a gated-off sluiceway that fed water from the Sound directly into the complex, not with a pump, but entirely through tidal action. Kept closed with a watertight door at low tide, that door was opened as the tide began to rise, with only two marine-mammal-proof gates to keep our cetaceous

133

friends captive. Eight feet wide and six feet deep, that tidal sluiceway was the key element in our plan. That and the fact that we were almost at high tide and the water was flowing in.

Though they were not visible in the darkness, as we stood next to Happy's tank, which also housed Flippy the porpoise, we could hear the two of them as they began to surface, blow, and softly let out a series of inquisitive whistles that surely would have meant something to the other marine mammals' ears. Rather than floating in sleep, both Happy and Flippy were restless. Maybe because they sensed what we were planning to do.

It was going to be super-simple. All we had to do was lift out the net that served as the initial barrier between them and the waters of the Sound and then open the sea gate that allowed the flow of salt water into their tank.

Except, as the Scottish poet put it, "The best laid schemes o' mice an' men / Gang aft a-gley." Which might be translated into modern English as "Oh crap!" Because just as Dennis and I were about to start turning the crank to raise said net, we heard a sound that was far too familiar to us three veterans of foreign wars.

A round being racked into the chamber of a rifle.

"*Down!*" I shouted, grabbing Sam's shoulder as I dropped to the floor.

Probably not necessary, seeing as how his own reflexes had been developed from being under fire a decade ago, with incoming coming from every direction from both friend and foe in that Balkan war that pitted neighbors against each other. Sam was on his belly at the same time as the two of us.

And just in time, as the sounds of two rapidly fired weapons mixed nicely with the accompanying chatter of concrete being chipped away by the bullets hitting above our heads. Luckily, the tank we'd been next to had a two-foot-tall solid lip, which was, for the moment, at least, providing us protection. From the way they sounded, both long guns had been fitted with muzzle suppressors—silencers for those who are fans of Hollywood films. But no "silenced" gun is fully silent—to the point that it becomes a little "poot!" in action films. Although the decibel level from the pressure wave of the rapidly expanding gases that propelled the bullets had been lowered, making the noise of those gunshots less likely to be heard or at least identified as gunfire from more than a hundred yards away, it was still plenty loud for those of us who were currently playing the roles of clay pigeons.

"If I knew you were comin', I'd've brought a gun," Dennis—who was close enough for us to be mistaken for Siamese twins—crooned softly into my ear.

Very funny. Also ironic, considering just how much my big buddy loved his firearms. Being caught in a potentially lethal situation was probably less distressing to him right about then than not being heeled himself.

Don't bring a knife to a gunfight, the saying goes. Except we didn't have even a single blade between the three of us.

Did you bring a weapon?

No, I brought the potato salad and the drinks.

Poor outing pre-planning, indeed.

Although it was still pretty much dark, aside from the dim light of the stars overhead and the muzzle flashes still coming from the same doorway we'd accessed, I had a map in my head of where we were. It's another of my gifts—being able to quickly take in and remember whatever terrain I've traversed.

I summed it up mentally:

1. The pool in which Happy had now dived deep to the bottom, one hundred feet wide.
2. The doorway where the shooters were emptying their weapons, fifty feet beyond the opposite edge of the pool.
3. The ten-foot-tall training platform to my right, jutting out into the roofless room, where Happy's trainer stood to hold up food for the minibus-sized adolescent cetacean to grab by leaping out of the water. That platform, situated right next to and above the doorway, was now occupied by our two assailants, who I had just mentally dubbed Rosencrantz and Guildenstern.

Okay. That was enough for me to make a quick plan.

Though we had no armory of our own to rely on, we did have two flashlights. No, not big enough to wield like clubs; just the small ones that fit in your pocket. But they were ultra-high lumen, so much so that you could light a fire by holding them close to a piece of paper, fry an egg, or melt the glass of your cell phone. If the two jokers now paused in their shooting, probably to reload, were wearing night vision goggles as I suspected, a sudden laser-like beam from one of our lights might temporarily blind them.

I put my right hand on the ground next to me as I began to shift myself to whisper my plan, pitiful thing that it was, to Sam and then Dennis. And as I did so, my hand found first one and then another element to add to my bright idea that was likely to end up with me as defunct as Buffalo Bill in the e. e. cummings poem.

As I quickly outlined what the three of us had to do, Dennis started chuckling when I whispered, "Like in that last game." Despite the fact that another round of bullets had started coming our way. Certain fond memories of our days at Dartmouth always produced those belly-deep rumbles from my best buddy, and none more than that of the last college game in which we played—me on defense at safety and Dennis on the O-line.

Our quarterback had fumbled the ball, but before any opposing player could fall on it, Dennis picked it up. Did he try to run with it? Nope, which was likely a good idea since endurance rather than speed was always his forte. What he did was unexpected—or at least not expected by anyone other than moi. Dennis, you see, though blessed with the exothermic physique so dear to the hearts of line coaches, also had an arm. In our games of tossing a pigskin back and forth when we were kids, it had always been Dennis who would say, "Go long."

And that was what he did. Dropping back another ten yards, he picked out a receiver fifty yards down the field and let go a perfect spiral, just before a group of defensive players from the other team hit him from three of the four cardinal directions—and bounced off like Dwight Eisenhower trying to tackle Jim Thorpe. The referee was so awed by the spectacle of my man Big D standing there nonplussed with a circle of groaning opponents on the turf around him that he did not throw the flag for a flagrantly late hit. Instead he turned to follow Dennis's gaze and watched, as did several thousand cheering fans, as the ball dropped into the grasp of our outside receiver, who took it in for the score.

Despite the odd circumstances, that TD counted, and our coach may have been as disappointed at not having the chance to draw up a deliberate play for the next game that would entail a fumble and a pickup and toss of the pigskin by my big buddy as he was to lose us two starters when we quit both the team and the school to exit stage left into the welcoming arms of the military.

"Might work," Sam said when I finished my speedily whispered instructions and handed him our flashlights.

"If not," I replied, "we'll always have Paris."

"Sta?" Sam said, which I assumed meant "What?" in Serbian.

"Never mind."

Our heads were so close together that we could feel each other's breath. "Ready?" I said. "You go on two, Dennis on three, me on four."

"One, two . . ."

Sam slid to his left, rose up to reach over the top of the tank's lip, and turned both flashlights in the direction of the gunfire.

"Three . . ."

Dennis rose to his knees, right arm cocked, and then fired the football-sized piece of broken concrete at the two men, who had been momentarily stunned by the high-intensity light.

It took only a split second for me to take the scene in, including the exact location of our two assailants. Of whom only one, let's say Rosencrantz, was now standing, Guildenstern having been hit square in the middle of his goggled face by Dennis's scoring pass.

"Four!"

And I was up, running to the right. Three strides and I was at the barely visible platform, which blocked me from the view of the sole remaining thespian. My momentum took me up the wall and onto the top of the platform in two strides. (Thank you, parkour training!) But I did not stop there. I launched myself at the sole remaining erect attacker, who was well illuminated and not looking my way. He had one hand raised to his face to lower the night-vision goggles, the other still holding the assault rifle. Which went flying as I swung my left arm down on his forearm at the exact second I hit him with a tackle that would have made the highlight reels. And although it hurt when my right shoulder struck the pavement, most of the rest of my body was cushioned by his as we went down hard. I rolled to my feet. He didn't.

Kicking the second rifle aside, I knelt and checked the pulses of both prone figures. Rosencrantz and Guildenstern were not dead, but they weren't about to stride the boards again any time soon. Concussions are not recommended for continued careers in either acting or assassining. Ambulances, not curtain calls, were the order of the day.

"*Clear!*" I shouted to Dennis and Sam.

They were each now holding a flashlight as they came up to me.

"I . . . know where the lights are," Sam said in a choked voice as he stumbled past me. Thirty second later, three banks of floodlights came on with a thud, and everything became as clear as day. Including that Sam had been hit in his large left arm in that last volley.

I tore pieces off the shirt of one of our unconscious party crashers, folded two for compression bandages, pressed them onto Sam's wounds, and wrapped a long strip around his arm. Standard NATO round, 5.56×45mm. The injury to his triceps was nowhere near as bad as it might have been with an expanding slug.

"Clean," he grunted through gritted teeth as he flexed his arm, opening and closing his fingers. "Missed the bone. Through and through. Nice match for the one on my other arm from '94."

So Sam had a gallows sense of humor, too.

He pointed toward the tanks.

"We need to let them go before anyone comes." He grinned as he pointed with two extended fingers at the bodies of our unsuccessful attackers. "Blame them."

The three of us worked fast, encouraged by various squeals, squeaks, and sprays of water from Happy and Flippy, who had come back to the surface and seemed to know what was going on. First, just in case their heads were harder than we thought, we tied the wrists of our two cold-cocked compadres behind their backs. Then we turned to the sea gates.

Flippy was the first to depart, a gray blur whipping. Happy—who barely fit through the sluiceway—was close behind on his little pal's tail. Neither paused to wave a single flipper goodbye. How sharper than a serpent's tooth it is to have a thankless cetacean.

"Don't forget to write," I yelled after Happy as he vanished into the dark waters.

"You crazy?" Sam said. "Orcas don't write letters." He looked at me straight-faced. "This is the twenty-first century. They use MySpace."

Yup, a sense of humor for sure.

As I searched the pockets of R&G, I turned up a fully loaded Glock with all seventeen rounds—including one in the chamber. I showed it to Dennis, who nodded and shoved it into his back pocket.

Then the three of us started getting our stories straight. We had seen the two guys looking suspicious, followed and overpowered them. But not before they'd succeeded in their mission of sabotaging the orca show by releasing Happy and Flippy.

Their wallets in hand—both bursting with Franklins—I discovered their identities to be William Smith and John Brown. Nothing phony about those names. Good American boys, despite the fact that their facial features and bad teeth practically screamed origins behind the supposedly defunct Iron Curtain, now being lovingly welded back together by Vlad the Impaler Putin.

As I frisked them, Sam was doing something next to the training platform. I turned in time to see that he'd just taken off a combination padlock and opened the lid of the long storage box I'd noticed that was fastened to the wall.

"We should put this in here," he said. "Otherwise our story about them coming to free Happy and Flippy may not stand up."

I looked at what he was holding: a lethal-looking harpoon gun. Tossed to the side by one of the two men we'd neutralized when they started shooting at us. A killer whale killer.

I restrained myself from walking over and kicking both unconscious men in the ribs. Instead, I picked up one of the assault rifles to carry it and two clips of unexpanded ammo over to the locker.

"Let's keep one of these."

"Better souvenir than a T-shirt," Dennis grinned.

27

The Morning After

Parting is only sweet sorrow
when you don't want to get out of town

When I woke at seven the next morning—after two hours of sleep—and got up to do my usual routine of stretching, tai chi, and the basic 200 (two hundred each of push-ups, crunches, front kicks, back kicks, side kicks, and roundhouses), I saw the message light blinking on my room phone. It was a call from the front desk.

"Your meeting with Chief Sea Antelope has been postponed. The new time is six P.M.," the recorded message said.

I had a feeling I knew the why of that postponement. More than one why.

First of all, part of Deep Bluewater was now a crime scene, yellow tape and all. That was going to make old S.A.'s day a lot more complicated than he'd expected. As word got out, it would surely be bringing more gawkers than gamblers. More to the point, I had no doubt that there would be a lot more questions for him today from the local gendarmerie than we'd had to answer. It was not our establishment that had been broken into by two thugs with ill intent. In the immortal words of Desi Arnaz, the Chief would have "a lot of 'splainin' to do."

Our own interviews with the local law people—which happened after Dennis had stashed the Glock in some convenient bushes—had been relatively routine. All three of us stuck to our simple story. The fact that Sam, Dennis, and I added up to well over half a ton of war veterans made it believable that we'd managed to disarm the two armed intruders.

After our individual statements, Dennis and I were escorted to an interview room with the requisite one-way mirrored wall and left there. Sam had already been allowed to go to an emergency clinic to have his gunshot wound properly treated.

As we waited, I contented myself with sitting in semi-meditation with my eyes closed—it being 2 A.M. Dennis, though, took the opportunity to stand in front of the mirror, making a variety of faces for the benefit of whoever might be watching from the other side. Childish, I suppose. But then again, there is this thing in Zen called Beginner's Mind, which suggests that seeing the everyday world with a baby's eyes can be a path to enlightenment. In which case my big buddy was clearly well along that road. Plus, in a gurning contest he would have been in the top tier.

Eventually, a young male detective came in. The fact that he was trying not to smile made me think he'd been watching from that adjoining room. He sat down and looked at us both, gave his name as MacDonald, and then mentioned, sort of offhand, that he was a member of one of the tribes farther up the coast. After repeating the questions we'd each been asked individually, he seemed to be buying everything we said. Until he circled back to our assailants doing all that shooting.

"So why did they bring a rifle with them?"

"Self-defense?" I suggested.

"And how did you three end up on the other side of the killer whale pool?"

"Just taking cover," Dennis said.

MacDonald almost smiled at that.

"And they set the orca free before you could stop them?"

"And the porpoise," I added.

At that point MacDonald raised an eyebrow. "My own clan's Skaana, killer whale," he said. "I've got to admit I like the thought of that blackfish swimming free."

"Me, too," Dennis and I replied in unison.

"Thank you for your service," he said, closing his notepad. "You're free to go."

"Just don't leave town?" I suggested, ever helpful.

He did laugh at that one. "Hell," he said, "you can go to Disneyland for all I care. But from what I've heard about why you boys are here, I doubt you'll be going anywhere for a while."

He checked to see if anyone was at the door. No one visible. Then he leaned across the table, his back to the mirrored wall, and spoke in a very low voice.

"Just between us, even though they've been officially written off as accidental, I still think those two deaths are suspicious. You find anything out, you've got a sympathetic ear here, okay?"

Dennis and I both made the subtlest of signs for agreement, barely lifting the index fingers of our right hands and dropping them half an inch.

"Good," MacDonald said. "And good luck with anything you might do to help . . ." He made a swimming motion with his right hand and the sign for big. "I wish," he whispered as he leaned forward to stand up, "we could just tell all those clowns out there on the Sound to get lost."

By the time we'd been dropped back at Deep Bluewater, it was 4 A.M.

"Good night, Jim-Bob," Dennis said as he disappeared into his room.

"Good night, Jon-Boy," I said to his closed door, realizing yet again just how much our lives were like those of the Waltons. Namely, not at all. That family in the old 1970s TV series lived a squeaky-clean life. Dennis and I, on the other hand, were always stuck with the dirty work.

By 8 A.M., the two of us were in the casino restaurant, enjoying the sight of an empty orca aquarium next to us. Like the day before, our waitress was JAN. Unlike the day before, she wore a broad smile as she approached our table.

"Ha? Dadatu!" she said. One of the few phrases in Lutshootseed that I knew. It meant good morning—and a bit more than that today, from the look on her face. She seemed to be channeling the Pollyannaish heroine of Robert Browning's poem "Pippa Passes."

God's in his heaven. All's right with the world.

"Good morning, Jan," Dennis and I both replied, then looked at each other. We were going to have to either decide who should talk first in situations like this or work on our choral accompaniment. His bass and my alto being not quite harmonic.

Jan giggled, a very musical giggle that made her look years younger. "I hear you boys were busy last night."

"Where'd you hear that?" I said.

"Oh, the moccasin telegraph has been working overtime," she said, looking at the empty seaquarium as she spoke. "Don't you just love the view this morning?"

"Only thing missing is a few guppies," I said.

Jan shook her head. "You are so funny."

I turned to Dennis. "Listen to the lady," I said. "She, at least, appreciates my sense of humor."

His answer was to roll his eyes ceiling-ward.

We were halfway through our double orders of steak and eggs, actually triple for Dennis, when my cell rang.

I'd been expecting the call—eating with my right hand while holding up my phone in my left—so I got it on the first bar of the jangling ditty guaranteed to make anyone within ten feet of any phone receiving a call reach for their pockets.

"Raven, 'Ha? Dadatu!'" I said.

My attempt at showing off fell as flat as a cake in an earthquake.

"Your Lutshootseed pronunciation is terrible," she said. "Unless you were trying to say 'Good morning' in Mandarin."

"Point taken," I said. "From now on it's English and Abenaki all the way."

"Thank you," she said.

"Nda kagwi," I replied.

Then came a long pause. Which is not uncommon in Skin-to-Skin conversations, especially in the case of someone who clearly listens to her elders—like Raven. Not at all like a lot of calls to and from non-Indians in which the person on the Anglo end of the line is suffering from verbal diarrhea.

I finally decided to be the one to break the silence. "So," I said, "what's shaking? Aside from the Seattle Fault?"

"Let's hope that's not happening," Raven replied. "Last time A'yahos woke up, a thousand years ago, she created a fifteen-foot-high tsunami."

To my credit, I knew who A'yahos was. The powerful supernatural spirit noted for such things as landslides, earthquakes, and rushes of water. Thank you, Google search engine.

"Unh-hunh," I said, breaking out my fluency in eastern Algonquin. Then, as Dennis began eyeing the remaining half of my second ribeye, I decided to get to what I assumed was the point of her call.

"You want to know about what happened last night?" I said, motioning for my pal the human garbage disposal to take the steak.

"I already know all about that," Raven said. "Grampop told me."

"Saw it on the news?"

"No, saw it his way. Know what I mean?"

I did. His way had to be "Original Indian TV," as my Uncle John calls it—seeing things happening far away in something like a dream or a vision.

Been there, done that. So my response was a second eloquent "Unh-hunh."

"So, you're free this morning, right?"

"Until six P.M."

"We'll be there in half an hour. Grampop found someone for you to meet. Nine o'clock sharp, okay?"

"Okay."

After breakfast, I was hailed by the desk clerk as we walked through the lobby. It wasn't Morris, but somehow he recognized Dennis and me.

"Mr. Neptune," he called, holding up something wrapped in red cloth. "This is for you."

I unfolded the cloth and discovered a beaded bolo tie with a clasp in the shape of a bear.

The desk clerk grinned as I put it on. "My running buddy, my cousin Morris, left this for you. His grandma, she's my aunt, makes them. She's a real artist. That one's a whole lot better than any of those that we sell to the tourists in the gift shop."

As we exited the casino exactly at nine, ready for the usual half-hour wait required by Indian Time, a Gigantopithecus with its left arm in a sling and bandages lumbered up to us.

"Hey, amigo," Dennis said, holding out his fist for Sam to bump it and then slap palms.

"Guys," Sam said, bumping my fist and then swatting my palm with a concussive thwat as loud as an M-80.

"You okay?" I asked, wiggling my fingers to restore sensation in them.

"I have been better," Sam said. "But I will be even better by eight o'clock tonight. That is when my plane touches down at John Wayne Airport. First flight I could get to the L.A. area. Just picked up my paycheck."

"What's the matter, don't you like our company?" I said.

"Yeah," Dennis added. "You got some kind of a problem with getting shot at?"

Sam chuckled. "Do such interesting things happen to you wherever you go?"

"What do you think, Podjo?" Dennis said. "How many times have people tried to off us since we've been here?"

"Let's see." I held up my fingers to count on them. "One . . . two . . . three thus far."

"Thus far?" Sam said. "And thus I will be far away before you get to four." He chuckled again. "But it's not you. Despite this"—he tapped his bandage—"it was good last night. But now, after we"—he looked back at the casino to make sure no one would overhear—"set the little one and his friend free, I decided it was time for me to leave Mr. Chief S.A. and all this behind me."

"Not a bad plan," I agreed. "Good luck, my friend."

Sam nodded. "Yes, my friends, I say good luck, stretno, to you both. Maybe we'll meet again down the road."

He reached into his pocket, took out a ring of keys, and tossed it to me. "The big one," he said, "is for the locker where we put the you-know-what. I think you may need it. Now I've got to finish packing."

As he turned and walked back into the casino, Raven's antediluvian Cherokee came rattling up. Exactly on time at 9:30.

Before it had stopped, her grandfather leaned precariously out the door. Holding on with one hand like a rider on a Frisco trolley, his glasses riding the tip of his nose, he waved at us.

"Let's go, boys," Luther George boomed. "Got someone for you to meet."

28

Home Team vs. Visitors

*No one can paddle a canoe
in two directions at once*

"**D**uct tape," I thought as we rattled along, "*is the rez car's best friend*."

Raven's jeep was not as bad as some I've seen—like the '79 Chevy driven by a buddy of ours named Brian Newell, a Passamaquoddy from Pleasant Point. Two years ago at Christmas, Brian's friends gave him a package containing four rolls of aluminum foil and some duct tape, with the message "Build a New Car." However, though not in total disrepair, Raven's ride was, shall I say, highly expressive. Its various rattles and bangs were contributing about as much to our conversation as anything that any of its passengers were saying.

Still, Chief George's voice was strong enough to make itself heard in a thunderstorm. Or maybe next to Niagara Falls, where there's a statue of the famous Seneca orator Red Jacket, Sagoyewatha—"He Who Kept Them Awake." The tradition is that the old speechmaker developed his deep, sonorous voice by practicing his orations while standing close to the roaring cataract.

"My great-niece Mary," Luther George said, pausing for a minute as the non-muffled muffler emitted something resembling a death rattle before somehow managing to hang on, "she's a lawyer. Georgetown and Harvard Law School. She was a tough little girl, playing soccer and topping the honor roll every year. But everybody liked her even though she kicked everyone's butt in every possible way. She's got this smile that just lights up the world."

Chief George grinned, maybe not intentionally showing us which side of her family Mary the lawyer had inherited that smile from.

"Of course, Mary's a tribal member," he went on. "Or at least she was before she decided to throw her lot in with us and get thrown off the rolls. Took her a lot of digging and finding her way through a string of dummy corporations and offshore banks. It helped that she was able to call in some favors from old classmates now in D.C. Anyhow, what she found out was what we'd been suspecting."

He held up his left hand and uncoiled his little finger from his fist. "The gist of it was that Deep Bluewater's entire existence is owed to its usefulness as a money-laundering operation for the Russian mob."

Which, I thought, *explains where that assassin on top of the building came from. And why the one he was targeting was Luther George, S.A.'s main rival.*

"Yup," Chief George continued, "that's who those outside investors are who put up the dough to help it all get built. And who are financing that giant expansion out on the peninsula."

It made perfect sense. Aside from, let's say, a megachurch, whose non-profit status and ability to generate large donations from the faithful make it a perfect front, few things are more perfect for cleaning large amounts of illicit gains than an Indian casino. Even if a large percentage of it went to the casino, the Russians still would come out of it way ahead.

We also listened for a minute as something else under our feet—maybe the drive shaft—concluded its soliloquy on the impermanence of all earthly things before it fell into semi-silence without falling off.

Chief George held up a second finger.

"The problem Deep Bluewater and Old Sherm are facing now, though, it's a double one." He held up two more fingers. "First is that unless that new luxury complex actually gets built—which is needed to handle the larger volume of cash that's supposed to be laundered—the casino's going to look like a losing proposition to them."

Another unspoken *unh-hunh* from me. From the looks I'd seen on the faces of Boris and Natasha, those Kremlin-oriented investors were not happy.

"The second problem, not unrelated to the first, is competition from other interests wanting to control the field. Home team versus visitor. Or in this case, visitors."

As a Native American casino, the usual rules of bankruptcy would not apply to it—but investors who no longer saw enough return on their capital would pull out, leaving the field open for a new player. And one of those potential teams, Luther George explained, was that good old-fashioned criminal enterprise that Americans all know and love on the silver screen—La Cosa you-know-who.

"As if that's not enough," Luther George said, "what's making that part of the equation more complicated is that my old buddy Sherm has a gambling problem of his own and the bad luck to match it. As a result he is up to his butt in debt to loan sharks with names like Vito and Marcello."

Chief George held up both hands and then crossed them. "It's like that old story we tell about a man who kept trying to please both his own people and the white folks. It was like having a man going down the river with one foot in two canoes that were side by side. Things went just fine until the people in those canoes started paddling in different directions."

Chief George shook his head, more or less in time to the rattling of the right front fender. "Poor Sherm," he said. "Seems he's currently suffering from a bad case of divided loyalties."

Then he chuckled. "But that's not the last ingredient in this greed stew—or maybe let's us call it a congee, seeing as how the other rival for our tribe's gaming affections is from the Far East. Trying to take the place of the current major stakeholders. Ever hear of Wo Hop To?"

I suspect that name wouldn't mean much to most westerners, but it did to Dennis and me. So much so that my big buddy turned toward me from his carving—which was turning into a respectable representation of a horse-headed snake—to share a meaningful glance.

We'd done a little work in Hong Kong, and though speaking the Cantonese dialect of Chinese was not our forte, we'd learned some words we would never forget. Such as Wo Hop To, the name of one of the major Hong Kong triads, the gangs that control everything illicit in that well-moneyed former British colony. Of the nine main triads, Wo Hop To was always mentioned first.

"Can you boys guess who's their representative hereabouts?'

Luther George turned his gaze toward the Sound, which was close on our right. A large white boat was just visible on the horizon.

"Oh," I said.

"Oh, for sure," Chief George chuckled. "Tony Oh is what he calls himself now. Except according to my great-niece Mary's sources, his real name is Heung Wah-yim."

Holy moley, Captain Marvel.

In 1987, there'd been a crackdown of sorts on the triads by the Hong Kong police when a man who'd been both a police officer and a triad member came to the authorities for protection. Eleven triad members ended up getting arrested, and Heung Wah-yim, identified as a triad head, was the most prominent among them.

So the Hong Kong triad Wo Hop To was being represented by Tony Oh, a supposed gourmet in a mega-yacht. True, his well-equipped boat with its thirty-person crew was equipped with sonar, cannons, harpoon guns, nets, and the like. Paraphernalia needed to pull in a leviathan. And sure, he would happily serve up a sea monster steak. After all, Southern Chinese cuisine includes everything that crawls, swims, walks, or flies. A traditional Chinese market looks like a doomed Noah's Ark. But his real interest was not so much in catching a Loch Puget Sound monster as it was in sabotaging Deep Bluewater's expansion plans and then stepping in to pick up what was left at a bargain price.

Unh-hunh, I thought.

That made his attempt to remove me from the field and send me to Davy Jones's locker by "accidentally" running over me much more understandable. If we were to solve those deaths and make it possible for construction to get back on track, we'd be setting back the triad's plans of moving in after the Russians gave up.

Unless the Sicilians got there first.

"Clear now?" Chief George said.

"Clear as mud or chocolate pudding," I replied.

"Yuck," Raven said as she turned the wheel to put us on a road that led down to a pier half a mile or so ahead. There was a single boat moored next to it.

"Sorry, it just seemed like a metaphor worth mixing."

Dennis started humming "I Can See Clearly Now," but had the grace to stop when I growled at him.

"Here," Raven said, reaching back over her shoulder to hand my tone-deaf pard a lock-blade knife. "There's a nice piece of driftwood under the seat in front of you."

Dennis dove for it like an osprey on a trout.

"Thanks, fellow music lover," I said to Raven as Dennis snapped opened the blade and started whittling. "Wliwini."

"Nda kagwi," Raven replied, and my jaw dropped.

Then she giggled. "Did I pronounce that right?" she said.

"Like a Native speaker," I said. "Where'd you learn to say 'Don't mention it' in Abenaki?"

"Overheard you say it, big boy."

"If you kids are through snagging," Chief George said, "I've got more to tell you."

Trying to come up with a fast reply to a loaded statement such as that was like a married man trying to figure out a way to answer the question "Are you still cheating on your wife?"

So, while Raven's knuckles whitened as she gripped her steering wheel tighter, I just said, "I'm listening."

Chief George grinned the way elders do when they've managed to embarrass us members of the younger generation. "Okay. I said there was someone I had for you to meet."

He nodded toward the forty-footer fitted out like a research vessel that was tied to the pier we were approaching. Aside from an outsized American flag flapping on top of a tall pole rising up from that dock, the boat, gently rocking in the tide, was the only thing moving.

"He's waiting for us there."

29

Calypso, Too

*The apple does not fall far from the tree
but it can roll a lot farther away*

The lanky man who hopped off that boat and came trotting up the pier to greet us looked like someone sent from central casting to play the part of Ichabod Crane or the skeletal main character in *The Nightmare before Christmas*. A good 6′5″, he was so skinny that he looked as if the first gust of wind that hit him would blow him away. But the grin on his face, which was widened by two pachydermish ears, was so broad and looked so sincere that I found myself sort of liking him.

"Man," Dennis said to me out of the side of his mouth as he more or less cleaned his thick glasses with his untucked shirt. "If that guy turns sideways, he's gonna vanish."

"That has not happened yet," the tall guy with the broad grin said as he reached us, proving that his hearing matched the size of his ears. Then, as he made my hand disappear in his own, which was big enough to palm a basketball with room to spare, he added, "But there were times when I was playing ball that the opposing teams wished I would disappear."

"Sandy here holds the school record for rebounds at UNLM," Chief George said. "Sandy Sanderson, I'd like you to meet my new friends Jacob Neptune and Dennis Mitchell." He winked at Raven. "Though it might just be that Jacob here is a-thinkin' of becoming my grandson-in-law."

"Grampop, you stop it!" Raven said. But her voice was almost as teasing as his when she said it. Which gave me pause to reflect on what might be a pleasant prospect—but was as unlikely with my lifestyle and the two of us being bicoastal as a sea otter marrying a bear.

Sandy, who had moved his grip from my hand to Dennis's, grinned even wider. "You are such a kidder, Chief," he said. "But I know you're not here to do a comedy special. Right?"

"Yes," Chief George nodded. "On your boat?"

Sandy Sanderson nodded. "Ah-yup. After you folks." He motioned toward the gangplank of the boat, which was, I noted, named *Calypso, Too*.

Although our new acquaintance had to nearly bend over double to fit through the hatch—which he did with considerable grace—the sizable room we stepped down into had an eight-foot ceiling. There were two long tables on one side with various books, charts, and gadgets neatly arranged on them. An impressive array of instruments, radar screens, and closed-circuit TV monitors covered a second wall. The other two sides were wide-windowed, opening onto the aft and port sides of *Calypso, Too*.

Sandy tapped the screen of one of the monitors.

"Saw her on this one just two days ago. Received from my little remote-control submarine, which is equipped with lights and cameras on six sides—front, back, right, left, above, and below."

"Her?" I said, though I was pretty sure I knew the answer.

Sandy replied using his own form of sign language, first making a sinuous motion with his right hand and then spreading both of his long arms wide enough to hug a sequoia. Then he held his right index finger up to his lips in a sshhing gesture.

"Got it," I said. "You actually got Her on video."

"Ah-yup. Just the tail, but that was enough."

Chief George, who had taken a seat in one of the chairs facing the monitor, spoke up. "We don't say Her name when we're on the water."

Dennis, who had taken a seat in the chair next to him and was back at work on his carving, nodded. "Makes sense," he said. "Don't trouble trouble and trouble don't trouble you."

Chief George leaned over and slapped Dennis on the knee. "Son," he said, "you got a wife back home?"

"I sure do," Dennis said, looking up from his carving and answering about twice as fast as usual.

"Too bad. Got me a great-niece who would like you just fine."

Chief George looked at Sandy. "So, let's us get down to business now. Tell him about yourself."

Sandy Sanderson gestured at the three other chairs in the room, which were arranged in a loose circle. I pulled back the one next to me for Raven and then took the one next to Luther George as Sandy folded himself down like a jackknife, his knees higher than his chin.

"Ever hear of Ivan Sanderson?"

I nodded.

"Really?"

"Unh-hunh. Read his book *Living Mammals of the World* in our school library on the rez when I was ten."

"I'm impressed."

I was about to add that Sanderson's book, published decades before I was born, was the newest book on animals in our school library. A school where most of the textbooks in our classrooms were so old that I ended up with a geography book with my dad's name at the top of the list of its twenty previous users.

But Dennis broke in before I could say that.

"You ain't seen nothing yet," Dennis said. "Wait till he starts talking about iambic pentameter."

Sandy wisely ignored him. "Ivan Sanderson was my great-uncle. The first real cryptozoologist, as far as I'm concerned. Admittedly, some of his ideas were a bit far out, but he was more often right than wrong."

"Like Malcolm Grattington?" I asked, unable to resist the impulse to show off a little.

"Puh-leez," Sandy said. "That old faker? He couldn't find a Mega-saurian if it came up and bit him in the ass. Everything he knows is from online research. The only way he got his book published was by doing it himself using print-on-demand."

"Hmm," I said.

"He's almost as bad as those"—he paused, seeking the right word and then settling on one made more meaningful by his speaking it as if he was spitting out something that had gone rotten—"*people!* The ones making their so-called documentary for the Pseudo-Science Channel, that *man* out there on his killer yacht. Those *people!*"

"So," I ventured, "why are you here? And who's sponsoring you?"

The grin returned to Sandy's face. "You might say the NBA. While other players were tossing their money away like free throws, I was investing. I majored in zoology with a minor in accounting. All of this," he waved his arm in a circle, "has come out of Apple and Amazon. This and a little house on a hill in Costa Rica." He leaned forward and raised an admonitory finger. "Do not buy beachfront property. In two decades it is all going to be underwater."

"Right," I said. "But getting back to that first question of mine, why are you here?"

Sandy sat up straight. "Do you have to ask?" he said, looking down on me, both physically and figuratively.

"I do. That's what I get paid the big bucks for," I replied, eliciting a deep chuckle from Chief George—which made Sandy relax a bit.

"Protection," he said. "I came here after all those others did. I believe that proving It . . ."—he looked at Chief George—". . . ah, She exists means we can get Her on the protected species list. And in the meantime I wanted to keep an eye on those . . ."

"*People*," I said helpfully.

"Exactly."

"Now," Chief George said, "tell him what else you found."

Sandy stood up so suddenly that I thought for a moment he was either going to go up for a rebound or burst through the ceiling like a rocket. "Easier to show him."

He walked over to another monitor and pressed his fingertip on it, bringing the screen instantly to life.

"Watch this."

He tapped an icon blinking in the lower left corner of the screen.

We all watched. And when the video he'd recorded with his mini-sub's remote cameras was done, I understood why Chief George had brought us here. There was no longer any mystery about what had killed those divers. My worst fears had been realized.

"They know you've got this?" I asked.

"Ah-yup, I'm pretty sure they do," Sandy replied.

"And that's why . . . ," Chief George prompted.

Sandy grinned. "Why they're trying to kill me."

30

On Video

What the right hand knows
the left hand soon learns

Sandy raised his hand. "Wait here a minute."

He opened a door in the back of the room, ducked his head, and disappeared through it. Ten seconds later, he came out with something in his hand. Four decades ago it might have been an alarm clock as the timing device, with wires connected to a couple of sticks of dynamite. Today, though, what with cell phones and more advanced forms of plastique, the whole thing fit into the palm of his large hand.

Dennis gave a low whistle.

"How much damage would this have done it I hadn't disconnected it?' the lanky cryptozoologist asked us.

"More than enough."

Sandy nodded. "I assume the plan was to wait till I was far enough out before they activated it. It was placed under the fuel tanks, so it would have been one hell of an early Fourth of July fireworks display."

"How'd you find it?" Dennis asked.

Sandy took a notebook-sized device off one of the tables. "My second degree was at RPI. This picks up any cellular signals, as well as other bugs. I check religiously every day."

Dennis raised an eyebrow at me.

Sounds familiar, he was thinking.

Yup.

"My guess," Sandy continued, "is that it was placed yesterday while I was out getting supplies. Well, not exactly a guess. You see, it was not

155

just my scanner here that alerted me to the fact I'd had an uninvited guest."

He slid his finger across another screen and then pressed one of the icons. What began to play was shot from a surveillance camera placed so that it was looking down on *Calypso, Too.*

"So small, it looks like a cleat," Sandy said, a bit of pride in his voice. "Designed it myself. Stuck thirty feet up on the flagpole. Which pole, you see, I did not erect merely due to an excess of patriotism."

As we watched, the small dark object moving out in the bay came closer and closer, revealing itself to be a sepia-hued whaleboat with a single person aboard, himself all in black.

"Nine twenty-three A.M.," Sandy said, stopping the video to point at the timer in the upper left-hand corner. "Exactly twenty-three minutes after I left on my grocery run." He turned to grin at us. "I make it a point to keep a very regular schedule. Just in case I'm being surveilled. I want to make it easier for anyone to try something like this fellow here is about to do. So that I can, as they say, catch them in the act. Best to be prepared now rather than sorry later, as my coach used to say. After all, paranoia . . ."

"Is the highest form of love," Dennis and I answered as one. Which made me realize I may have quoted the loathly un-sainted Manson a bit too often.

"Ah-yup," Sandy said, turning back to the screen and restarting the recording. "Observe."

We observed as the midnight-clad intruder tied his boat to Sandy's, then vaulted up and over its side, landing without a sound in a low crouch that looked all too familiar to me. It was the Harimau stance I'd worked long and hard to master myself during my years of silat. Tiger ready to leap. I could see the sinewy strength practically throbbing from him. He was about my size, which I calculated from my memory of that part of the deck, which I'd observed just before entering the boat's main room. Having the eidetic memory I was blessed or cursed with does come in handy at times. He was also possessed of the impressively long musculature that comes with the kind of martial arts training that lasts decades. No overdeveloped bodybuilder, weightlifter biceps. The only thing about him that was not as streamlined as a shark was the bulge of the bag fastened to his belt.

As gracefully as a big cat, still moving low in that same way I'd learned, the figure disappeared through the hatch. As the counter on the screen ticked off the seconds, he was nowhere to be seen—until a mere half minute later, when he reappeared. The bulge in his waist pack was gone, and in another thirty seconds, so was he. A black speck at the end of the wake left by his motor—which was probably electric since it was as silent as he had been. The only sounds we'd heard through the entire video were the calls of gulls and the soft slapping of waves against the hull.

Then we heard a low buzz. It was the cellular device attached—but no longer connected—to the packet of plastic explosives.

"I hear you knocking," Dennis hummed, "but you can't come in."

"Hmm," Sandy said. "It appears that they may have been hoping to get five for the price of one."

I was out of the cabin in one bound and up on top of the roof of *Calypso, Too* in another catlike leap before the buzzing stopped. Far out in the bay, too far for me to make it out as anything more than a tiny dark line against the horizon, was a boat. Too far for me to recognize it with my eyes as the same whaleboat that had carried the assassin. But I have other ways of seeing, and that second sight told me with even more certainty than normal vision who was out there and—like an especially unwanted telemarketer—dialing our number with one hand. While looking our way through a pair of high-powered binoculars with the other.

I tapped my chest with both hands, put my right fist against my left palm, and bowed slightly. Then, spreading my arms as wide as the span of an eagle's wings, I made one of those "Come and get me" gestures that you'd see Bruce Lee doing in his films. Followed by another gesture, this one not from Asian martial arts, but a more universal sign involving an outstretched arm and a middle finger.

Instead of answering my challenge and getting larger, the man in his barely visible boat turned toward the south, until it was obscured from sight by a headland. Maybe arcing his way back to shore?

Later, I thought. *Later.*

What I should have been thinking was *sooner*.

31

What You Assume

The best gift may be
knowing what to give

A ssuming that the danger had passed was not exactly what we
did then. We just assumed that it was not as imminent a threat
as a high-explosive charge blowing us all into smithereens.
Which is a word I love. It means small pieces, and it was swallowed by
the ever-hungry English language sometime in the early eighteenth
century. Its derivation is probably from the Irish word "smidirin."
Which I need to put into a poem one of these days.

Although at that moment "assumptions" was tapping harder on my
shoulder.

I took out the small notebook with the stub of a pencil thrust
through its binding rings and wrote "ASSUMPTIONS" at the top of a
new page.

> What you assume
> will be is not
> often the same
> as what happens.
> It's like the dream
> that comes, unbidden
> when you close your eyes
> and find yourself
> either flying or falling
> and it is only

> when you land
> that you find out
> which it is.

"Interesting," Raven said.

I hadn't noticed her looking over my shoulder.

"When I grow up," I said, "I want to be a poet. Think I have a shot at it?"

"Stranger things have happened, cowboy."

Cowboy. As I stowed my notebook away, I thought how much better that sounded than "Mr. Neptune." Maybe I wasn't about to get published in the *Atlantic Monthly*, but it seemed I was not ready for a walker yet in her eyes.

If Dennis had started singing "Cowboy Take Me Away" just then, I would not have told him to put a sock in it.

Cowboy.

Buoyed by that, and the possible prospect of our relationship developing beyond the stage of being near-co-blow-up-ees, I vaulted up from the deck, turning in midair to land on the pier with my right hand held out toward her.

"Ma'am," I said, using my best early Clint Eastwood accent.

And though she was clearly in good enough shape (more than good enough) to disembark on her own, she grinned, took my hand, and allowed me to hoist her up.

Shaking his head, Chief George waved aside my hand—which I had reluctantly removed from his granddaughter's grasp—and did his own surprisingly graceful jump up to land beside us.

Never one to let pride get in the way of practicality, Dennis ignored us all. Still whittling away at the piece of wood, which was taking on the appearance of a Chinese dragon, he used the gangplank five feet to our left. Nonchalantly, even though it did bend ominously while his considerable weight was on it.

"Good luck, friends," Sandy said. "I'm off. Going to cruise up the coast a hundred or so nautical miles. After nearly being blown up real good here, I think a little Canadian air may be a bit more healthy."

"We'll let you know what happens," Chief George said. "You take care of yourself."

"You take care of *him* . . . or *Her*," Sandy replied.

"Best we can," Chief George said.

Dennis and I untied the lines and tossed them to Sandy, who wrapped them quickly and neatly around two sets of cleats. He turned, disappeared into the hold, and then reappeared with a captain's hat on his head and something in his hands.

"Can you take care of this for me?"

He tossed the little explosive device my way. Unlike nitro, plastique does not explode on impact, so none of us ducked as he did that. I snagged it out of the air with one hand.

"You never know when a little demolition might come in handy," I said.

"Ah-yup," Sandy grinned as he climbed the ladder up into the wheelhouse, started the engine, backed out of the berth, and then roared away full throttle, leaving a much wider wake behind him than was left by the assassin's black rubber boat. And heading north—in the opposite direction from that taken by our unsuccessful exterminator.

As we rattled and rolled away from the empty pier in Raven's shake-mobile toward the road leading south, Dennis looked up from his whittling.

"Is it my imagination, or did we just get away from that bad situation a little too easy?"

He placed the water dragon in my hands. One of his best yet. It seemed as if it was about to float from my grasp and start swimming across the sky. I looked toward the front seat ahead of me, where Chief George was holding on to one of the roll bars over his head with both of his long, sinewy hands.

Dennis nodded.

I leaned forward and reached over the old man's shoulder to place the carving in his lap. He let go of the roll bar to take it in both hands.

"Saw one of these when I was on Okinawa," he said. He held it up and touched it to his forehead. "Gonna keep this on the shelf in front of my desk."

Then he turned back to look again at the road ahead of us.

No 'Thank you' to Dennis. Which was exactly what Dennis and I expected. The gift is for the one who receives it, not the giver. That's one of our old ways of looking at things.

"People who expect all sorts of grateful words," Uncle John used to say, "they're giving that gift just to get praise for themselves." Then he grinned. "But don't giving things make you feel good?"

I didn't have much time, though, to ponder the relative mutual benefits of philanthropic behavior. Because just then, as we were approaching a bend in the road around a stony hill, a familiar feeling came to me—sort of like a spider crawling up the back of my neck.

I leaned forward to make myself heard over the anvil chorus of Raven's rattlebox jeep.

"*Stop!*" I said.

And she did. Most emphatically.

Of all the various parts of her vehicle, it seemed the brakes were in the best working order. Although we did not stop on a dime—unless that dime was as long as the thirty-foot skid mark we left on the road—it was abrupt enough for me to end up upside-down between Raven and Chief George.

"Whoa!" Chief George said, totally unrattled by our screeching halt. "If I'd knowed you were coming, I'd've baked a cake."

Had Dennis not braced himself with both hands as I'd leaned forward—somehow anticipating what I was about to request (be careful what you wish for)—that front seat would have been too crowded for anyone to say anything other than "Whoompf!"

Which is pretty much what I said when I hit the floor headfirst, having ducked my head just enough for my nose to not make an attempt at changing the station on the car radio.

After Chief George climbed out, I was able to follow, doing something like a slug attempting a slow forward roll out of a clown car. This whole being-a-hero business ain't always easy. As I attempted to regain my breath and my dignity—while Raven and her grandfather waited for an explanation—Dennis filled in for me.

"My man Podjo here," he said, slapping me on the back in a comradely way that slowed the return of my normal respiration, "he's got the best danger radar I ever saw. Saved my bacon more than once."

I straightened up, pulled a few strands of my ponytail out of my mouth, and took, thankfully, a normal breath.

I turned to Raven.

"Is that Barrett M82 still under your back seat?" I asked.

32

The Higher Ground

Something not seen
may still be there

It was. Since we'd last seen it, it had been neatly wrapped in a Pendleton blanket and shoved far enough under that it was not dislodged by either the semi-seismic nature of travel in Raven's jeep or the sudden stop we'd just experienced. Which had actually wedged it in further.

But with Dennis's help, I was able to pry it out.

And after being unwrapped, it appeared to be in the same shape it had been in when I confiscated it from its former owner. Maybe the scope might need readjusting, but I didn't plan to be making any real long-distance shots with it. In fact, my hope was that I would not need to fire it at all. Good enough. I checked the clip to make sure it was full, then reinserted it.

"How far?" Dennis asked.

"Maybe a quarter of a mile around that bend. Too far for anyone to have heard us stop. But just in case somebody decides to come looking . . ."

I unhooked the spare tire from the back and leaned it against the side of the jeep to create the impression that a blowout had been the cause of our stop. And now, having discovered that we were missing a jack, we were probably all heading back to see about finding some help at the gas station we'd passed a mile back.

"Over there," I said, looking down toward the bay, "just downslope there's some big trees."

162

Raven nodded. "Grampop and I will wait down there until you get back."

Chief George held up his cell phone. "No problem. Got me a new game I just downloaded that I want to try out. Better than whack-a-mole." He grinned. "I'll leave that to you."

As they began to make their way toward the concealment of the big trees, Dennis and I exchanged a glance.

We had done this sort of thing often enough that neither of us needed to talk about our plan.

All Dennis said was "Got my little friend here," as he reached into his back pocket to pull out the Glock we'd confiscated from Guildenstern. Plus the bullet he'd ejected from the chamber before putting the clip back in. A wise choice unless he'd wished to accidentally shoot himself in the butt while being bounced around in Raven's cement mixer of a Renegade.

Dennis racked in a shell, pulled out the clip, clicked in the extra bullet, and replaced the clip. A full seventeen 9mm rounds were now at his disposal.

I nodded, and then we both headed out.

To do what?

It was pretty simple. Move off the road to our left, spread out about fifty yards apart, and then start up that hill in front of us. Essentially, we would, like Stevie Wonder, seek the higher ground and then take it from there.

It wasn't all that easy. Although we were not struggling up sand dunes in hundred-degree heat, as we'd done in Kuwait, or wading hip deep in mud while watching out for caimans and anacondas, as we'd done in a part of Amazonia that I will not identify for various reasons, the slope we were climbing was steep and rocky, and finding footing was not all that easy. No need, though, like in the Southwest, to worry about snakes being under any of those rocks we were clambering over. I've never been bothered by snakes in general. And the only poisonous one in the state of Washington was the western rattler, whose range was far to the east of us.

Within ten minutes we were near the top of the hill. A glacial drumlin, like all the hills in the lowlands below the mountains. Deposited when the great mountains of ice withdrew. None of those hills are more than six hundred feet high, and the one we were on was probably in the four-hundred-foot range. We'd made our way through dense shrubs, serviceberry, ocean spray, Pacific madrone, white-tipped asters blooming here and there as bright as big snowflakes, and occasional small Douglas firs seeking to replace the coastal giants cut down decades ago. We both stopped just below our parts of the summit. Never crest a ridge while standing up. Unless you want to be dragged back down it in a body bag.

I could see Dennis off to my far right. He signaled that he would take a look.

Okay, I signaled back, watching as he crawled the last few feet and then lifted up just enough to see over the ridge, looking through the bright green clumps of madrone that kept him camouflaged. He slid back down and signaled to me again. This time I couldn't quite make out what he was trying to tell me. But it was easy enough to find that out.

I pulled out my phone and dialed his number. It rang only once before I saw him reach into his pocket and pull out his own Nokia.

"Oceanview Surveyors," he replied, his voice dozens of decibels below normal.

"What?" I said.

"No sign of any unfriendly," he said. "But I got a great view of Mount Rainier. Lovely today, isn't it?"

"It is," I said. Patience has always been important with my big buddy, who loves to draw things out in ways that used to drive our superior officers batty. "But what else can you see in addition to that poetic vista?"

"The bay," Dennis replied, pausing again, and I waited, taking the opportunity with his second long pause to study the Sound stretched out before me. It was a beautiful sight. Made more beautiful by the sight of a pod of five orcas. Distant, but distinct enough for me to see their erect dorsal fins as they breached the water. None of them, to my disappointment, had a dorsal fin that flopped over. No sign of Happy or his porpoise companion. Nor was there any sign of a horse-headed sea serpent. Though, if the object of so much attention was behaving as such beings are said to behave in all our traditions, that was no surprise. Not being seen is a specialty of most such beings. Unless they want to be seen.

"And," Dennis finally said, "can you guess what I can see pulled up onshore down there? Where you can't see it from your viewpoint—and where we wouldn't have seen it from the road?"

I didn't have to say it, but I did anyway.

"A black rubber boat."

"You got it, Podjo. Your radar was in perfect working order. Has to be our dude who planted the bomb."

Harimau. The tiger man.

Several questions inserted themselves into my mind at that point. Pretty simple ones, but all with potentially disastrous outcomes if Dennis and I came up with the wrong answers.

Was our silat-trained ambusher alone?

How was said once-stymied assassin armed?

Where was he—if indeed singular—set up along our route?

And, assuming we figured out those first three, what would our best approach then be?

Oh, and how long would Tiger Man wait for his quarry to come rumbling along in Raven's jeep before he got suspicious and either bailed or came looking for us?

A way more complicated problem than which of those two roads diverging in that yellow wood we ought to take.

"What I think," I said to Dennis after two or three minutes of cogitation while he hummed (not helpfully) the theme music from *Jeopardy*, "is that the place where our tiger is hiding is in that little hollow fifty yards from where the road comes out from behind this hill."

"Makes sense," Dennis said. "Clear field of fire, just enough elevation, plenty of cover. But how do you *feel* about it, Podjo?"

Feel. I knew what he meant. Not just what I was being told by my five senses, but by that inner voice that spoke wordlessly to me in times like this. A kind of tingling. Or maybe like that feeling you get of the hairs standing up on the back of your neck when you know that someone you can't see is watching you. Hard to describe, except I could feel that he was there.

"So what we can do is this."

As I laid out my simple plan, Dennis unh-hunhed his assent about each step.

Stay out of sight.

Stay split up.

Move down the hill so that we come on that place from two sides.

But stop if we see anything, feel anything wrong.

I didn't say anything about being quiet as we made our way. That was a given. From our years of working together, I knew the only person who could move through challenging terrain more quietly than me was my bear-sized friend. Which should not be that surprising to anyone with firsthand knowledge of the woods. It's the little creatures, the mice, the squirrels, that make the most noise, rustling through the leaves and debris on the forest floor. While the deer, the bear, even the moose can move as silently as shadows.

When I was in Africa, I learned that the same thing held true there with the continent's impressive megafauna. From Cape buffalo on up to elephants, unless you were fully aware, they could be on you before you had a chance to run. Like that time in Namibia when a rhino ambled quietly up to where I was lying in a ghillie suit under an acacia. I'd actually heard him when he was thirty feet away, but decided to just stay where I was and not scale that tree, leaving my rifle behind as most guys would have done. Luckily he was a friendly guy, just snuffled at my feet like a giant pet pig and stood by me for a while. Until he lifted his head, sniffed the air, and then went galumphing off, showing no sign of ever having seen me. Which made it easier for me to get the drop on the poachers who appeared a minute later. They were the ones I was after and who had been trailing the big male—who the park game wardens had nicknamed Clyde. The killer squad, men from nearby South Africa led by a Yemeni, had been hoping to get Clyde in their sights to harvest his horn—worth its weight in gold. They quickly raised their hands and dropped their weapons after my first shot removed the AK-47 from their leader's hands, along with his trigger finger.

Thinking back on it later, I concluded that maybe that companionable rhino knew what I was doing and had just dropped by to give me a bit of encouragement.

It took another ten minutes for Dennis and me to drift like smoke to the positions we'd decided to take. A hundred feet away from each other, we were both slightly up the hill from the place we'd figured out our tiger was hiding. I could see Dennis and he could see me, though we were still concealed from our dangerous quarry, who was halfway between us. Which meant that each of us was within fifty feet of that unseen adversary. Not across from each other, but at right angles so there'd be no chance of either of us catching a stray round. And holding the higher ground.

As we watched, I saw no sign of motion. No trembling of leaves from that out-of-place pile of brush—freshly cut, I could see as I looked at it through the scope. But no motion really meant nothing. If you're a halfway decent sniper, you can stay in place without moving for hours. If you're a really good one, up that to days. And be prepared to thoroughly soak your underwear after you've completed your assignment.

No, everything I could see and everything I could feel was telling me that Tiger Man was there.

And just in case, I'd made a plan to make sure of that. That was why I had picked up several heavy baseball-sized stones on my way. I raised my index finger toward Dennis and saw him nod. I removed three of those rocks from my pack, hefted them, and chose the two weightiest ones. With an underhand motion I lobbed the first of them up in a high, high arc, followed by a second stone launched before the first one hit.

The accurate tossing of heavy round objects has always been one of my talents. Which is why—after the first few games I played—I found myself banned from bocce by the old men in the small southern Italian mountain town where Dennis and I spent two months rooting out a gang of kidnappers and rescuing the niece of a prominent Sicilian politician whose relatives in Boston had recommended us to him.

Those two stones were not at all like an arrow shot into the air to fall to earth I know not where. They landed with consecutive branch-breaking crashes right where I'd planned—in the center of that patch of brush that had looked, from our vantage point, out of place and a little too thick. And while neither igneous seemed to have hit the person within that quickly constructed shooting blind, they did produce a satisfactory result. A black-clad figure came rolling out from beneath it, without his rifle—which we later found. Its plastic stock broken in two pieces, its bolt bent, it had been knocked out of his grasp by stone number one.

"Freeze!" I shouted, standing up and leveling the M82 at him.

The late summer weather of the Puget Sound was apparently too warm that day. For, rather than freezing, he loped toward me in a low crouch. I had no more than a millisecond to take in the fact that he was brown-skinned and long-limbed, tightly muscled, my size—and about to throw a four-bladed knife at me. He flicked his wrist, and that knife came spinning in my direction—with more accuracy than I would have preferred. Had I not deflected it upward with the barrel of the rifle, it would have effectively opened the third eye in the middle of my forehead (site of the pineal gland, which in the tuatara, a marine iguana native to the Galapagos Islands, actually is able to sense light) spoken of in Tibetan Buddhism.

There was no time either to continue to consider the connections between vertebrate anatomies and esoteric spiritual beliefs or to congratulate myself on my self-defense skills. Because then, with an impressively feline final leap, Tiger Man was on me.

33

Silat

Do not bring a knife to a gunfight
unless you are really good with a knife

O r, to be precise, he was over me. Briefly. For as he leaped, hands clawed out to twist from my grasp the rifle I was holding across my body after using it like a short staff to deflect that knife, I rolled backward, placing my feet in his belly. That version of a balloon sweep, as it is called in Brazilian jiu-jitsu, was pretty near perfectly executed. It sent him flying over and beyond me. Most people, who do not know how to fall, would have ended up thudding down hard on their backs when that move was done against them.

Tiger Man was not most people. He twisted in midair and landed in a crouch on one knee, left hand on the earth, right hand still held up, fingers curled back like claws in matjan. Tiger paw.

Luckily, while hoping for the best, I'd planned for the worst and already rolled back up to my own feet.

Pentjak silat has been called the deadliest and most varied of all the Asian fighting arts. First brought to Indonesia centuries ago by monks from the mainland, it quickly began to evolve as it spread from island to island, until it was everywhere on the vast archipelago of thousands of islands that stretches more than three thousand miles from the Indian Ocean to the Pacific Ocean. By the late twentieth century, when my own training in silat began, it had become the official national sport of Indonesia. Virtually every inhabited island—and sometimes every village—had its own style of Pentjak. Pentjak—the art. Silat—the application of that art in fighting. And a dizzying variety of weapons—knives of all sorts, double sticks, staffs, sais, throwing stars, you name it, they had it—had been incorporated.

Then there were the silat fighters themselves. The best were men and women with no fear of either pain or death. Their dedication to their art was all that mattered. That was why the first president of Indonesia, Sukarno, the man who led the island nation's struggle against the Dutch for independence, never traveled anywhere without a cadre of silat body-guards. One of my gurus—the Indonesian word for an advanced teacher—told me about something he'd seen in 1960 when he was a boy and Sukarno was at a rally in Jakarta. A hand grenade was thrown from the crowd. As that grenade hit the ground, one of Sukarno's bodyguards threw himself on top of it, instantly followed by a second bodyguard, who leaped on top of the first man, then a third, a fourth, a fifth, and a sixth man joined the pile before the grenade could detonate. When it did, all six men were killed, but their bodies had completely absorbed the force of the blast.

In the split second I thought of all that, two of those weapons I just enumerated—seven-edged throwing stars—came flying my way, attempting to incorporate themselves into my corpus.

Ching! Ching!

I blocked them with my rifle, still held across my body, sending deadly little pinwheels flying harmlessly past me to each side. In the split second after I did that, I saw that my adversary was not yet done with pro-ducing edged weapons. He'd now pulled out from somewhere a very sharp-looking curved-blade kris. Then he growled like a tiger.

A tiger with a kris? Yup, just what you'd expect from an expert in Harimau baranti silat, a style of Pentjak in which weapons play a big part. Sometimes small curved ones held in the palm. And sometimes the kris.

Found and revered in the islands of Southeast Asia—from the Phil-ippines and Malaysia to Indonesia—the kris is the favorite close-range killing weapon on the islands of Sumatra and Java. There, those who make the long knife are known as Empus—men said to take the half-forged blade from the fire while in a trancelike state and then shape it with their bare hands.

I'd learned a lot about the kris during my years of studying silat. It is made of an alloy combining nickel, iron, and pieces of meteorites, with the waves on the blade standing for a fire serpent. And each double-edged kris is said to have a soul, and a deep hunger for human blood.

Every part of the kris, from its handle and hilt to its blade, is meant to say something about the status of the one to whom it belongs . . . until it is passed on down to the next in the family line, for a true kris may be passed from generation to generation. From what I could tell about this kris's current owner by the way it was being pointed at me, he planned to use my blood to quench that blade's thirst and do so lekas-lekas—which means feverishly quick in Bahasa Indonesia.

Rule of thumb in fighting: Charge a gun. Run away from a knife.

As if I had time for that.

He came at me low, looking to sweep my legs from beneath me at the same time he swung his arm up with the blade to slash my throat. I countered that attack by not being there, leaping backward and to the side, spinning in midair so that I came down on my own hands and knees. Oh, and about that kris? As I'd spun, I'd struck that knife and its owner's knuckles with the barrel of my gun. And wherever that knife went, it was not in Tiger Man's bleeding right hand any longer.

However, he had quickly recovered. Ignoring the injury to his hand—which looked to have at least one broken finger—he was now crouched exactly as I was, ten feet away from me.

As our eyes met, he grinned. Not a friendly grin.

"Baik, pertempuran bergerak," he growled.

"Terima kasih," I replied. The least you can do is say "thank you" when someone compliments your fighting.

I knew there would not be enough time for me to raise my rifle and fire it before we engaged again. Like a tiger, he had paused only to ready himself to attack even faster, his left hand held back, his right held out in front of him. That bleeding right hand twitched slightly then, a subtle clue to me about what that attack would be.

Ah, what it would have been, that is.

Because just as he was about to make his move, someone else, who'd approached as silently as a cloud drifting in, landed on him like a boulder.

Dennis, of course. Imagine a hippo doing a belly flop into the Zambezi or a humpback whale in one of its high arcing leaps out of the ocean off the Gulf of Maine. Then imagine the force of said tonnage landing. That may give you a mental picture of what Dennis looked like as, arms spread out, he took flight. On a smaller scale than either hippo or whale, but still landing with such devastating force that it made me grit my teeth and cringe.

In one of the stories Aunt Mali told me that I loved best, Azban, the Raccoon, decided to race a great rolling rock. He was so fast that he not only overtook it, but was actually able to get ahead of it. However, winning was not good enough for Raccoon. He began to zigzag back and forth in front of the boulder, looking back over his shoulder to taunt the big stone for being so slow. And because he was not looking where he was going, Raccoon did not see the root sticking up from the hillside that tripped him. He fell, and that big stone rolled right over him, leaving Raccoon as flat as your hand and unable to move.

When Dennis rolled off, I sort of expected our man in black to look like Raccoon. But, although he seemed to have been pushed down some into the earth, he wasn't flattened out. However, he also was not moving.

"You okay, Podjo?" Dennis asked as he rose to his feet and brushed off his knees with his left hand, the right still holding the Glock he had not let go of. "You're bleeding."

I lifted my finger to my left cheek, which had begun to burn a little as a slight breeze touched it. There was a cut there, but it felt as if it was only an inch or two long and not that deep.

"I'm okay," I said.

I took the handful of paper napkins Dennis pulled from his pocket and pressed them against the wound. That first four-bladed knife Tiger Man threw had come closer to getting me than I'd realized.

"He was too close to you for me to take a shot. And I figured it would be better anyhow if we could take him alive."

"Really?" I said, eyeing the recumbent figure, who on second glance did look flatter than he'd been before he was pile-drivered.

But when we rolled him over, we saw that it was not having Dennis's three-hundred-plus pounds land on him that had killed him. What had killed him was the knife he'd been concealing in his left hand, which had been driven deep into his belly as he was driven down to the earth.

He had no identification on him—just more knives. Four that we located. Then we rolled him back onto his stomach.

"What now?" Dennis said.

I pointed at our deceased foe and swept my right hand to the side, then held my palm toward the ground.

Let him stay here.

Dennis nodded.

It was better to leave the body as it was for now, out of sight from the little-used road in a place where there was not likely to be anyone going.

Better in more ways than just saving us the trouble of lugging over two hundred pounds of literal dead weight.

A second reason to leave Tiger Man where he lay was to not let the one who'd sent him—and I was pretty sure I knew who that was—realize that his pet assassin had been taken off the board.

A third reason was that letting the authorities know about this death would result in our spending hours, if not days, in the local jail while forensics teams examined the site, as we were grilled again and again to see if there were any holes in our story.

A fourth reason was that our being in the hands of the authorities would not leave our hands free to protect Chief George, who was clearly in need of protection after two—well, actually, three—attempts on his life.

And ours.

Three was more than enough.

One of my tried-and-true methods has always been to come in, stir things up, and then see what happens. Sort of like poking a beehive with a stick. Then, depending on what shows itself as a result, doing what needs to be done.

What needed to be done now was to stop being a decoy. Enough of playing the part of both the staked-out goat and the tiger hunter. Enough of setting Dennis and me up as targets. Time to take the fight to the enemy. I was pretty sure that, though I didn't know everything, I had gathered sufficient knowledge to do that.

Like Uncle John used to say about farming: Nobody ever knows it all, but if you know enough, you can bring in a pretty good crop.

As I'd been thinking all that, Dennis and I had been retracing our steps back to the jeep. We had covered our deceased assassin with the same branches he'd used to make his shooting blind—just in case something like that copter we'd seen the day before flew over low enough for its passengers to take note of a body.

As we reached the road, Dennis turned to me.

"What now?" he asked.

"Now," I said, "it's our turn."

Dennis grinned as broad as a jack-o-lantern. "About time!"

34

Message in a Zodiac

Don't look a gift horse in the mouth
unless you intend to ride it

Chief George and Raven were waiting by the jeep.

"Grampop said he had a feeling we ought to come up out of the woods and be ready to go," Raven said.

Chief George smiled at me. "One of them feelings," he said. "You know what I mean."

I certainly did.

Neither of them asked—at least with words—what had transpired while we were gone. But Dennis answered whatever question they might have been thinking with two eloquent gestures: An index finger held up to indicate one enemy. And then the side of his hand drawn across his throat.

"Okay," I said, climbing into the jeep. "Let's go."

We didn't go far. I had Raven stop when we were just around the bend in that hill. Dennis and I got out and looked toward the water. From the landmarks I'd picked out from the hilltop, this was the right place.

"Down there," I said, pointing with my chin toward the Sound.

"Yup," Dennis said. "Down there."

"Want me to come with you," Raven said, climbing out from behind the wheel and joining us. The way she said it was not a question.

Chief George leaned back in his seat, put his feet up on the dash, and took out his phone. "I'll man the fort," he said.

He looked at the bulge in Dennis's pocket. "Want to leave me that hogleg of yours—jes' in case I get visited by any hostiles."

Again, not a question.

Dennis took out the Glock, spun it in his hand, and held it out butt first to Luther George, who put down his phone to take the automatic. He hefted it like one long familiar and comfortable with the feel of a gun in his hand, ejected the clip, and slid it back in again. "Not as heavy as my old .45, but it'll do," he said. Then he put it on the seat next to him, picked up his phone, and began working his thumbs across the keypad.

There was no real path down to the Sound from the road, but I saw the subtle signs of someone having forced his way up through the brush. Scuffed soil. Green leaves on the ground. Small broken twigs. Our defunct opponent might have been a martial arts expert, but it seemed that he had not been wilderness trained the way Dennis and I had been by Tom Nicola and Uncle John.

As we made our way, me going first followed by Dennis and then Raven, Chief George's granddaughter held out her hand several times for me to help her down. Having seen how she moved (and I do not mean that in a lecherous way), agile and strong, I had no doubt she didn't really need to take my hand. But I was glad that she did. Her hand was warm in mine, and both of us may have held on for a second more than needed each time. And when she stumbled slightly as a mossy rock shifted under her foot and I found myself catching her with my arms around her waist, I lost my breath for a moment.

And these lines from my second-favorite Northwest Coast poet came into my mind:

> I knew a woman, lovely in her bones,
> When small birds sighed, she would sigh back at them;
> Ah, when she moved, she moved more ways than one . . .

Yeah, old Ted Roethke knew how to say it.

And as for me—I was ready to measure time by how a body sways.

"Children!" Dennis said from above us, imitating the voice of one of our old grade-school teachers, "no time for that now!"

As we broke apart, the thought came to me that once this whole thing was over—which I now hoped would be soon—I needed to take a little vacation break here on the scenic Northwest Coast. Accompanied by a certain local guide.

The little smile Raven gave me as I was thinking that let me know that she'd either been reading my mind or just having the same thought at the same time.

The black Zodiac boat that Tiger Man had been in was still moored there. It had been tied up to a small cedar and tucked in so close to shore that it was invisible not just from the road, but until you were almost on top of it. It was angled into a bend in the shore in such a way, in a miniature cove, that even from the Sound it was out of sight. The only reason Dennis had caught sight of it from the hilltop was that he was high enough up and at the exact right angle to see over and through the brush and trees that had concealed it from other eyes.

It was almost exactly the same as the Zodiacs used in Special Forces training. Dennis and I had been in almost identical ones plenty of times in the past. The Evinrude motor on the back would get you up to fifty knots in almost no time at all. Small enough for one person to handle and big enough to carry six men on a mission, the Zodiac, with its inflatable rubber sides and rigid frame, was an almost unsinkable craft. Perfect for getting into a hot zone fast and out at equal if not greater speed. Paddled with the motor off, it moved through the water easily and silently.

As we looked the boat over, Raven was the first to spot something.

"Here," she said, reaching into the Zodiac. She'd found a hidden compartment. Inside it were a cell phone, a cache of ammunition, extra knives, and a bulging wallet filled with hundred-dollar bills and several credit cards. There were also two passports—an Indonesian one and a British one. The identical photos on them were of the one I'd been calling Tiger Man. Salim Praja.

Salim Praja—a name that meant a lot. Indonesia has hundreds of different ethnic minorities. During my time on Java, where there are still remnants of the old caste system that placed royalty at the top and the commoners on the bottom, Praja was a name reserved for the warrior class. Which fit our man and the role he'd been playing for someone above him on the social ladder. The name Salim was a different story— and explained why our deceased warrior appeared to have Chinese features. When Suharto, the successor of Sukarno, was president, members of the Chinese minority were ordered to drop their Chinese surnames. But some just Indonesianized their names. Thus Lim became Salim.

A buzzing sound came from the cell phone.

"Avon calling?" Dennis said.

I picked it up, hoping it wasn't password protected. As soon as I pressed it, a message appeared on the screen.

HOW WAS YOUR LUCK? ROLL ANY SEVENS?

Talking indirectly, of course. I took a wild guess that rolling a seven was code for, to use another euphemism, neutralizing a target.

ROLLED FOUR, I replied.

The response appeared almost immediately.

GOOD. RETURN TO BASE. FISHING GOOD!

Followed by a set of coordinates. And the last two words: MEET HERE.

I turned off the phone, thinking about what I'd just read. Those first seven words carried a boatload of meaning. The first meaning was that my wild guess seemed to have worked. The late Salim's employer thought the four of us, Chief George, Raven, Dennis, and I, had all been removed from the table. The second, if I was interpreting it right, was that the fishing being done was for Her, as Raven referred to the Big One. And that saying the fishing was good meant it was either caught or about to be.

Clearly, there was only one place Dennis and I needed to be now—as fast as possible.

The compartment also contained a change of clothing and a black balaclava like the one Salim Praja had been wearing, as well as a variety of helpful items that could be used to restrain a prisoner. A flat lead-filled sap, rope, duct tape, a couple of sets of handcuffs. All good stuff.

I looked at the black clothing. *My size?* I wondered.

"You thinkin' what I'm thinkin', Podjo?" Dennis said.

"If the shirt fits," I said as I picked up a black long-sleeved shirt, "put it on."

Dennis was right. We had the same size, the same build, the same dark skin, even the same eyes. Cover most of my face, and Salim and I would be hard to tell apart—at least at first glance.

"Want to turn your back?" I said to Raven as I started to take off my shirt.

"Nope," she said. "Chippendale time."

As Dennis began to hum "Da-da-da, da-da, da-da," I finished stripping off my shirt and squeezed myself into the tight black one from the compartment in the Zodiac. I put the balaclava on my head and pulled it down over my chin so that only my mouth and eyes were showing.

"Yup," Dennis said. "You'll pass."

"And you'll lie flat in the bottom of the boat with this over you," I said, lifting up the large black rain poncho that had been left draped over the seat and placing the M82 with its knife-scarred stock in the bottom of the boat. I was getting fond of that rifle, especially seeing as how it had saved my life a couple of times within the last hour. No way were we going on our little expedition without it. And if we got out of this still breathing, my intent was to ship it back home to add to the collection of firearms dear to my heart in my gun cabinet.

Dennis climbed in and pulled the rifle next to him. As I started to cover him with the poncho, Raven put her hand on my shoulder to turn me her way.

"For luck," she said, pulling my head down toward her and kissing my cheek.

I thought of saying something along the lines of "Maybe I'll get luckier after I get back." But instead I opted for just nodding. Playing the strong, silent type is always a better idea than hopping away with your foot in your mouth. Plus my heart was pounding so much from that kiss that I might have had a hard time speaking. Why is it that falling in love never happens at a convenient time for me?

Dennis shifted under the tarp so that he was closer to the back of the boat where I took a seat. Our combined weight lifted the prow up from the shore enough that all Raven needed to do was give us one hard push to send us far enough out into the water for me to drop the motor.

She lifted a hand and I did the same, hoping this was a see-you-later scenario and not a farewell forever.

I dropped my hand and tapped my chest. Raven smiled and did the same.

Wowie Zowie, as Frank Zappa so brilliantly expressed it. But this was no time for snagging.

Get serious, Neptune, I thought at the same time the lyrics for the late, great Buddy Holly's "It's So Easy to Fall in Love" were playing somewhere in my medulla oblongata.

I started the motor, backed us up, turned, and we were on our way.

35

One Big Yacht

*It doesn't matter when you arrive
as long as you arrive on time*

What was it my Aunt Mali said to me when I was a kid?
"I love you many big boats."
That's yachts and yachts for you landlubbers and lovers
of puns as awful as those so many of my older relatives inflicted on me
when I was little.

But right now there was just one yacht on our minds as I steered the
rubber whaleboat across the Sound.

According to the message we'd received on Salim's phone, the big
white boat was not where it had been when we'd first seen it from Sandy's pier. As I followed the coordinates, using the instruments in the
Zodiac, I realized where we were headed. Up the coast toward the headland where the casino extension was under construction.

Where the Big One lived.

If that was where we'd find the yacht, we had over twelve nautical
miles go. A trip that would take us, cruising along at thirty knots, at
least twenty minutes. But, to our surprise, we found out we were not
alone. Five minutes into the trip, a porpoise leaped in front of us, then
started coasting along next to us. Not an unusual thing for a porpoise
to do.

What was unusual was what happened next. With a leap that took
his whole body out of the water, an orca with a bent dorsal fin came to
join him. The two of them swimming along side by side left no doubt
that they were our buddies, Happy and Flippy. At fifteen feet long,
weighing a mere three tons, Happy was only two-thirds what his adult

size would be. But still damn impressive as he swam along no more than six feet from the Zodiac.

"Hey, guys," I shouted. "Great to see you!"

In response, first Flippy and then Happy responded. Flippy with a tail walk and a chittering cry, and Happy with another one of those big leaps, which landed him on his side—and sprayed us with a wave of salt water that soaked us and made Dennis and me laugh out loud.

At least we'd done one good thing so far.

I killed the motor, so Dennis could wipe his glasses clean and both of us could say a proper hello to our two finny friends.

As soon as the boat drifted to a stop, Happy surfaced and pushed his head against it. I reached out and placed my palm on his smooth side. He rolled to expose his white belly, like a dog asking to be petted.

Dennis leaned over me to rub his hand on Happy's back.

"Remember what Sam told us?" he said. "About how smart these guys are?"

I nodded. It was clear that our two cetaceous chums not only recognized us but seemed grateful for what we'd done to free them.

They stayed with us until we came in sight of the yacht, half a mile offshore from the partially built new casino. We could see the two arcing towers of the main building rising up like blackened wolves' teeth, framing the white ship.

Happy and Flippy surfaced to look at us one more time, as if wishing us luck. Then they dove to vanish in the 450-foot-deep water.

Dennis peeked out from under the tarp and whistled softly. "That is one big yacht."

I twitched the tarp back over him. "Wait," I said.

The huge white ship was not alone. Two much smaller boats were on either side, perhaps a hundred yards off the prow. The glints of metal and glass coming from each boat—like shimmers of light reflected from a diamond—told me who they were. The film crew from the *Creature Catchers* show. Had they been called to witness something spectacular, or were they just there on a hunch? There was no way to tell.

I headed straight for the yacht as if I knew what I was doing. Which I didn't, but luck was on my side. As I approached its huge bulk, I could see its name written on the side in both Chinese characters and English: *Pure Harmony.* The boat was massive. Not as big as the supertanker *Seawise Giant*, of course, which at fifteen hundred feet was the longest ship ever built, but damn impressive nonetheless. It was the size of a cruise ship, with a helipad on a raised part of the deck. And below that helipad was my lucky break. Someone, a tall guy wearing a uniform as white as vanilla ice cream and holding a flag in each hand, was semaphoring to me from the aft deck. Arms held wide apart and lifted up. Attention!

I was supposed to head to the port side. I did so, and there it was, a sort of cargo net that I guessed I was supposed to pull into. As soon as I killed the engine and let my momentum carry me in, the net started to rise. It lifted the Zodiac and its cargo (Dennis and me) high, high up, to be swung onto the deck and deposited.

The winch was being run by a single operator. The same guy who'd held the flags. Up close I could see that everything about his spotless uniform was Moby Dick white except for the design of two leaping porpoises on his breast pocket. I could also see all kinds of activity going on in the fore part of the boat, but aside from Flag Guy, no one else was back there.

Sometimes—maybe all the time—it's better to be lucky than good.

Flag Guy came up to me speaking Chinese. Which made sense since he looked like a member of the Shanghai Sharks basketball team. He was certainly tall enough, a slightly shorter version of Yao Ming, the 7'6" All-Star who'd been playing for the Houston Rockets for a few years by then. This littler Yao looked to be a mere 6'10".

I motioned for him to come closer, half turned away and gesturing as if there was something in my hand I wanted him to see.

He bent over to look.

Sadly, what I did next would have gotten me enough technical fouls to be thrown out of the game forever. However, my own chosen athletic pursuits not being part of any organized sport, my actions served my purpose well. They resulted first in Little Yao being bent even further over from my quick blow to his diaphragm. Then, secondly, in his being unconscious from the rear headlock that cut off the flow of blood through the carotid arteries on either side of his neck to his brain. Held just held long enough for him to go sleepy-bye without any permanent damage.

No one seemed to be around—or looking our way from the distant front of the big boat where all the activity was taking place.

I levered the flag man up until the top of his long body was over the side of the Zodiac. Dennis reached up to help me pull Little Yao the rest of the way from inside the rubber boat. After making use of the handy ropes and other restraints left by the late Salim, including duct tape over our unconscious power center's mouth, we decided that no further giftwrapping would be needed to ensure that this present would not be opened before Christmas.

"What now?" Dennis whispered.

I looked at the door some fifty feet away from us.

I thought a moment. Getting stuck onboard this yacht was not such a good idea.

"Let's find another place to stow our flag man."

Together Dennis and I pulled Little Yao out of the boat and placed him behind a locker bolted to the deck beside the door I'd just noticed. Then we used the winch to lift the Zodiac out and lower it back into the water. I climbed down the net, tied a long line to it that I'd fastened to the railing, then backed the boat out of the net, grabbed the net, and let Dennis winch me back up, without getting my feet wet.

Okay, quick exit strategy in place.

"What now?" Dennis asked.

"We start below."

The passageway we entered was just as empty as the entire aft deck of the boat had been. But the room it led to first was different. It was the size of a conference room. There were no people there, but it was far from empty.

It was distinguished by two large salt-water tanks and a sort of canvas stretcher apparatus that could be lowered and lifted up through a hatch in the ceiling—up onto the deck, I guessed. The tanks were empty, but I felt certain I knew what had been in them. Especially when I saw resting on a wall shelf, below a TV screen, two hand-held devices that looked like television remotes, only vastly more sophisticated.

Dennis looked at them and growled.

"Yup," I said, picking up the first device and stomping my foot on it as Dennis reduced the second one to its constituent parts by crushing it between his paws.

"And now?" Dennis said, wiping bits of plastic off his palms.

I put my hand on the wall of the room, feeling the deep vibration of an engine somewhere below us.

"Deeper," I said.

Both Dennis and I knew our way around a ship well enough to be able to locate the engine room. Which was where we started to run into a few folks, their white uniforms indicating their status as crewmen. But only one or two at a time. And we came upon each of them at a fast enough speed to prevent them from either resisting much or escaping.

Plus the rifle I was holding was a definite inducement for them to raise their hands rather than use their fists.

Luckily, we'd thought ahead and brought our favorite gifts for those who are into bondage. Which we exchanged for firearms—two nice little fully loaded Glocks with a spare clip for each.

By the time we reached the part of the engine room we'd been looking for, we'd left half a dozen people cocooned, cuffed, and trussed up in various ways—and we were running out of duct tape.

One of the men we had subdued was, while not in the greatest shape, big enough to generously donate to our clothing drive, so Dennis now also had sufficient garb for my big buddy to resemble, at least at a quick glance or a distance, a member of the crew. Although the bulge of the Glock in the pocket of his new coat did spoil its clean lines.

It's amazing how easy it is to sabotage a ship's engines. All it takes is the right knowledge—which I am not going to impart to the public just in case someone hearing this has a hard time on a Carnival cruise (we told you not to eat the fish!) and decides to exact some revenge. A wee bit of sand from a handy fire bucket poured in here, a wrench left behind applied there, a valve broken, a line cut. Little things mean a lot.

By the time we reached the door that opened onto the foredeck, the engines of *Pure Harmony* had shut down and the boat was, to all intents and purposes, adrift.

I placed the rifle off in a corner, where it would be easy to reach if we were coming back that way. Then we opened the door and emerged into the hazy sunlight of a typical Puget Sound afternoon.

No one seemed to notice either us or that their ship was adrift. The several dozen people we saw as we stepped out were not looking our way at all. They were clustered together on the foredeck staring over the railing. Everyone's attention was on the water in front of the boat. More precisely, they were trying to see what was struggling in the two big drift nets still being pulled in there. Waves and white foam were being thrown up, and the sound of thrashing in the water was loud.

I couldn't see what it was, but something else I could see there in the front of the ship, raised on two turrets, gave me a sinking feeling (not the thing to have on a boat). It was further evidence that *Pure Harmony* was far from a pleasure cruiser. Pleasure cruisers are not equipped with large, permanently mounted harpoon guns tipped with explosive grenades.

36

Shoot Him

*You have to know something
to know what to ask*

The sound of whatever was trying to escape that net was not the only thing to be heard as we approached the crowd at the bow—none of whom were leaning out and proclaiming "I'm the king of the world." Instead, in Cantonese, the southern variant of the Chinese language that I'd picked up a smattering of while in Hong Kong, they were shouting such things as "Se keoi laa!" which means "Shoot him!"

That was a phrase I knew well, having heard it shouted behind me in the New Territories as I was following Dennis rather rapidly out the window of a warehouse.

Uh, just before it exploded. Our bad.

The people in the prow of *Pure Harmony* were not the only ones taking in the spectacle in the ocean below them.

The two small boats from the *Creature Catchers* show were there as well, positioned at either side of those nets. In the larger thirty-foot cabin cruiser was a film crew of six men, with cameras and booms trained on the action and recording it all for posterity—and the ratings required by their corporate overlords. It looked to me as if the way they were framing their shots, they'd have the immense black aluminum, steel, and glass dorsal fins of the partially built new casino in the picture.

There were only two men in the other boat, a twenty-foot-long Chris-Craft Calypso. The first man, acting as captain, was in the center console at the steering station, holding the boat in place. The other man—tall, blond, and dressed in khaki camouflage—was standing, quite cine-matically, in the seating area in the bow, and pointing at the two nets where salmon were leaping and obscuring the view of whatever was below them trying to escape. Clearly Khaki Guy was as much a focus of those cameras as whatever was churning the water.

But the camo-clad cable star was not the person I was looking for. That man was on the yacht, standing at the front of the crowd.

Our paths had never crossed during my time in Hong Kong, but it was easy for me to recognize him. It wasn't just the way everyone in that small milling crowd was still standing back from him, being care-ful to not intrude on his space—aside from two armed bodyguards with black bandanas around their necks. What made him stand out was also the imperious, privileged way he was carrying himself.

It was Heung Wah-yim, the triad boss who was going by the name of Tony Oh. His clothing was the same white color as that worn by every-one else on this ship—except for me. But his suit was cut in a way that screamed bespoke, and no one else was wearing white diamond rings on every finger.

I gestured with my lips toward the harpoon guy closest to us.

Dennis adjusted his glasses, nodded, and started walking that way.

As I continued forward toward Tony Oh.

"*Dailo!*" I shouted. "*Yao fan!*"

Two ways of saying "boss" in Cantonese—the first more appropriate perhaps for a gang boss, the second a more muted, polite way. Or at least that was what I recalled. I didn't learn all that much Cantonese.

But I think my accent was pretty good, because when he turned my way, he didn't act surprised. He was seeing me as his man, the not so dearly departed Salim. So he didn't give the order for either of the body-guards next to him (subtly recognizable by the AK-47s slung over their shoulders) to "Se keoi laa!"

Instead, he opened his arms to embrace me.

And that is when everything started to happen at once.

The first thing happened when I stepped into his embrace, wrapped my own arms tightly around him, pressed the Glock I'd slipped from my pocket under his chin where no one but the two of us could see it, and whispered in his ear.

"Salim is dead. You want to stay alive, do what I tell you."

I'm quite sure he understood what I said. English is one of the major languages of currency in Hong Kong, and any international criminal like Tony Oh had to be fluent in the tongue of money.

But it seems that neither the Glock 19 nor I was as persuasive as I'd hoped. For the second thing that happened, without a moment's pause, was that Tony Oh shouted the three words in Chinese I did not want to hear just then.

"*Se keoi laa!*"

37

Something Large

Words certainly can hurt you
if the wrong person says them

"**S**hoot him!" the triad boss had shouted.

Fortunately for me, that command was inexact enough that the two harpooners on their raised turrets—and not his bodyguards—assumed those words were addressed to them. Which meant the third thing that happened was that they pulled the triggers of their guns.

The harpoon that was fired from the port-side turret hit something large and writhing in the net. As the grenade exploded, sending a spray of blood and flesh into the air, the watchers on the yacht cheered. A part of me felt the pain of whatever was there in that water, felt its pain and then felt its spirit leaving it in a way that hurt my heart. It almost made me pull the trigger of the Glock. But I managed to keep myself from sending Oh to his ancestors. And I was not in total despair because of what was happening to my other side.

The grenade-tipped harpoon fired from starboard had not been nearly as precise in striking its target. That was because, at exactly the moment when the trigger was being pulled, Dennis had barreled into the harpooner, throwing off his aim.

Instead of hitting what was in the second net, that grenade sailed on past it, hit the exact center of Khaki Guy's Chris-Craft right at the water line, and then exploded. The concussion threw the intrepid cable star into the water as the boat broke in half and started to sink. Fortunately for him, he did not land in the net, and there was plenty of space between the net and the shore for the filming boat to come around and rescue

186

him. As well as the boat's captain, who had jumped out of the center-console cabin and into the water almost as soon as the harpoon hit.

The fourth thing that happened was that after Dennis took down and knocked out the harpooner with what would have been a highlight-reel sack on a football field, he dropped down to the base of the winch lifting that second net and hit the button that released it. As the freed net sank, something came swimming out of it. Although it was underwater, and in the midst of a roil of escaping king salmon so it was indistinct, I could still see that its body was long and mottled green and snakelike, its crested head bigger than that of any fish I'd ever seen. And then it was gone.

To say that all this created more than a little confusion would be an understatement. With everyone's eyes on either the two nets or the sinking boat and the *Critter Catchers* personality being rescued, no one was looking my way. I spun Tony Oh around, my left arm around his neck so tight that I was cutting off his breath, the Glock in my right hand pressed into that spot where the nape of the neck meets the skull. Then I started moving backward toward the hatch where we'd entered.

I had almost reached that door when someone did look my way. Two someones. Both of them holding AK-47s that were being swung in our direction. The triad boss's bodyguards.

They started to move apart, guns leveled, aiming to flank me.

Not good. For them, actually. Because they had not noticed Dennis taking out the harpoon man or releasing the net, they also did not notice him—still dressed in the egg-white uniform of a crew member—coming up behind them, spreading his arms wide to cup their heads in his huge palms and then slap them together.

Had Dennis been a cymbals player, he would have garnered praise from his conductor, even though the resultant sound was more of a crack than a ringing clash. Excedrin headache numbers two and three for those bodyguards when they woke up.

I went through the door, dragging Tony Oh, who was now semiconscious from my rear naked choke. Dennis followed, shutting the door and locking it before he picked up the M82, holding it under one arm as he cleaned his glasses with a black bandana he'd pulled from around the neck of one of the fallen bodyguards.

"Se keoi laa?" he said.

"I know, déjà vu all over again. But enough Cantonese review for now. Let's book."

We made our way quickly through the ship, pleased to see our various previous acquaintances still as neatly packaged as we'd left them.

The various "Ooomps" and "Oorghs" they grunted at us through the duct tape still stuck across their mouths were likely their way of expressing their deep gratitude to us.

When we reached the door that led out onto the aft deck, Dennis opened it slowly and looked around. Seeing nothing, he stepped out, pointing in first one direction and then another with the M82.

"Clear," he said.

But as I stepped out, still moving backward with the limp triad boss still in my grasp, I saw two things that made me realize that my big buddy's assessment of the situation had been slightly flawed. The first was that I no longer saw Little Yao's feet sticking out from the place where we'd stowed him behind the box. The second was the very tall person dropping down on me from the place he'd been crouching on the roof of the yacht.

38

One Good Arm

The seen does not include
the unseen yet to be seen

Hadn't we left the flag man tied up? Wasn't he well secured with duct tape wrapped tightly around his arms and legs?

Yes, but we'd done a quick job of it. And as useful and efficient as duct tape may be in training your children to sit still (joke, joke—do not call Child Protective Services), there is a simple two-step way to escape it.

1. Raise your arms over your head.
2. Swing your arms down fast while pulling your wrists apart.

The result is that the tape will tear, which explained why I had an immense basketball player falling on me like a praying mantis on a moth.

As Little Yao's body hit mine, I had no choice but to let go of Tony Oh. But instead of hitting the deck with the full weight of a nearly seven-foot-tall attacker on top of me, I managed to grab his arm and twist enough as I fell that I landed partially on top of him.

Not his desired result. His head hit with a loud *crack!* But the fall was not exactly ideal for me, either, since I hit my elbow and shoulder hard enough to send a shooting pain through me. When I got up—and he stayed down—I could barely move my left arm.

Which made it most inconvenient when Tony Oh—who had apparently been imitating a North American marsupial—came rushing at

189

me, head down, catapulting me backward over the railing before Dennis could reach me.

But I did not fall alone. Even though I could only grab his collar with one hand, it was enough to take Oh with me as I fell, and we hit the water together.

The fact that he was on top drove me deeper. I'd taken enough of a breath and then closed my mouth tightly, so that I didn't swallow any water. But when I came up, Oh was waiting to grab me by the shoulder and apply the same chokehold I'd used on him. Either he was a fast learner or he'd had similar training to mine. Which, with one arm immobilized, was not enabling me to do as much as I'd have liked to keep from being choked out and drowned before Dennis could get to us.

I kicked hard, managing to drive us back up to the surface long enough for me to see Dennis sliding down the rope into the Zodiac. I understood his thinking.

Podjo can handle himself against just one crime boss. Rather than diving in to help, better for me to get the boat ready for us to make a getaway.

Except his buddy Podjo had only one good arm right now. And Tony Oh was on me as tight as the Old Man of the Sea was on Sinbad. His legs wrapped around me from behind, his arm around my neck, the palm of his other hand cupping the back of my head. Textbook Gracie jiu-jitsu, damn it!

Ever heard of dirty fighting? Folks, that is only when you're in a competition that has rules. In reality, when it's life or death, it's all dirty. That is why I stopped trying to pry his arm from around my neck. Instead I twisted my hips to the side, reached down as far as I could, and then struck with a tiger-claw fist at the area that is referred to in the martial arts of India as the "golden zone." Struck, grabbed, and twisted.

Tony Oh's scream as my last-ditch technique threatened to turn him into a eunuch coincided with his releasing my neck and my pushing myself away from him. As I did so, a motion from above on the yacht caught my eye. A man I'd not seen before, who appeared to be Chinese like the rest of the triad boss's crew, was leaning over the railing. He was wearing a lab coat and thick eyeglasses, and staring intently at a black unit in his hands a little bigger than a cell phone. And working a joystick on it.

Uh-oh!

Tony Oh was coming toward me, reaching out to grasp my throat. But I grabbed his shoulder first, pulled him into me, and turned both our bodies in the direction where I'd seen a fin break the water. A split second later, I was thrust back violently in the water as a bottlenose dolphin wearing what looked like a metal skullcap hit us beak first.

It was the kind of carefully aimed strike that would have killed a shark. One reason why even most sharks steer clear of schools of cetaceans of all types, all of whom are fierce in their defense of their young. The blow from its beak would have ruptured most of my major inner organs— just like those divers at the casino construction site. But instead of yours truly, the brunt of that force was absorbed by Tony Oh, who I'd held between me and the finned attacker. Oh violently coughed up blood, convulsed, and then went limp.

But it wasn't over. That radio-controlled dolphin—which looked to be twelve feet long and was clearly one of the ones that normally resided in the tank inside the yacht—was starting to circle back. Another fin fifty yards away showed me he was not alone. The shock of that deadly marine mammal's strike had knocked half of the wind out of me. I was coughing, trying to regain my breath, weakly treading water.

If they came at me from two sides, Tony Oh would not be the only one to sleep with the fishes that day.

39

A Friend, Indeed

Making friends pays back
more than it costs

As the porpoise closest to me surfaced, I could see its eyes. They looked crazy, as if the animal was in constant pain. People talk about the smile of the dolphin, and it is true that they often look—and act—as if they are having a ball, as if it's better to be a dolphin than a king. But not this one. Whatever was going on in its head was causing it agony.

I'm so sorry to see you like this, I thought.

And for a moment it seemed as if I was touching its mind. But then whatever contact there might have been between us was broken. It dove, and I knew what was next. When it was deep enough, it would turn and come up like a rocket from below, breaking me, driving me up out of the water.

Dennis and the Zodiac were now a quarter mile away. Some kind of current had been pulling at me. Dennis was trying to start the motor. Even if he was only yards away from me, it would be too late.

I released my grip on Tony Oh's dead body, letting it drift from me. I took a deep breath, looked down, and did a shallow surface dive.

At least I can see my death coming at me, I thought.

But what I saw was far different from what I expected.

A large black shape had intersected the dolphin below me. Grasping the bottlenose by its tail, the orca shook it like a dog shaking a rat. It did so with such violence that the metal cap on the dolphin's head tore loose. And when the orca—who I knew had to be Happy—let go, the dolphin steadied itself in the water, then turned and swam away.

Happy didn't follow the bottlenose—which I hoped was now free of its cerebral implant and might survive. It wasn't its fault that it had been turned into a killer.

The young orca came up gently beneath me and lifted me up to the surface, where I hung half on his back, my good arm around his dorsal fin. A friend, indeed.

I looked around for the other metal-capped dolphin. It was gone. And Dennis was standing in the Zodiac, the M82 to his shoulder. Underwater, I hadn't heard the shot, but I could see, draped over the rail of the yacht, the motionless body of the man in the lab coat, the control box gone from his open hand.

Happy stayed until Dennis reached me. My cetacean pal waited until I was fully in the boat. Then he lifted his head out of the water and made a sound that was half whistle and half chatter.

I wish I could have replied that same way. But I did the best I could.

"Thanks, pal. Good luck to you," I said.

As Happy dove, Dennis put something around my shoulders. The white coat he'd been wearing. I hadn't realized I was shaking. Shock is like that.

"You okay, Podjo? That current was crazy, carrying you away like that."

That current? I looked back toward the headland where the casino was being built. I could see that the water level had gone down on the shore. Was still going down.

"Dennis," I said, "point this boat out to sea and open her up. Fast!"

There's this traditional story that a Hopi/Apache friend of mine named Michael Lacapa told me about the Four Worlds that existed before this one. In each of those worlds, someone did something wrong, and that world was destroyed.

This one time, Michael told me, Coyote was going along. He was next to the river. When he looked into that river, he saw a baby in the water. That baby was so cute that Coyote couldn't resist picking it up. He hid that baby under his blanket and kept going along.

Then there was this big noise. Everyone in the world heard it. And the water started rising everywhere. It looked as if everyone was going to drown. So the Holy People planted Big Reed. That reed grew up and up, and the people climbed up inside it because it was hollow. They climbed out until that reed pierced the sky and came to another world.

But when the people climbed out of Big Reed and looked down through the hole, they could see that the water was still rising.

"The Water Monster is really angry," the people said. "Who did something to get the Water Monster so upset?"

That was when the baby under Coyote's blanket started to cry.

"What do you have there, Coyote?" the people said.

"Nothing," Coyote said. "I've got nothing here."

But when they opened his blanket, they saw that baby.

"Oh no," they said. "This is the Water Monster's baby."

They carefully lowered the baby into the water. Then the water went down, leaving the people up there in the new world they had entered.

Somebody made the Water Monster angry by doing something to his baby. Don't ask me how I knew that something like that was going on. I just knew. And as Dennis and I roared away from the headland, we saw it coming toward us from out to sea. A wave bigger than the giant ones you sometimes get on the west side of Oahu in the Hawaiian Islands. We headed into it, rode up it, and came out the other side.

"Okay," I said, "we're okay."

We turned the boat to look back, in time to see that wave, a mile away from us now, lift up the big white yacht and carry it toward shore, on up onto the point, right into the middle of the partially constructed casino, where it was left on its side in the middle of the wreckage between the two collapsed orca-fin towers as the water receded.

40

The Ends of the String

When one end of a string is tied to the other end,
it can form a circle

In the weeks that followed the destruction of the construction site by the combination of that sudden high water and the grounding of Tony Oh's yacht, which had come in like a massive broom sweeping everything before it, there were a lot of explanations of what happened.

They called it a rogue wave, a mini-tsunami caused by an undersea earthquake, and finally just an anomaly that affected only a small part of the coast. It was, in short, something that happened which could not be explained. Unless you believed in certain legends. "Last time A'yahos woke up, a thousand years ago," Raven had said, "she created a fifteen-foot-high tsunami."

Way to go, A'yahos.

The harpooned sea serpent that washed ashore a few days later, still tangled in *Pure Harmony*'s net, was another story. It was over thirty-six feet long, with two long antler-like fronds growing out of its head. The Internet and the news media had a field day with it.

MONSTER STORY PROVEN REAL
CREATURE OUT OF SALISH LEGENDS REALLY LIVES
PUGET SOUND'S LOCH NESS MONSTER

Those were just a few of the headlines.

Until an actual ichthyologist from the University of Washington took a look at it.

"*Regalecus glesne,*" she said. "An oarfish. Seldom seen, usually stays in the deeper waters, but every now and then one shows up and gets mistaken for some mythical creature."

Interestingly enough, no one talked about what I'd seen caught in and escaping from that second net. And I was not about to tell anyone about it. Or that no way was it a second oarfish.

Speaking of creatures, everyone from the *Creature Catchers* show also survived. Although after the show's host and the captain of the harpooned Chris-Craft were rescued, it was too late for them to head out to sea as we did. They were swept onto the casino headland along with *Pure Harmony*, barely escaping being crushed by its bulk. Their boat ended up stuck for thirteen hours twelve stories up on what was left of one of the orca-fin towers before a fire truck with a long enough ladder could get them down.

As for the stranded yacht, it was a total loss. Registered in Hong Kong, it had been insured with Lloyd's of London, and the heirs of Tony Oh collected a settlement that covered two-thirds of what it had been worth when it was still a Japanese whaling ship and had not yet been refitted as a combination research vessel, floating laboratory, and the world's most exclusive private restaurant.

Unlike some of the popular images of tsunamis, huge waves such as the one that dragged *Pure Harmony* across the casino site like a scouring pad don't always move that fast. What kills people is usually the debris that floats with them. No one on the crew manifest of *Pure Harmony* lost their lives, though they were as shaken and stirred as a martini. However, two people did end up missing—one of the scientists onboard and the reclusive billionaire himself. When the wave receded, it apparently took them back into the depths with it.

As for Salim, the Tiger Man assassin, his body was never discovered by the authorities. That was because—as Raven explained it to me later—Chief George's great-nephew ran a funeral parlor with its own crematorium. She didn't mention how the remains got there, and I didn't ask.

The casino project was abandoned. Unlike the yacht, it wasn't covered by insurance—the policy that was supposed to have been taken out on it had never been paid for. Somehow the money for the premiums had all ended up in and been withdrawn from the bank account of the CEO of Deep Bluewater, Chief Sea Antelope. A number of people were quite miffed about that, including the Russians, the IRS, and the employers of people with names like Vinny the Pipe and Luigi Bones. That all came to light two weeks later—at virtually the same time Mary,

Luther George's lawyer great-niece, presented conclusive proof in federal court that the ballot count for the last tribal elections had been rigged, and that Old Sherm had actually lost by a landslide. Chief George became chief again, and all those purged from the rolls returned to full tribal membership. The Russian money-laundering pipeline through the casino was shut down for good. The federal prison where the former chief is serving twenty years has him in the special security unit—at his request. For obvious reasons.

I had only been in the hospital for twenty-four hours when a nurse escorted two visitors into my room.

It was good to see them. Dennis had left that morning to head back home—leaving me to recuperate for as long as it took. He'd started missing Patty Ann, their kids, and the countless puppies as soon as our case was wrapped up. I knew the feeling. After eight hours stuck on a narrow cot with no one to talk to, I'd been getting mighty lonely myself.

"How ya doin'?" Chief George asked as he sat in the chair by the bed.

"Better now that you two are here. You know, when they say a good guy can't get a break, now all I have to do is point to this," I replied, tapping the cast on my right arm.

Raven was looking at the chart hung at the foot of my bed. "Plus a cracked sternum, two broken ribs, and a dislocated shoulder."

She was, I should mention, looking amazing. Some people were made to wear skinny jeans.

"It only hurts when I laugh. Or cough. Or breathe."

I chuckled at my dry, manly sense of humor and immediately regretted it. It really did hurt.

"Well, cowboy," Raven said, sitting on the bed and making my sternum hurt even more (though it was worth it to smell her perfume), "looks like you're not going to be doing any riding for a while."

"Hey, I'll be back in the saddle before you know it."

"Oh, I'll know it," she replied, putting her hand on my wrist.

Chief George held up both hands. "If this goes any further, I am going to have to leave the room."

"Sorry," I said.

"I'm not," Raven said in a way that made me thank my lucky stars that I've always been a fast healer.

Her grandfather reached out and put his hand on my good shoulder. "Getting serious now, we owe a lot to you, son. My people and me, we can't thank you enough for what you did for us and . . ." He looked out the window, which had a great view of the Sound.

I followed his gaze, and neither of us said anything for a few minutes.

"I'm glad it all worked out," I said.

"Me, too," Chief George replied. Then he left the room.

But Raven didn't.

And that's a good enough place to end this story for now.

CPSIA information can be obtained
at www.ICGtesting.com
Printed in the USA
LVHW091221091220
673704LV00003B/210